BUSINESS OF SPORTS

THE WINNING FORMULA FOR SUCCESS

VINIT KARNIK

Popular Prakashan
www.popularprakashan.com

IISM International Institute of Sports Management
KNOWLEDGE SERIES

Published by
Harsha Bhatkal for
POPULAR PRAKASHAN PVT. LTD.
301, Mahalaxmi Chambers
22, Bhulabhai Desai Road
Mumbai - 400 026
info@popularprakashan.com

First Published May 2022
First Reprint June 2022

Author: Vinit Karnik with Vishnu Govind

(4540)
ISBN: 978-81-956093-6-9

Cover design: PealiDezine
Layout: Anjali Sawant
Typesetting: Satyawan Rane

PRINTED IN INDIA
by Repro India Ltd.
Lower Parel
Mumbai - 400013

Contents

Chapter 6

Sports Consumer Behaviour

Chapter 7
Promotion in Sports Marketing

Chapter 8
Five Pillars of the Indian Sporting Industry

Chapter 1

Introduction to Marketing and Sports Marketing

INTRODUCTION

Successful companies operating in today's time have one thing in common: they are strongly customer-focussed and heavily committed to marketing. These companies share an intent for satisfying customer needs in definite target markets. They aim to help build enduring customer relationships based on creating value.

Technological advances, economic, social and environmental challenges are some of the deciding factors which have shaped how customers these days are reassessing and engaging with brands. New digital, mobile and social media developments have revolutionised how consumers perceive, engage and interact with the surrounding environment which leads to the development of new marketing strategies and tactics. It is more important now than ever to build strong customer relationships and long-lasting engagements based on real and enduring customer value.

Marketing is a multi-billion-dollar global industry that has a definite impact on the economy. This includes construction of sports infrastructure, sporting goods and services, licensed sports products, live sporting events and so on.

Let us consider sports events. The sports industry has widespread effect on different industries. When families drive to play and watch cricket, football, hockey and other sporting activities and events, it has a supportive impact on automobile industry. These sports events generate business for restaurants, hotels and service stations. Sports marketing has also created job opportunities, ranging from say a marketing executive for an IPL team franchise to a parking lot attendant job during IPL games. Stadiums and entertainment venues have to be constructed and maintained, which in turn require facility managers, security personnel, hospitality and maintenance crews. Athletes require coaches, trainers, managers and medical staff. Athletes also hire agents to manage their engagements, handle social media accounts, publicity and negotiate contracts for them.

The sports industry today reaches over and above the field of play; from food, merchandise at the stadiums to media rights and sponsorships.

The industry also offers a compelling proposition to different industry participants from broadcasters and streaming platforms seeking viewers and advertising revenues to broadcasters and streaming platforms looking for subscribers, big and small sponsors who want to move from traditional media, event organisers, athletes and spectators.

We will discuss more in detail about Sports Marketing in various verticals of the industry, posing exciting new challenges for both customers and marketers, in the subsequent chapters.

But first, let us understand the basics of marketing.

WHAT IS MARKETING?

Marketing involves an exchange of offerings that hold value for customers or clients. It has within its purview the activities, processes and structures involved in the creation and delivery of the same. The offerings can include an entire bundle of tangible and intangible goods as well as services.

Four components can be extracted from the above definition of marketing –

1. **Create:** The system of collaborating with customers and suppliers to create offerings that satisfy their needs and demands.
2. **Communicate:** Describing those offerings and understanding the wants of the customers.
3. **Deliver:** Ensuring that those offerings reach the consumer in a way that optimises value.
4. **Exchange:** Assigning trade value for those offerings.

Marketing is not just a promotional function. It includes every activity that an organisation undertakes to promote the buying or selling of a product or service. Marketing includes a full range of activities that an organisation undertakes to make certain that customers' needs are met and the organisation, in return, receives its value for doing so. The organisation needs to receive enough value, in return, that is worth the time and investment made to provide the service or product being offered. Marketing not only includes advertising, promotion, public relations (PR) and sales but it is also an activity that helps an organisation perform related activities thoroughly. One could think of advertising, promotion, PR and sales as being influenced by a marketing strategy.

One common misconception is that sometimes people do not differentiate between marketing and sales. Sales and marketing are both components of an organisation's marketing strategy. Sales include selling the organisation's products or services to its customers, whereas marketing is the process of communicating the value of a product or service to customers so that the product or service sells.

Marketing includes every activity that organisations generally undertake to satisfy customer needs –

- Ideate a product or service and define its characteristics and benefits.
- Decide the pricing of the product or service.
- Identify the target market.
- Build awareness of the product or service amongst potential customers.
- Convince people to buy the product or service.
- Deliver the product or service to people who buy it.
- Manage and maintain relationships with customers after the product or service has been delivered.

In the marketing concept, we need to achieve the twin objectives of meeting organisational goals as well as the satisfaction of customer needs. Effective application of this marketing concept will further guide all the organisation's marketing activities. The marketing concept always puts the customer first: as the most important goal. Satisfying the customer's need must be the goal of everyone in the organisation. But the organisation also needs to ensure its survival and growth fuelled by profits. A proper balance between customer satisfaction and company survival has to be established.

Often, "customer" and "consumers" are used synonymously and are easily confused with one another. A *customer* is a person who purchases the goods or services of a certain producer or a business by paying a price in exchange. However, the customer is not always the consumer. The customer might pay the price and buy the products but those products may be consumed by a different person. A *consumer* is a person who consumes or uses goods or services. The customer can be the consumer, but not in all cases. The consumer will know the nature and genuine quality of the product or the service.

The marketing concept focuses on getting the right goods or services or ideas to the right people at the right place, time and price, using the right techniques of promotion and utilising the right people to provide the customer service associated with those goods, services or ideas. This concept is referred to as the "right" principle and is claimed to be the basis of all marketing strategies. The marketing concept is also a way of finding out the wants and needs of potential customers (consumers or organisations) and then providing goods and services to meet the expectations of the customers.

To encourage exchanges, marketers follow the "right" principle. If a representative from Speedo International Ltd, a distributor of swimwear and swim-related accessories does not have the right swimsuit for an elite swimmer (potential customer) when she/he wants it, at the right price, the swimmer will not exchange money for a new swimsuit from Speedo.

Think on the above example: What if the price of the swimsuit had been 30 percent higher? What if the store had been less accessible? Would the swimmer have bought anything? The "right" principle tells us that the marketing concept controls many factors that determine marketing success.

WHAT IS SPORTS MARKETING?

Initially, sports marketers only focussed on sponsorship deals as a marketing strategy for their organisation. But thanks to dissemination of advertising and increase of new channels, it has led to fresh opportunities for brands, teams, athletes and clubs. It has led organisations to cultivate deeper relationships and engagement with the fans.

Sports Marketing is the application of marketing concepts to sports products and services, and the marketing of non-sport products through an association to the sport. Sports Marketing has two key features –

1. It is the application of most general marketing practices to sport-related products and services.
2. It is the marketing of other consumer products or services through sport.

Like any type of marketing, Sports Marketing seeks to fulfil the needs and wants of sports consumers. It fulfils wants and needs of consumers by providing sport services and sport-related products to consumers. However, Sports Marketing is different from conventional marketing. Sports Marketing can also assist the consumption of non-sport products and services by its association. It is important to understand that Sports Marketing means the marketing of sports along with the use of sports as a tool to market other products and services.

Theoretically, before any kind of sales, a sports product or service must hold a place in the mind of a consumer. But in reality, a consumer needs to be aware of the availability of any sports product or service to respond to it in one way or the other. The process of creating awareness amongst consumers and initiating a response towards the sports product or service is termed Branding. When a sports brand has grasped a place in a consumer's mind, the sports product or service is said to be positioned in the mind of the consumer. The positioning may have a favourable or non-favourable image, depending on the perception of the consumer.

The significance of successful branding and getting hold of strong market positioning is not merely a single, one-time operation. Sports Marketing suggests the establishment of an ongoing relationship between a sports brand, product or service and its users.

Sports Marketing academicians, as well as organisations involved in it have put forth various definitions of Sports Marketing over the last couple of years. There is no one generally accepted definition. Due to the evolving nature of the Sports Marketing area and different viewpoints, various definitions with different viewpoints arise. This section discusses three different approaches to the definition.

The first approach has the following perspective –

"Sports Marketing involves the use of sports to market products."

The above definition gives rise to questions like:

- Who is using Sports Marketing?
- What kind of products can be marketed through sports?
- What if the product itself is sports?
- How is sports used for promotions?
- Is sports the only distinguishing feature of Sports Marketing in comparison to conventional marketing?

Here's another way of defining Sports Marketing; this time it is from the perspective of the sports organisation.

'Sports Marketing involves the process by which a sports organisation creates value for itself by creation and exchange of products with customers."

This is an approach that is consistent with marketing practises across sectors. Generally, when we refer to marketing within a category of products, the understanding is that the discussion pertains to the marketing of products in that category. This definition approaches Sports Marketing from a similar perspective.

Let us now look at a more comprehensive approach. The definition given below, blends the earlier definitions, thereby giving room to the possibility that there is a widening in the scope of Sports Marketing.

'Sports Marketing involves the application of marketing processes to the business of sports goods and services, influencing the business of non-sport goods and services by associating them with sports and enhancing the public perception of sports properties."

The above definition takes two unique approaches within the broad concept of Sports Marketing into consideration:

1. Marketing OF sports.
2. Marketing THROUGH sports.

We can thus summarise that Sports Marketing can involve the following business scenarios –

a. Marketing of sports products, like gears, facilities, accessories, etc.
b. Marketing of a brand or its products by associating with sports, like sponsorship.
c. Marketing of sporting organisations to build a following, raise funding, etc.

This definition implies that Sports Marketing, although based on general marketing principles, needs specific applications. This then leads to the question of how Sports Marketing differs from other forms of marketing. The next section will examine the unique characteristics of Sports Marketing.

SPORTS MARKETING UNIQUENESS

In Sports Marketing, given the various scenarios involved, the range and scope is such that different products, when marketed, bring different marketing aspects into play.

The uniqueness of Sports Marketing as a function, can be seen as a consequence of the variety in the following –

1. The Sports Product.
2. The Sports Industry.
3. The Sports Consumer.

According to an article, sports is considered as a part of the entertainment industry. There are various similarities as people watch sports to be entertained. However, it also differs on various aspects from other entertainment sectors or ordinary businesses.

Sporting organisations often operate in a closed, competitive environment. Sporting organisations try to contest on and off the pitch but also need each other to create sporting competition. The sports industry and sporting organisations sometimes have an 'unhealthy' relationship with the principle of profitability. Every company in the ordinary business sectors aims to generate profits. Sporting entities like football clubs, however, have a huge motive of winning on the field, a goal that may align at some level with the need for maximising profits, though the two are not quite the same. In the sports industry, some teams and organisations are not focussed purely on profits as a factor to be successful like a business in other sectors. They are in this environment for the "sport" and do not look at their marketing activities as a business entity selling a service to the consumer. They are not profit-oriented. For example, Reliance Foundation Youth Sports or RFYS, a non-profit and Corporate Social Responsibility (CSR) initiative driven by Reliance Foundation aims to offer a platform for Indian youth at school and college level. RFYS provides a platform for schools, colleges and athletes to display their skills and passion for sports. It also aims to support the sporting ecosystem by aiding in skill development of teachers, infrastructure, digital empowerment and creating sporting heroes. They also provide scholarships and opportunities to deserving athletes to get scouted by teams, coaches of schools and colleges. RFYS launched an academy in 2015 called Reliance Foundation Youth Champs to offer an opportunity for talented players across India build successful professional careers in football. In October 2020, several athletes under this programme were scouted by professional teams of the Indian Super League (ISL). Muhammed Basith PT, Aritra Das and Birendra Singh were signed by Kerala Blasters Football Club (FC) whereas Aqib Nawab and G Balaji made it to Chennaiyin Football Club.

Winning competitions is important from a business perspective for popular sports teams, since it is a big driver for fan appreciation and popularity. Financial performance has a co-relation with sporting performance and latter does not come with guarantees. A sports product is defined as a 'good, a service or any combination of the two that is designed to provide benefits to a sports spectator, participant or sponsor.' Sports products as provided by sporting organisations can be divided into two: i) base product or core product ii) product extensions. The base product will be the initial event, game or competition and the product extensions will be all the goods and services that are related to the core product.

For example: Take the case of Bengaluru FC. Bengaluru FC is an Indian professional football club based in Bengaluru, Karnataka competing in the Indian Super League. The match between Bengaluru FC and other teams or the football camps held is the base product or core product. Availability of merchandise, catering, hospitality, broadcasting, endorsements of football players, PR or information services are product extensions from a Sports Marketing angle for Bengaluru FC.

The base product is a combination of all characteristics of a service (intangibility, inseparability of production and consumption, perishability), whereas the product extensions can be goods or services related to the core product. The core product can be distinguished between participant sports and spectator sports. The differentiation makes sense as both forms target different consumer groups. In the case of participant sports, sporting organisations try to stimulate as many people as possible to become active in a specific sport, whereas in the case of spectator sports, sporting organisations are trying to attract people to attend the event/game.

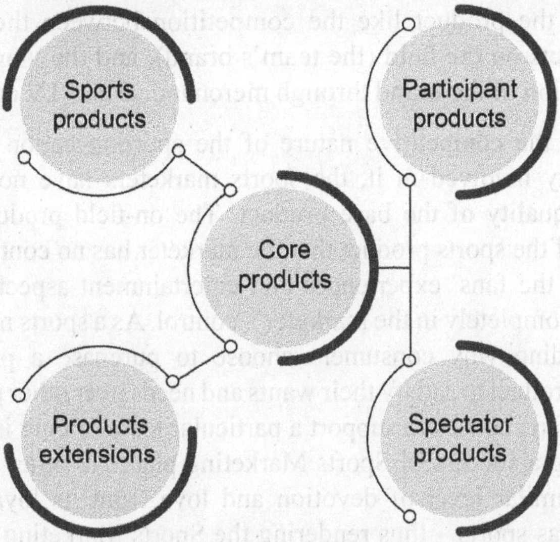

Figure 1.1 – Types of sports products

Organisations in the traditional industry sector aim to monopolise a situation to determine the market whereas sporting organisations are concerned at retaining some level of parity between them. Otherwise, sports as a product would have a possibility of losing much of its appeal and value.

The sports customer expresses his or her personality and values to others through the choice of a particular team/product and its distinguishing attributes and brand personality. This makes branding and public relations important in the Sports Marketing mix. Personal involvement and self-identification of fans are driven to a considerable extent by public perception; hence managing how the team/product is perceived amongst fans is an important aspect of Sports Marketing. A product that aligns with a particular sport or a potentially desired lifestyle can inspire life-long loyalty of a brand. Example – The Adidas brand.

Marketing sports product presents several challenges for sports marketers due to the uniqueness of the game. While marketing any sports product, sports marketers are illuminating several key points of the product like the competition between the teams, the products on the field (the team's brand), and the viewership/ consumption of the brand through merchandise and TV contracts.

Owing to the competitive nature of the sporting action and the spontaneity involved in it, the sports marketers have no control over the quality of the base product. The on-field product is an element of the sports product that the marketer has no control over. However, the fans' experiences and entertainment aspects of the sport are completely in the marketer's control. As a sports marketer, understanding why consumers choose to purchase a particular sporting product to satisfy their wants and needs over other products or why a fan chooses to support a particular team or club is vital to developing a successful Sports Marketing plan. No other industry inspires similar level of devotion and love from its loyal brand followers as sports – thus rendering the Sports Marketing concept unique as compared to a general marketing concept.

THE SPORTS MARKETING MIX

A good marketing strategy is a must-have to truly build brand loyalty. The 3 Cs of marketing, a strategic marketing concept, is a very widely accepted concept for marketers. This model takes into consideration 3 areas to develop an effective marketing strategy –

1. The Consumer.
2. The Company.
3. The Competitor.

These three components are dynamic and fully dependent on each other. In case, there is a change in any one variable of any component, it affects the other two variables as well.

The heart of the sporting market is the sports marketing mix. The 3Cs of marketing – the consumer, the company and the competition are central to the Sports Marketing mix. For effective implementation of a marketing plan, we need to get a good understanding of the interplay between the three Cs and the relationship they have with the elements of the marketing mix.

As a rule, in marketing, the marketing mix is always viewed as the 4 Ps of marketing – product, price, place, promotion. However, in Sports Marketing, there is a need for an expanded role that publicity/ PR plays.

Hence, the Sports Marketing mix has evolved into the 5 Ps of Sports Marketing:

1. Sports Product.
2. Sports Price.
3. Sports Place (Sports distribution).
4. Sports Promotion.
5. Publicity or PR.

As all the 5 Ps and 3 Cs need to be considered in association with each other, it does not matter in what order you define them.

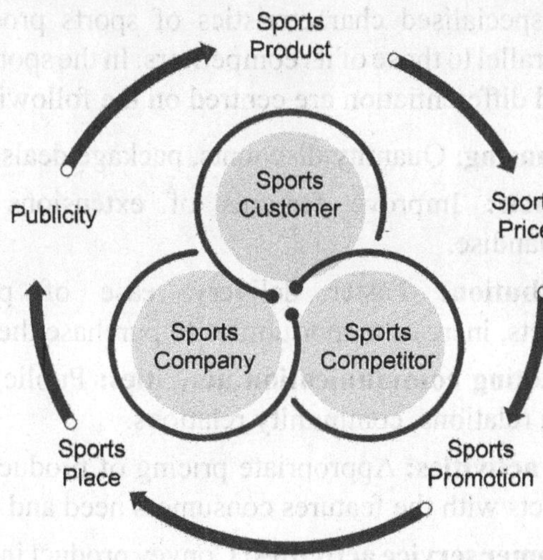

Figure 1.2 – 5Ps and 3Cs model

Sports Marketing mix (5Ps) and its relation to 3Cs of marketing

Sports customers and consumers are the reason why any sporting business takes place and are the driving force behind all the marketing activities. Marketing is all about brand building. Sports customers need to understand what to expect from a company. Strong values and ideals of the company are important, to ensure that all marketing that a business carries out is done in alignment to its values and ideals. Irrespective of the industry the company is in, competition is always prevalent. Competition should be evaluated and the drive to innovate needs to continue to gain an edge over the competitors.

The successful interaction of the marketing mix with the target market, as well as between the components themselves, is important to any successful marketing effort. This interaction has a complete effect on the sports marketing professional's decision-making process. The 5 Ps of the Sports Marketing mix can be utilised if they are in alignment with the 3 Cs of marketing. (Fig 1.2: The 5Ps and 3Cs co-relation model of Sports Marketing)

Differentiation is the concept of creating and demonstrating distinct and specialised characteristics of sports products and services as parallel to those of its competitors. In the sports market, efforts toward differentiation are centred on the following:

- **Purchasing**: Quantity discounts, package deals.
- **Products:** Improve features of extensions such as merchandise.
- **Distribution:** Faster delivery, ease of purchasing products, increase opportunities to purchase the product.
- **Marketing communication activities:** Public relations, media relations, community relations.
- **Sales activities:** Appropriate pricing of products, selling products with the features consumers need and want.
- **Customer service activities:** Convey product information to the sport's customers, availability to effectively and efficiently deal with customer problems and queries.

Sports Product

The core of a marketing mix is the product. A sports product is anything that satisfies a need or want of a sports customer. A product does not always refer to a physical, manufactured item. A product can also refer to services, people, places, ideas and the benefits that a sports organisation offers consumers. In relation to sports, two important concepts have implications for Sports Marketing. As shown in Fig 1.1, the first is the base (core) product, defined as the actual game or event. The sports marketer has no control over the outcome of the game. The sports marketer is in no position to determine and promise the sport's customers about how good the game will be or how well specific athletes may perform or the outcome of the game. The second concept is the importance of product extensions related to the core product to the overall marketing effort. The marketer has complete control of the product extensions and can ensure to achieve acceptable levels of quality.

Many sports organisations often offer a service in form of some physical activity, entertainment or an experience. Instead of a physical product, the sports organisation might offer intangible product benefits such as lifestyle, social group or even a belief system. Packaging the sport product includes presenting the product or service in the best possible manner. Marketers must present the product in different ways because consumers differ. Packaging the core product of sport, the game, or event will require providing information before the point of purchase. For example, sports marketers might package the game or event as family entertainment and offer family ticket plans. Marketers might package sports as a good place to make business connections and offer business ticket plans. A sports organisation that wants to keep an image as one that cares about the community might offer group discount plans for social service and charitable organisations.

Sports Pricing

The price of a product is a representation of what consumer hands over in exchange for a sporting good or service. A sports price should reflect the value of the sports product. Although price is generally thought of in financial terms, the price may include various aspects like cost of time or social costs the customer has to give up to obtain the sports product. The opportunity cost of lower waiting time in a queue or being in a group yoga class or gym fitness class instead of one-to-one training is also considered while determining the price.

A sports marketer's biggest challenge is to determine the right price for the end consumer. There are various ways to manipulate the price of the sports product:

- **Promotional pricing:** Annual membership for a 30% discount price if taken within the next one week.
- **Special sale pricing:** For seasonal sports equipment or discount if the quantity purchased increases.
- **Long-term pricing:** Monthly gym membership package INR 3000; 3 Months package costs INR 8000; 6 Months package costs INR 15,000 and Annual package costs INR 25,000.

Sports pricing can get very complex and critical for the success of the marketing activity. But the price is one aspect that can be readily changed; either increased or decreased. Sports organisations often alter their pricing strategies –

- **To attract a different segment of consumers:** For example, students may get a student discount on the event ticket but the general public may not get one.
- **According to the market environment**: For example, lowering prices during a recession or depending upon the economic conditions.
- **Based on the team's performance:** For example, increasing prices as a team's performance considerably improves.

Additionally, sports marketers must also determine how consumers perceive the value of the product when compared to all competing products in the sporting market to set an appropriate price.

Sports Place (Sports Distribution)

The place is the means of delivering the sports product to the consumer. It is also known as distribution, i.e., distributing the sport product to the consumer. The sports marketer will have to analyse the various types of distribution methods and choose the one that will deliver the product to the right place. The right place is determined based on where the consumer is, shops she/he will travel to or what websites she/he will visit.

Sports place should be characterised by –

- **The location of the sports base product:** Stadium, arena.
- **The point of beginning for distribution of all the product extensions:** Ticket sales at the stadium, sales by a toll-free telephone number or internet.
- **The geographic location of the organisation's target markets:** Global, national, regional, state, communities and cities.
- **Accessibility of the sports product for the target audiences**: Through various channels such as time, day, season or month in which the sports product is offered, as well as the media distribution outlets consumers may use to receive the sports product's experience.
- **Accessibility of the physical location of the sports product**: Event, highway systems, parking, walkways, ramps.
- **Attractive physical appearance:** Well-maintained, pleasant and properly painted.
- **A pleasant, convenient and functional environment**: It should have quick and easy access to concessions, clean restrooms, smoke-free and odour-free environment.
- **Safe and pleasant surroundings**: It should have adequate public safety, security personnel and attractive neighbourhood.

- **Availability of sports products and services:** They should be available on online platforms and e-commerce space.

Factors like ease of access, aesthetics, provisions to make the fans comfortable, nice ambience, clean and hygienic facilities, etc. play a major influence on perceptions in the mind of the fans about the stadium. Higher the perceived quality, more the sports fan's gratification. Satisfaction of the sports fans not only increases their likelihood of staying in the stadium for a longer period and spending more money but also ensures their return to the stadium more often.

Sports Promotion

Promotion means creating awareness. In simple words, promotion is the process of making people aware of a product or a service. A variety of methods may be involved in creating awareness and grabbing the attention of potential consumers to inform them or educate them about something.

In the Sports Marketing space, promotions cover a range of inter-related activities. The activities intend to attract attention, stimulate interest and awareness and encourage the consumers to purchase the sports product. Promotion is all about communicating and educating sports consumers. It not only involves advertising and educating the consumer about the product but also persuades and reminds them about it. Persuading the consumer to develop a favourable opinion about a sports product in alignment with the positioning strategy and stimulate the consumers to try the sports product should be the aim of the sports marketers.

Sports Promotion involves the following elements –

- **Advertising:** Advertising involves paid, non-personal communication and activities about a sports product or service through different media formats like print, TV and digital. This is aimed at attracting attention towards the sports product.

- **Sponsorship:** Sponsorship is a mutually beneficial relationship between a company and the sports organisation. Normally, it involves contribution in monetary and non-monetary resources from the company against possible publicity opportunities, like developing brand image, loyalty, etc.
- **Public relations:** Public relations is a bouquet of activities, communications and media coverage that convey who the sports organisation is and what they have to offer; all in the effort to enrich their image and prestige.
- **Licensing:** Licensing involves creation of strategic alliances in which the manufacturers of a sports product permit a second party to manufacture that product in return for specific royalties or payments.
- **Personal service:** Personal service involves one-on-one communication between a representative of the sporting organisation and the sports consumer intending to achieve the promotional objectives which range from providing information about products and services, catering to their needs and enabling generation of sales.
- **Sales promotions:** These include the benefits of reduced costs that are presented to motivate a sports consumer to purchase the specified sports product or service.
- **Ambience:** It utilises the design of visual communications — such as lighting, colours, music — in an environment to entice the sport consumer's perceptual and emotional responses to purchase the sports product or service.

Sports Publicity (PR)

The publicity of sports includes activities that are utilised to promote awareness and establish a connection with the public by disseminating information through various mediums and media outlets. Due to the expanded role of publicity in the sporting industry, this aspect has evolved into the 5th P of Sports

Marketing and has been broken away from being a small part of a promotion. Sports publicity successfully combines sports with the products that sporting teams promote. Sports as an industry can be promoted. Athletes, fans and some organisations are frequent consumers of products that are advertised through sports publicity.

Sports Publicity (PR) promotes teams, individual players, brands, leagues and sporting organisations through earned media channels including broadcast, print, radio and online media outlets. Sports PR focuses on reporters, editors, producers, writers and anchors at mass media outlets such as Star Sports, ESPN, Sony Sports, sports websites and sports journals. Athletes today are screened with a microscope held by the media, their fans and the lay public. Therefore, PR strategy has an extremely vital role to play. Sports PR works to develop and maximise an athlete's potential image, allowing the player to focus solely on perfecting their specific sport.

The basic framework on which marketing mix is built, the 4Ps, with publicity being the 5th P in the case of sports, can be developed further to explain the marketing process in a detailed way. Experts in the past have articulated a few additional Ps that play a pivotal role in Sports Marketing mix. They are –

- **Positioning**: Understanding the sports customer's consumption motivations, external environment influences, segmenting audiences and positioning the sports products and services accordingly.
- **Platform**: Responding to sports customers by developing several benefits delivered as products, services or experiences to meet their needs on an accessible platform.
- **People**: Those who are involved in selling a sports product or service, designing it, managing teams, serving sports customers via effective implementation of platform and promotion.
- **Profits:** Satisfying sports customer's basic needs and wants while pursuing a dual goal of organisational profitability.

It is not unexpected that after the 4Ps, the first P in the Sports Marketing mix is positioning. Positioning leads to gaining an understanding of the customer's needs, motivations and influences. The term "Customer-focused" and "Customer is the king" strategy has to be applied by an organisation to ensure the focus is on what the customer needs.

Although the Sports Marketing industry does not completely focus on profits, the P for profits is still an important aspect to be considered. Profits are fundamental to marketing. The Sports Marketing concept has a dual focus of meeting sports customers' needs while achieving organisational goals such as profitability. The sports marketer should have an understanding of the following while designing a strategy –

- The kind of promotions that generate the highest incremental revenue or
- Implementation of any dynamic pricing drive ticket revenue.
- Spending capacity of fans.

Offerings of an online campaign yielded the highest click rates, call-to-action and sales.

<u>Example: Indian Premier League's Marketing Mix (5Ps/ Product, Place, Promotion, Price, Publicity) – (MBA Skool Team, 2020)</u>

Indian Premier League (IPL) is a professional T20 cricket league founded by Board of Control for Cricket in India (BCCI) in 2008. It is scheduled every year from March to May. The league has ten teams namely –

1. *Mumbai Indians*
2. *Delhi Capitals*
3. *Sunrisers Hyderabad*
4. *Royal Challengers Bangalore*
5. *Rajasthan Royals*

6. *Chennai Super Kings*
7. *Kolkata Knight Riders*
8. *Punjab Kings*
9. *Gujarat Titans*
10. *Lucknow Super Giants*

Several marketing strategies like marketing investment, product/ service innovation, focus on customer experience, etc. have facilitated the growth of IPL as a brand.

Here is the elaboration of the marketing mix of the IPL –

IPL Product Strategy

IPL is a cricket league based in India including cricketers from all over the world. A total of ten teams play each IPL season and every team plays opponent team twice, once on their home-ground and once on the opponent's home-ground. The tournament's structure has been created in such a way that 56 matches are played in the league. The top 4 teams then advance to the semi-finals, qualifiers and finals. These 56 matches between the participating teams are the core product of the IPL and its marketing strategy. The value-added experience provided to the fans through merchandise, catering, hospitality and other marketing activities like broadcasting, cricketer endorsements, PR or information services are the extensions of the core products of IPL.

IPL's Pricing Strategy

IPL's pricing and revenue strategy depends on media rights, title sponsor and other sponsorship rights, broadcasting and streaming rights, advertisements, franchises, merchandising and ticket sales, etc. According to Bhasin (2019), income from IPL will approximately be around US$ 1.6 billion over a period of 5 to 10 years. Until 2017, the revenues were directed to a central pool. 40% of the revenue went to IPL, 54% to the franchisees and 6% as the prize money for the winning team. After 2017, 50% of the revenue went to IPL, 45% to franchisees and 5% to prize money. According *to India Today Web Desk (2020), the revenue of IPL 2020 is INR 4000 crore.*

IPL's Place and Distribution Strategy

IPL's place or distribution strategy contains a set of methods through which IPL delivers its products to the customers. IPL's distribution channels fulfil various purposes like easy ticket booking services, easy access to the match venues, availability of merchandise, food, beverages, etc. at the venue and overall atmosphere of the game.

IPL's Promotion Strategy

IPL's promotion mix is a mix of various promotional tools like – Advertising, Sales Promotion, Personal Selling, Public Relations, Direct Marketing and Digital Marketing. Promotions of IPL takes place through TV ads, jerseys, radios, live podcasts, social media posts, banners, hoardings and billboards.

Here are few components of promotional campaigns of IPL over the previous years that have proven advantageous to the brand's promotion –

- *Franchisee model creates a great win-win situation for both IPL promotion and the brands involved.*
- *Media rights helped create a solid viewership base and improved fan base.*
- *Title sponsor's name attached to the IPL brand not only creates brand awareness to aid the company's name reach every household but also recognised by everybody. For example, VIVO IPL 2021.*
- *Branding opportunities like strategic timeout, where commercial ads are run leading to generation of revenue for IPL as well as advertisers. This is another well-established promotional strategy by IPL.*
- *Contests for fans through various media and by various entities associated with IPL are also beneficial ways of*

promoting and creating a buzz about the brands. This also helps increase sales and viewership.

IPL's Publicity (PR)

Many cricketers and teams playing in the IPL are included in advertisements, press conferences and campaigns to promote the game. The snapshots of their previous matches, emotions of wins and losses are strategically placed to promote the brand. Well-known personalities like Shah Rukh Khan, Preity Zinta, Neeta Ambani who own teams are also seen promoting the IPL and their respective teams through various media outlets.

Example: Nike Inc.'s Marketing Mix (4Ps/Product, Place, Promotion, Price) – An Analysis (GREGORY, 2018)

Nike Inc.'s marketing mix (4Ps) ascertains the profitability and growth of its athletic footwear, apparel and equipment business. Let us focus on the company's product line that specialises in shoes that are designed to satisfy the needs of professional basketball and football athletes. Although the products manufactured are targeted to a specific market, say, basketball and football players, these products are also marketed to consumers around the world, for athletic as well as leisure activities, based on the specifics of Nike's mission and vision statements. Nike's 4Ps evolve according to the dynamics of the global sporting goods industry. Such evolution is a significant success factor that enables the business to utilise its marketing mix to respond to market trends and changes that influence local, regional and international market demand for its products.

Nike Inc., through its marketing mix, strengthens its core competencies to protect its business from the strong force of competition. The company competes with various firms involved in the footwear, apparel and athletic equipment markets. For example, Nike operates in the same markets as Adidas, Puma, Under Armour, ASICS, etc.

Nike's Products

This element of the marketing mix includes the organisational outputs offered to target consumers. These outputs are known as the Nike's product mix. Nike Inc.'s growth arises with the changes in its product mix. For example, Nike continues its investment in research and development to manufacture new products and enhanced versions of its current products as per changing trends. Originally a distributor of shoes, the company diversified its products into various shoes, apparel and equipment for different sports. Based on Nike Inc.'s standard strategy and rigorous growth strategies, the business also integrates new technologies into its product lines to improve product effectiveness and customer satisfaction.

Nike's Prices and Pricing Strategies

This element of the marketing mix identifies the prices that Nike applies to maximise profits while attracting the desired share of the multinational market it operates in. Nike's investments in technology are connected with a strategy to offer its products at a premium. Although Nike chooses to offer their products at a premium, it also considers current market conditions in setting its price points and price ranges. Based on the above considerations, the following pricing strategies are applied in Nike Inc.'s business:

***Value-based pricing strategy**: Based on consumer perception about the value of its products. This value is used to determine the highest prices that consumers are willing to pay for the company's sports shoes, apparel and equipment.*

***Premium pricing strategy:** Involves high prices. The high pricing is based on a premium branding strategy that institutes Nike products as higher in value and quality than other competing products.*

In 2014, the business successfully increased its selling prices and generated higher sales and revenues. This trend continues, as the company enjoys increasing sales revenues while steadily increasing its prices. Based on the market analysis of Nike Inc., such a trend is linked to the socio-cultural and economic changes in the industry environment. The business alters its price ranges according to such changes. In this element of the marketing mix, Nike Inc. successfully uses its pricing strategies to maximise its profits while emphasising high value in promoting its products and brand.

Place/Distribution in Nike's Marketing Mix

This element of the marketing mix outlines the location/ venues where the company's products are sold, accessed or distributed. Nike Inc. sells its sports shoes, apparel and equipment through a large number of outlets worldwide. The following form Nike's distribution strategy, arranged according to significance –

- ***Retail stores**: Retail stores are the most important platforms where Nike products are sold because they are strategically located and easily accessible in various markets around the world. These retailers include large firms like Lifestyle, as well as small local and regional stores.*
- ***Nike's online store:** Customers can purchase Nike's sports shoes, apparel and equipment through the company's online store.*
- ***Niketown retail outlets (company-owned):** These outlets are company-owned and help gain access to market information that supports corporate strategic management about marketing strategies and tactics for current, new and emerging products of the competitors.*

Nike Inc. regulates the distribution and sale of its products, majorly through its online store and Niketown retail outlets. However, the company has limited control over the distribution and sale of its products via other retail outlets.

Nike Inc.'s Promotion

This element of the marketing mix involves the tactics that Nike uses to communicate with its target markets. The company depends on the valuable promotion of its products to maintain a strong brand image. It uses promotional tactics to communicate to the target customers about its products and persuade these consumers to purchase them. The following are Nike's promotional activities –

- ***Advertising:*** *Nike heavily relies on advertisements involving high-profile celebrity endorsers, such as professional athletes and sports teams.*
- ***Personal selling:*** *Sales personnel at Niketown retail outlets are trained to persuade target consumers to buy the company's products.*
- ***Direct marketing:*** *Direct marketing activities involve direct communications with colleges, local sports teams and other organisations.*
- ***Sales promotions:*** *Nike sometimes applies discounts and special offers to attract more customers and generate more sales. These offers and discounts form the organisation's sales promotions.*

Nike Inc.'s Publicity (PR)

Nike Inc. sponsors and provides financial support to other organisations like community-based network to promote its athletic shoes, apparel and equipment. Based on the tactics included in this element of Nike's marketing mix, the business depends on its relations with high-profile endorsers like elite athletes to succeed in promoting its business and products to the national and international sporting goods market.

BENEFITS OF SPORTS MARKETING

Sports Marketing generates certain impulsive purchase behaviour amongst fans during sporting events. The number of new memberships at sports clinics, recognition and sales of sports products are generated during certain seasonal sporting events. These create large benefits for the companies that use these events to advertise.

Benefits are not only created for the athletes but also the leagues and the managers because of a significant increase in new memberships and fundraising for the sports teams included. The marketing of events is effective and help a sports customer understand what is available for their entertainment. Marketing strategies can also elevate sports teams and an athlete's social status as well.

Sports Marketing is not only advantageous for athletes, teams and associations but also for companies that sponsor and promote sports.

- **Advantages for the athletes:** Athletes, teams and organisations enjoy direct revenue from their endorsement deals. Being the face of a brand makes them more and more accessible to people who do not follow sports. This can encourage people to follow sports for the sake of this athlete or team leading to the increased revenue from ticket sales. Sports Marketing creates awareness and interest in a sport which leads to benefits for everybody associated with it. The benefit from the media rights also grows with promoting sports.
- **Advantages for sponsors**: Business organisations benefit from sponsoring sporting teams and events because they receive revenue from the deal. Additionally, they can utilise this event or team to endorse their products in return. Followers of sports or fans of a particular team will be informed about the product through the endorsement and take an interest in them. Using the endorsement of a celebrity athlete is a positive way of ensuring increased sales and profit. By entering into deals with sports organisations, sponsors can promote major

events and associate themselves with the event, which benefits sponsors in the long run.

- **Advantages for viewers:** Viewers can gain awareness of different sports and sporting events through Sports Marketing. Sports Marketing allows fans to interact with their favourite athletes through promotional events. It also focuses on raising interest and participation in sports among viewers.
- **Advantages for venue location:** The cities and countries which host major sporting events benefit impressively as a result of Sports Marketing. The event is often promoted with an emphasis on the country or city which is hosting it, such as the Olympics. The city or country receives its revenues directly because of the taxes. Additionally, a major sporting event such as a World Cup leads to an increase in tourism. Fans of the sport or a particular team or athlete often travel to this particular location to view the event in person. If the event is promoted well then it ensures revenue from the tourism industry.

SUMMARY

Marketing involves an exchange of offerings that have value for the customers or clients. It has within its purview the activities, the processes and the structures involved in the creation and delivery of the same. The offerings can include an entire bundle consisting of tangible and intangible goods as well as services. Marketing includes a full range of activities that an organisation undertakes to make certain that customers' needs are met and the organisation receives value in return. The marketing concept always puts the customer first: as the most important goal. Satisfying the customer must be the goal of everyone in the organisation. But the organisation also needs to ensure its survival and growth fuelled by profits. A proper balance between customer satisfaction and company's survival has to be established.

Sports Marketing is the application of most general marketing practices to sport-related products and services. It involves the marketing of other consumer products or services through sport. Three aspects make Sports Marketing unique – The Sports Product, The Sports Industry, The Sports Consumer. Sports products as provided by sporting organisations can be divided into the base product and product extensions. The core product will be the initial event, game or competition and the product extensions will be all the goods and services that are related to the core product.

The 3 Cs of marketing, a strategic marketing concept takes into consideration 3 areas to develop an effective marketing strategy – The Consumer, The Company, The Competitor. As a rule, in marketing, the marketing mix is always viewed as the 4 Ps of marketing – Product, Price, Place, Promotion. However, in Sports Marketing, there is a need for an expanded role that publicity/ PR plays – Sports Product, Sports Price, Sports Place (Sports Distribution), Sports Promotion, Publicity or PR. The 4 Ps and 3 Cs together need to be considered in co-relation with each other. The order in which they are considered is not as relevant.

Sports Marketing is advantageous for athletes, teams and associations as well as companies that sponsor and promote sports.

Chapter 2

Marketing in a Sporting Environment

INTRODUCTION

A group of organisations involved in producing various products and providing different types of services are termed as an industry. The working environment of the industry has a large influence on the activities of any business. The music industry is known for its genres like rock music, country music, jazz, classical, etc. The television industry includes sitcoms, soap operas, talk shows, movies, reality shows, etc. Similarly, the sports industry also has various verticals. They are either categorised based on sports like cricket, football, hockey, kabaddi, swimming, badminton, tennis and athletics or based on various areas like sports events, grassroots development, performance development, sports analytics, etc. The sports industry comprises key players that operate in the industry –

- Sporting national governing body, sports associations and federations.
- Sports leagues, franchisees and clubs.
- Sports consultancy firms.

- Sports talent management firms.
- Sports events and operations.

A business environment is a combination of organisations, people and factors that may be controllable or uncontrollable by the industry affecting their activities. It includes external forces, factors and institutions that are beyond the control of the business and affect its functioning. These include customers, competitors, suppliers, government and social, political, legal and technological factors, etc. While some of these factors or forces might have a direct influence over the business, others might operate indirectly. Thus, business environment includes all elements which have a direct or indirect bearing on its functioning. Each key player in the sports industry is also influenced by controllable or uncontrollable factors that affect their operation in the industry. They need to study and gain a good understanding of the factors affecting their environment to develop strategies that will grow their business. This will also help them gain an advantage over the competitors. All the marketing strategies and decisions should be based on the respective industry standards, data, norms and trends.

The external environment of the industry along with the internal environment of the business has an impact on the business enterprise. This unit gives an insight into the sporting industry and the environment which affects the organisations, players and customers.

THE SPORTS MARKETING ENVIRONMENT

The marketing environment of a company has several internal and external factors which can potentially impact the way it builds its relationships with its target customers.

In the sporting context, the Sports Marketing Environment includes the influences or variables of the external and internal environment of a sports organisation that controls the marketing activities' capability to build and maintain a relationship with the sports customer. A range of environmental forces affects an organisation's marketing strategies and tactics. Few of the forces are controllable whereas a few are uncontrollable by the sports marketer. It is vital to modify the organisation's marketing activities as per the shifting sporting environment. This modification will help the organisation take advantage of the positive factors and manage the negative factors. An organisation's Sports Marketing Environment can be divided into two types –

1. **Internal environment**: The internal environment focuses on the specifics of the internal nature of a sporting organisation. It includes all the factors and forces prevalent within the controllable environment of a sporting organisation. These factors affect the choices, activities and decisions of any organisation. This environment includes the various factors of the organisation like employees, finances, production of sports goods, objectives, strategies, etc. It also includes the Sports Marketing mix, namely, sports product (athlete, apparel, sport event, etc.), sports pricing, sports place/ distribution, sports promotion and publicity. For example, associations and federations, say Indian Olympic Association's (IOA) internal environment includes factors like their objectives, various initiatives/schemes, employees, structures, processes, internal revenue management, relationship with external stakeholders like associations and federations, etc. Meanwhile, a sports league like Pro-Kabaddi League's (PKL) internal environment consists of their objectives, various teams participating in the league, workforce including coaches, support staff, management employees, revenue generation strategies, promotional activities, strategies to reach out to PKL fans, athlete publicity, etc.

2. **External environment**: The external environment focuses on the external factors and forces beyond the controllable environment of a sporting organisation. These

factors include technological advancements affecting the industry, political or legal factors like Gross Domestic Product (GDP) as well as social and economic factors like an economic recession or global pandemic. For example, IOA's external environment includes supporting governing policies by other sporting governing bodies like Sports Authority of India (SAI), political forces, technological forces, economic situation, laws, climate, social and cultural forces which affect the decision making for activities planned by it. On the other hand, leagues like PKL, are affected not only by political forces, technological changes, economic situation, laws, climate, social and cultural forces but also by the operations of other leagues like IPL, ISL and emergency events like pandemic, war, etc.

The external environment is further classified into –

- Micro Environment.
- Macro Environment.

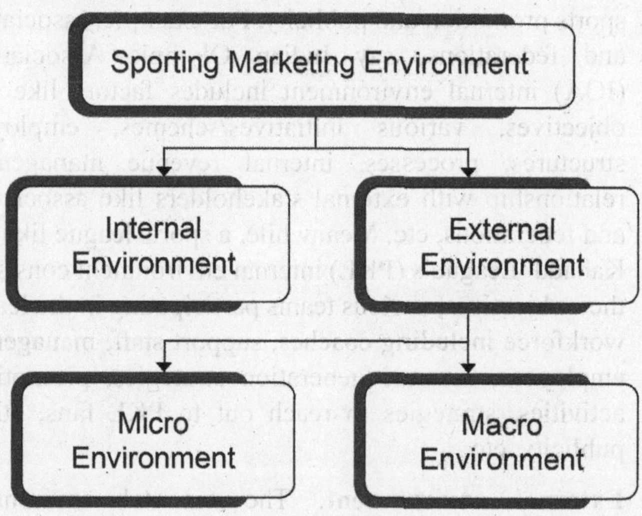

Figure 2.1 – Classification of Sporting Environment

MICRO AND MACRO ENVIRONMENT IN SPORTS

The Micro Environment

The Micro Environment includes external forces that are closely associated with the company. These forces affect the capacity of the organisation to serve its sports customers and are directly related to the business. These include –

- **Suppliers**: Businesses that provide the resources required by a sporting organisation and its competitors to produce sports goods and services are the suppliers. Sports marketing managers must keep a tab on the availability of resource supply as supply shortages, labour strikes, delays and other factors can affect the business in short run and negatively affect customer satisfaction in the long run. The price trends of suppliers also need to be monitored. Rising supply costs may force a price increase of the sports products and services which may harm the sales of the organisation.
- **Market intermediaries**: Market intermediaries include all the parties involved in distributing the product or service of a sporting organisation. These include physical distribution firms, marketing-service agencies and financial intermediaries.
- **Customers**: Sports customers consist of a target group of the organisation. The marketer needs to keep up with the constantly changing needs and requirements of its customers and should keep in touch with these changing needs by designing and implementing an appropriate strategy. The customers may be B2B or B2C, local or international and their reasons for buying the sports product will play a large role in how the marketer approaches the marketing of their products and services to these customers.
- **Partners**: Partners are all the separate entities and firms like advertising agencies, banking and insurance

companies, market research organisations, transportation companies, etc. that conduct business with a sports organisation. Marketers are also increasingly treating their suppliers as partners to create and deliver customer value.

- **Competitors**: Competitors are the players in the same market who targets similar customers as that of a sporting organisation. Organisations selling the same or similar sports products and services as the marketer's organisation is a market competitor. The way the competitor sells their products, their pricing strategy and their product differentiation needs to be taken into consideration. The marketer needs to leverage all of the above to reap better results and get an advantage over the competitors.
- **Public**: The sports organisation's micro environment also includes the public. A public is any set of customers that has an actual or potential impact on a sporting organisation's ability to achieve its objectives and serve its customers. The various categories of public that can make an impact come from the areas of media, government, finance, citizen-action, internal as well as general.

The Macro Environment

The Macro Environment constitutes all the external factors and forces which influence the sporting industry as a whole but do not have a direct effect on the business of a sports organisation. The marketing decisions of a sports organisation are developed with the factors in the macro world. These factors cannot be influenced by the marketer as they are external and uncontrollable. The strategies have to be developed in a way to monitor the external environment and moderate the effects of these factors on the organisation's business.

The factors of the Macro Environment are grouped as follows –

- **Demographic environment**: It is the study of population in terms of age, gender, size, location, occupation, race and other statistics along with the characteristics of each element.

- **Social and Cultural environment**: It studies the changing preferences, tastes, purchasing behaviour and priorities of customers.
- **Legal environment**: The legal environment establishes how a business should operate in a society within the existing framework.
- **Political environment**: It consists of government agencies, pressure groups and laws that influence and restrict the various organisations and individuals in a given society.
- **Economic environment**: The economic environment consists of factors that affect the consumer's spending patterns and purchasing power. It studies the demand for products in economy and can impact both the organisation's strategy along with the consumer's decision-making process.
- **Technological environment**: It incorporates the variables that lead to innovative work and advancement in communication technology. It also studies the induction of innovation in the business environment and barriers that may affect technology.

Demographics involve the study of population trends. It critically examines factors that influence population rise or decline, evaluates different age groups in a population, and analyses important factors like its population size, density, age structure, birth rates, death rates, sex ratio, etc. In the sporting industry, demographic parameters are used to study large fan bases which could be seen as target markets. Organisations use demographics to decide their next course of action or strategy.

The growth of sports franchises has used the study of demographics to develop a marketing strategy to place professional sports teams. The sports marketers or owners look at the demographics of a particular sport to decide the best place to create or relocate a sports team. The demographics of a particular sport, average viewership age group, population of that area, etc. may also be considered.

Sports marketers can do extensive demographic studies in different aspects pertaining to fan behaviour — like how they attend games at the stadium, how they purchase fan merchandise, or how they vary in income, lifestyle and attitudes. Organisations also conduct a study on the demographics of their consumers while introducing a new product. For example, Gatorade is a popular sports drink consumed worldwide. Their initial product was just the drinks but they began variation and expanding their product line based on the study of the demographics, likes and needs of the athlete. Gatorade used this information to then market their products. Expansion began with the introduction of new flavours in the sports drink and continued with the launch of protein powders, bars, shakes, chews and equipment.

The economic environment in sports is dependent on the macro and micro economic factors like spending habits of fans, their purchasing capacity, incomes of athletes and fans which leads a sports organisation to adjust its marketing strategy accordingly. The socio-cultural environment takes into account fan behaviour, preferences and needs characterised by cultural differences.

The technological environment creates new technologies which lead to the emergence of new products and new market opportunities. Some technological changes evolve over some time whereas some changes are sudden, strong and disrupt the pattern. The sports marketer should be aware of the general trends that influence the marketing strategies and predict the trends in the near future. There are several technological advancements seen in recent times that hold the potential to influence Sports Marketing in a significant way, be it traditional or non-traditional sports –

1. Rapid growth of Gaming and ESports.
2. Increase in application of Artificial Intelligence across sectors.

3. Use of sensors and data analytics to evaluate performance.
4. The blockchain as an important part of life.
5. Online fan engagement to be a competitive space.
6. Virtual and Augmented Reality will be embraced.
7. Betting and Fantasy Sports are on the rise.

All organisations have to operate in a regulatory environment and adhere to the local, state and national legislation. The sports marketer's role is to understand the guidelines the legislation imposes and steer the organisation accordingly. Organisations have to adhere to the same while planning and implementing marketing activities. These forces can vary in their scale and can affect organisations differently. Changes in the government at a national level may have a noticeable impact on the marketing activities of quasi-government sporting authorities than for the privately-owned smaller sports firms.

To sum it up, the micro environment affects the working of a particular business to which they relate to whereas the macro environment affects the functioning of all the business organisations operating in any industry.

DOMAINS WITHIN THE SPORTING ENVIRONMENT

As discussed in Unit 1, Sports Marketing involves the application of marketing principles to promote sports goods and services, as well as the marketing of non-sport and sport-related products and services through an association with sport. This involves the marketing of sports bodies, their codes, their personalities, their events, their activities, their actions, their strategies and their image. (Van Heerden,1998). This leads to two unique approaches in the Sports Marketing Environment, namely,

- Marketing THROUGH sports.
- Marketing OF sports.

Fullerton & Merz (2008) designed a model (Fig 2.1) that showcases the Four Domains of Sports Marketing to identify strategies and tactics used by sporting organisations in these four key domains. This theoretical model has the following four domains –

1. **Theme-based**

In this domain, traditional marketing strategies are used to incorporate a sports theme into the marketing activities for non-sports products. This might involve the usage of a sports-related platform to advertise non-sports products. An important aspect of theme-based strategies is that the sports marketer's efforts are not projected upon an official relationship with any specific sports property in its effort to create the sports overlay for its marketing efforts.

The sports marketer's actions are not directly relevant or have any sort of direct relationship with a sporting organisation is one of the key components of a theme-based strategy. This type of domain has the lowest level of integration with the sports industry as compared to all the other domains.

The elements of the Sports Marketing mix (5Ps) can also use a theme-based strategy by incorporating sports into them. Organisations embed sports themes into their product strategies to connect with the customers. The Indian Premier League (IPL) games are a very good example of how organisations use technology and various mediums for promotional and publicity strategies. The TV audience views different advertisements of various products throughout the season in IPL themes. Pricing strategies for these organisations might be different and they might have a strategy where they offer discounts to customers if they have tickets to a particular match in IPL. Organisations may have a booth to sell their products at the stadiums where the IPL matches are held.

Example: Bournvita's campaign on #Taiyaari Jeet Ki

In a promo campaign, Bournvita, a brand of malted and chocolate malt drink mixes manufactured by Cadbury, a subsidiary of Mondelez International, shows an inspiring story of a fighter son and a supportive mother. This advertisement begins with the son being injured due to an accident that stops him from participating in professional swimming. It depicts how his mother supports and teaches him to have faith during adverse situation. She helps him figure out his progress towards the path of recovery. The catch-line of the ad, "Himmat tab nahin dikhaye jaate jab dikhana aasan ho," which means that displaying courage and bravery in comfortable situations is easy and has no point.

2. **Product-based**

In this domain, the efforts of the sports marketer to market sports products using traditional marketing strategies when she/he has no official relationship with the sports entity/ organisation/ individual used in its marketing efforts. The organisation using these strategies is very unlikely to have a sense of a sports theme beyond the offering of the product. These strategies may involve initiatives by sports marketers for equipment and attire to reduce prices and provide incentives for the retailers.

For example, Indian retail brands like Nivia sports, Cosco, Shiv-Naresh, etc. have utilised traditional forms of promotion by –

- *Distribution of flyers and business cards.*
- *Publishing articles based on interviews with journalists, students and others.*
- *Supported community, sports and other special events.*
- *Submitted own press releases used by others in blogs, articles, radio broadcasts, etc.*
- *Paid for sections in trade magazine business listings.*
- *Paid for Ads in local newspapers, magazines and radio broadcasts.*
- *Promotional merchandise. For example, pens, keychains, t-shirts, tote bags and their goods.*
- *Engaged in celebrity promotions.*

3. **Alignment-based**

In this domain, the sports marketers of non-sports products who officially associate themselves with sports properties via one or more of the four forms of sponsorship namely; traditional sponsorships, athlete endorsements, licensing agreements and venue naming rights.

Many organisations offering non-sports products align themselves officially to sporting organisations to represent a high level of integration within the sports marketing environment. Digital marketing has expanded the market exponentially. This has expanded avenues for sporting organisations to develop and expand their traditional marketing strategies. For example, Vivo bagged the title sponsor of Indian Premier League (IPL) in a 5-year deal to market their non-sports brand.

Example: Old Pepsi Ad India – Sachin Tendulkar – "Yeh dil maange more"

Pepsi, a carbonated soft drink manufactured by PepsiCo Inc, came up with a very popular advertisement around the early 2000s when Sachin Tendulkar was at the peak of his career. Millions of people all over the world started looking up to this cricketer from Mumbai who was refining the game of cricket and eventually went on to be called "God of Cricket". The ad shows children playing gully cricket wearing Sachin's mask and were surprised and spellbound with admiration when they found that their hero was also one of them hiding behind a mask. Every child wanted to be like him.

Example: Panini FIFA partnership

Panini, an Italian company produces stickers, books, magazines, comics, magazines, trading cards and other products through its publishing subsidiaries. They have had a long partnership with FIFA and have held the official license for the production of the World Cup sticker collection since 1970 in Mexico. As technology advances, Panini diversified its strategy and adopted the digital way by introducing the Panini sticker album app. Along with physical sticker collections, they also released free digital sticker albums for avid football fans. This strategy generated higher levels of awareness among fans and increased demand for their products.

4. **Sports-based**

This domain is characterised by the official partner of a sports property who are selling other related sports products.

Due to the role of sports in both the product and integration components, this domain may reflect maximum dependence on sports-oriented initiatives.

A marketer of a sports-related products might enter a traditional sponsorship contract with a sports team, event and or athlete. This strategy of choosing any one element to sponsor may seem easier and cost-effective. But it is speculated that a strategy focusing on sponsoring all three elements (team, event and athlete) is more beneficial than focussing on one. This speculation has proven effective in terms of reaching out to the target audience.

Example: Star Sports – Mauka Mauka – India v/s Pakistan WC 2015

Star Sports, is a sports channel owned by Star India Pvt Ltd, a subsidiary of The Walt Disney Company India. Star Sports launched a Mauka Mauka advertisement, during the 2015 ICC World Cup to promote the India vs. Pakistan match and show that Pakistan gets another Mauka (opportunity) to beat India. The 40 seconds ad was made by an advertising agency called Ogilvy India which was an extension of the 'Patake kab phodenge' campaign (When will we burst the firecrackers). The ad featured a Pakistani fan awaiting his chance to burst crackers after his team wins against India. Years pass and he ages but India keeps defeating Pakistan in all World Cup matches. He keeps waiting for his mauka to burst the firecrackers but is dejected as Pakistan always loses to India. Many users on social media platforms openly expressed their displeasure over its tone which goes against the spirit of the game. However, the ad generated over 1.7 million YouTube views within a day after it was released in 2015. The music of the Mauka song went viral with people making it their ringtones during the World Cup. The success of this ad encouraged Star Sports to produce a whole series of the campaign during the World Cup 2015.

Example: Adidas

Adidas, the largest sportswear manufacturer in Europe, and the second-largest in the world employs a strategy where they sponsor all three, i.e., team, event and athlete. Adidas has a record-breaking 10-year kit deal with Manchester United that costs them approximately £750Mn. They also sponsor many other events and tournaments including FIFA, UEFA and tournament ball for 7 different Olympics games. They have also sponsored different Indian athletes from a variety of sports like Hima Das – athletics, Rohit Sharma – cricket, Kuldeep Yadav – cricket, Nikhat Zareen – boxing, Siddhanth Banthia – tennis and many others. They have also sponsored many international athletes like Stuart Broad – cricket, Lionel Messi – football.

Fig 2.2 below represents the diagram of the four domains in the Sports Marketing Environment –

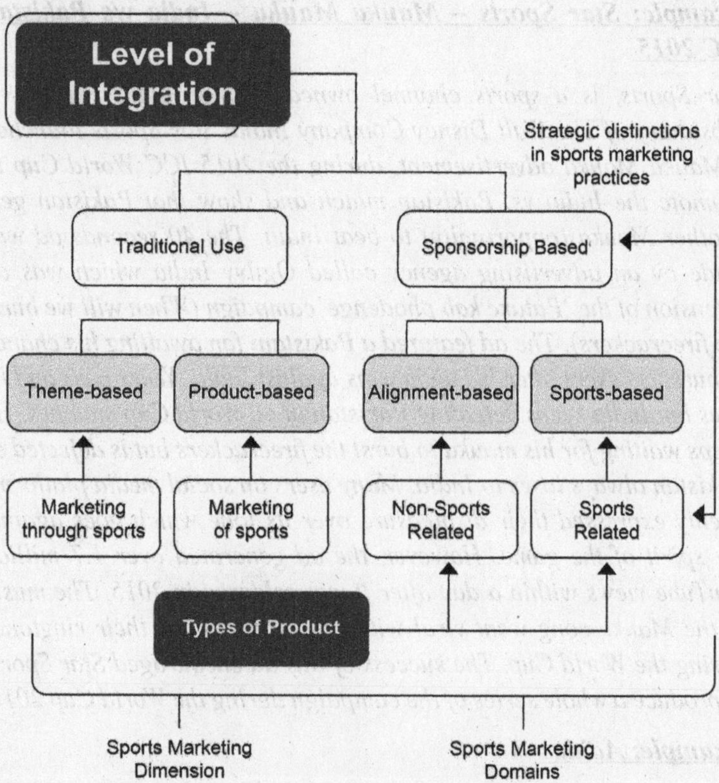

Figure 2.2 – Four Domains of Sports Marketing

Source: Fullerton, S./Merz, G.R.: The Four Domains of Sports Marketing: A Conceptual Framework, in Sports Marketing Quarterly, 2008, 17, p. 90 108.

The first two domains, theme-based and product-based are more traditionally used, while the latter two, alignment-based and sports-based are more sponsorship-based.

SWOT ANALYSIS

A SWOT analysis is a commonly used framework developed by Albert Humphrey at the Stanford Research Institute (SRI) to assess the internal and external environments of any organisation. SWOT analysis is generally a part of an organisation's strategic planning process. It provides help with planning and decision-making because it allows the organisation to understand the current situation and provides a way to generate strategic alternatives. SWOT stands for Strengths, Weaknesses, Opportunities and Threats. A SWOT analysis is an effective framework for ascertaining strengths, weaknesses, opportunities and threats that an organisation faces. It is vital to leverage strengths, minimise threats, take advantage of opportunities available while managing the threats.

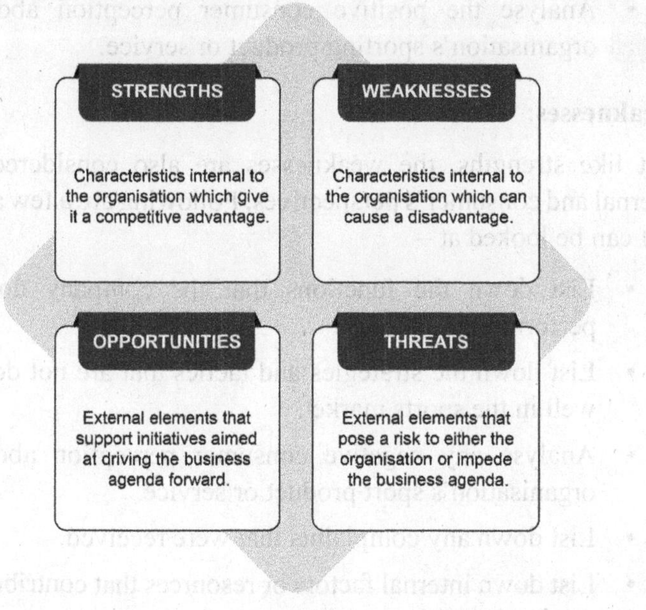

Figure 2.3 – SWOT analysis framework

Conducting a SWOT analysis

There are various ways to conduct a SWOT analysis. Regardless of which way an organisation chooses to structure the SWOT analysis, the sports marketer has to begin by asking a series of questions.

Strengths:

The strengths are considered from an internal and consumer's perspective. Following are a few aspects that can be looked at –

- List down the advantages of the organisation.
- List down the selling proposition adopted.
- List down the unique resources available with the organisation as opposed to its competitors.
- List down the low-cost resources the organisation has access to.
- Analyse the positive consumer perception about the organisation's sporting product or service.

Weaknesses:

Just like strengths, the weaknesses are also considered from internal and consumer's perspectives. Following are a few aspects that can be looked at –

- List down the functions that the company does not perform well.
- List down the strategies and tactics that are not doing so well in the sports market.
- Analyse any negative consumer perception about the organisation's sport product or service.
- List down any complaints that were received.
- List down internal factors or resources that contribute to a weaker brand image.

Opportunities:

Opportunities are considered from an external perspective. Following are a few aspects that can be looked at –

- List down any good opportunity that may be available in the marketplace.
- Some trends that the organisation can capitalise on.
- Changes in technology or market dynamics that the organisation can take advantage of.
- Changes in behaviour, lifestyle, social patterns, etc. that the organisation can take advantage of.

Threats:

Just like opportunities, the threats are also considered from an external perspective. Following are a few aspects that can be looked at –

- List down any obstacles that the organisation might face.
- Study the competitors and list down what the competition is doing better.
- Analyse if a technology change is threatening the position of the organisation.
- Analyse the threats and risks that the organisation's weaknesses might lead to.
- Analyse if changes in behaviour, lifestyle, social patterns pose a threat to the organisation.

Case study: SWOT analysis of Decathlon

With presence in more than 45 countries, Decathlon, a French sporting goods player, is one of the largest sports goods retailers in the world. Founded by Michel Leclercq in Lilly, France, in the year 1976, Decathlon's expansion journey started a decade later, with entries into other European markets — like Germany, Spain and Italy. It has also expanded to major Asian countries like India, China, Malaysia, the Philippines and employs over 82,000 + personnel of 80 different nationalities.

Their product mix has a wide range — from sports goods like tennis racquets to bicycles to advanced scuba gear! With an average store size of 4,000 sq. feet, they own over 20 brands and have R&D facilities all over France, dedicated to developing innovative designs. Each sporting group or brand has a dedicated design tool and product development section. As of January 2020, Decathlon had 1,647 stores in 57 countries.

Below is the SWOT analysis of Decathlon –

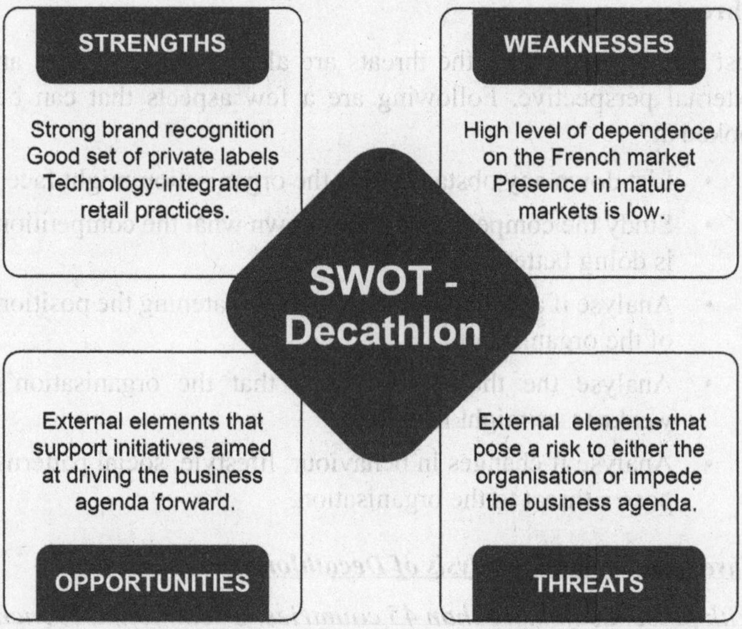

Figure 2.4 – SWOT analysis of Decathlon

<u>Case study: SWOT analysis of Wimbledon Championship</u>

The Wimbledon Championship is the oldest and most prestigious tennis tournament in the world. It has been held at the All-

England Club in Wimbledon, London, since 1877 and is played on outdoor grass courts. Wimbledon is one of the four Grand Slam tennis tournaments, the others being the Australian Open, the French Open and the US Open. Wimbledon is the only major tournament still played on grass courts which are traditional tennis playing surfaces.

SWOT - Wimbledon

STRENGTHS

- High on traditions, like white clothing, involvement of royalty, strawberry & cream etc.
- The fast grass courts that have witnessed the skills of some of the greatest serve and volley exponents of the game, like John McEnroe, Boris Becker, Pete Sampras, Roger Federer etc.
- High-quality coverage in different parts of the world.
- Cherished by many pros as the one tournament they all want to win.
- Well disciplined Ball Boys and Ball Girls with best in class training.

WEAKNESSES

- Slowing down of the grass courts in recent years which makes the players stick to the baseline.
- Extremely short grass court season beacuse of the small gap after the major European Clay season.

OPPORTUNITIES

- Unlocking of revenue through sponsor branding around the court.
- Use of Wimbledon brand to nurture more young talent into the game using pull of the tournament.
- Rekindling the serve and volley brand of tennis by making the courts faster.

THREATS

- Challenges in holding on to the tag of the premier in tennis in a more globalised and commercialised eco-system.
- Other Grand Slam tournaments.

Figure 2.5 – SWOT analysis of Wimbledon Championships

PESTLE ANALYSIS

PESTLE analysis, also known as PESTEL, PESTLIED, STEEPLE, SLEPT, etc. arises from a scanning tool ETPS which is thought to be created by Harvard professor Francis Aguilar in his book, "Scanning the business environment" in 1967. Over the years, many variations of the term have been used.

PESTLE analysis is a framework for assessing the important features of any business environment. In a PESTLE analysis, each component of the external environment identified falls under the following headings –

- Political.
- Economic.
- Social.
- Technological.
- Legal.
- Environmental.

The PESTLE analysis framework is intended for the sports marketer to identify growth opportunities or potential threats. PESTLE is useful for the following reasons –

1. Assists in recognising business or growth opportunities for the sporting organisation.
2. Provides warning of significant threats that may arise much in advance.
3. Aids in shaping the strategy that should be undertaken and the modification of an existing strategy.
4. Reveals the direction of change within the sporting industry.
5. Assists in developing an objective view of a new environment.
6. Assists in breaking free of assumptions when an organisation enters a new market, region or country.

It is a great idea to conduct a comprehensive situational analysis before putting any sports marketing strategy or tactics into place. PESTLE analysis needs to be undertaken frequently because the conditions in the environment change very frequently. This repeated analysis of all components helps the sports marketer identify changes in the macro environment and adjust the organisation's strategy and tactics accordingly. Successfully monitoring and creating an effective response to the changes in the macro environment, the sports marketer will be able to employ strategies to differentiate her/his sporting organisation from its competitors and potentially create a competitive advantage.

Below are some of the categories of external factors that affect the sporting organisation –

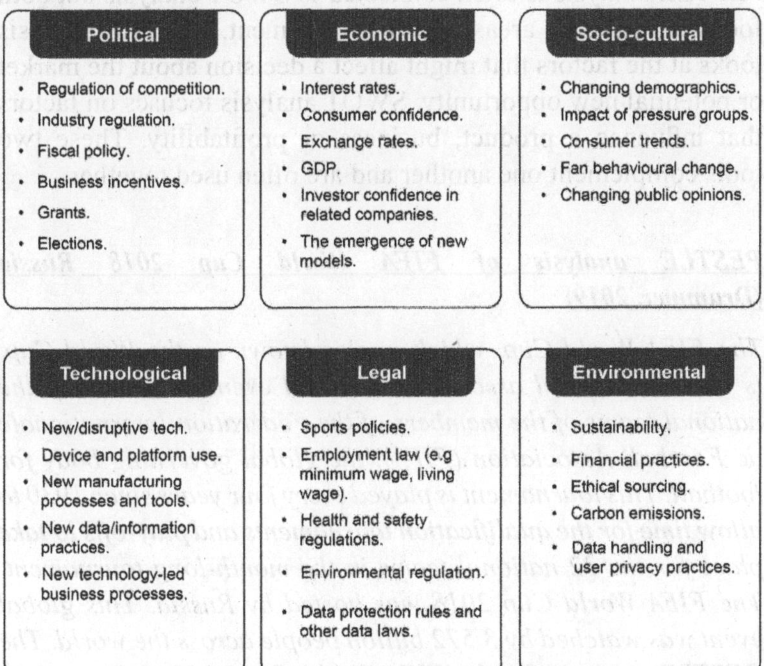

Figure 2.6 – PESTLE analysis – Categories

\Ref: https://www.targetinternet.com/how-to-conduct-a-pestel-analysis/

The above categories are starting points to help analyse and monitor the external marketing environment in a structured manner. The outcome of these assessments can further be used to identify weaknesses and threats aiding the analysis of the SWOT of a sporting organisation. The sports marketer can also take ideas/ data from team members, consultants, research companies, fans, consumers and other stakeholders involved. The analysis should consider the current situation as well as predict future developments that might affect the organisation. Although it is difficult to predict certain factors, especially social trends or sports events, adding a quantum layer to the analysis with multiple outcomes will be useful.

PESTLE analysis is often connected to SWOT analysis but both focus on different areas of the environment. PESTLE analysis looks at the factors that might affect a decision about the market or potential new opportunity. SWOT analysis focuses on factors that influence a product, business or profitability. These two tools complement one another and are often used together.

PESTLE analysis of FIFA World Cup 2018 Russia (Drummer, 2019)

The FIFA World Cup, which is also known as the World Cup, is an international association football event contested by the national teams of the members of the Fédération Internationale de Football Association (FIFA), the global governing body for football. This tournament is played every four years since 1930 to allow time for the qualification tournaments and play-offs to take place for the 32 national teams in the month-long tournament. The FIFA World Cup 2018 was hosted by Russia. This global event was watched by 3.572 billion people across the world. The PESTLE analysis for the FIFA World Cup of 2018 focused on the event from a micro and macro perspective that would affect the games.

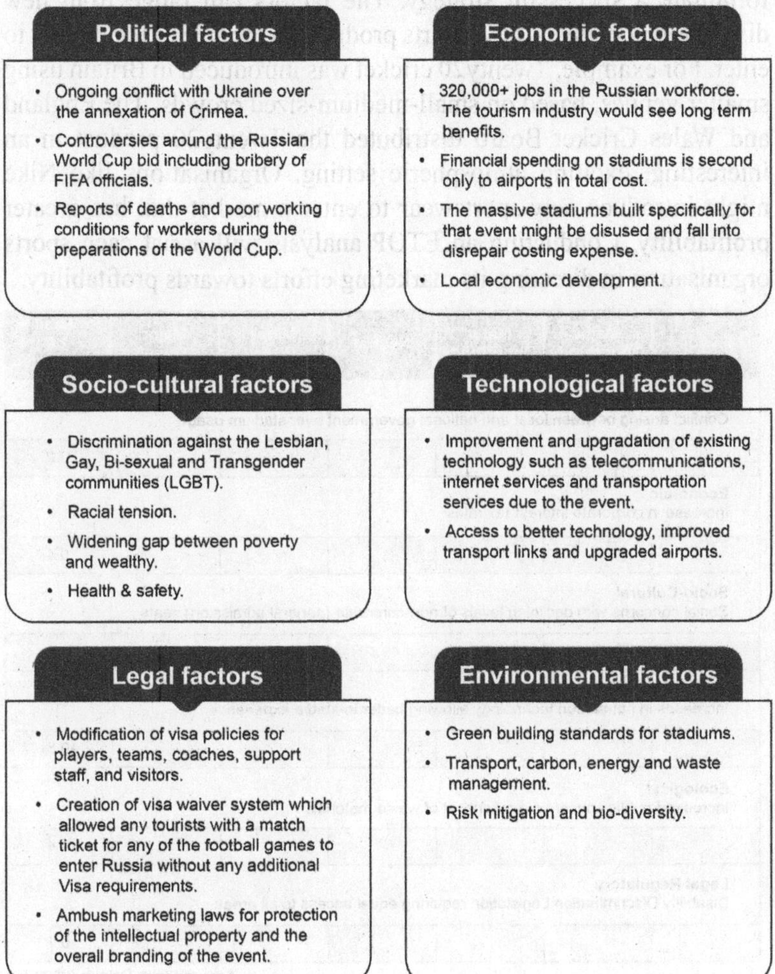

Figure 2.7 – PESTLE analysis of FIFA World Cup 2018 Russia

ETOP ANALYSIS

Environmental Threat and Opportunity Profile – ETOP was introduced by Palmer (2000). This concept allows the sports marketer to evaluate the potential of every opportunity. The greatest potential depends on factors that the sports marketer considers to formulate a successful strategy. The factors can range from new distribution channels, new sports products to the size of the market to enter. For example, Twenty20 cricket was introduced in Britain using smaller venues, based on small-medium-sized crowds. The England and Wales Cricket Board distributed the Twenty20 product in an interesting, exciting atmospheric setting. Organisations like Nike might introduce new sportswear to enter a market that has greater profitability. Conducting an ETOP analysis will assist each sports organisation in directing its marketing efforts towards profitability.

Factor	Major Opportunity	Minor Opportunity	Neutral	Minor Threat	Major Threat	Probability of Occurrence
Political Conflict arising between local and national government over stadium usage						
						0.2
Economic Increase in corporate interest tax rates						
						0.4
Socio-Cultural Social concerns with declining levels of non-corporate (general admission) seats						
						0.6
Technological Increases in flat-screen technology allowing better in-stadia experience						
						0.8
Ecological Increased public concern over disposal of waste materials						
						0.4
Legal Regulatory Disability Discrimination Legislation requiring equal access to all areas						
						0.1

Adapted from Palmer (2000:50)

Figure 2.8 – ETOP applied to National Sporting Facility in any given country
Source: Kitchin, P. (2007). Understanding the Sports Marketing Environment.

Fig 2.8 shows a basic application of all the environmental forces affecting the marketing activities of a national stadium in any country. The above demonstrates that a range of environmental forces may contain threats as well as opportunities for a sports marketer. For example, even though the structures of the stadium require few adjustments under the legislation of discrimination, the sports marketers could use this as an opportunity to feature the innovations of the stadium and the leadership role in the management of the facility. On the other hand, to improve the financials of the venue, increasing the proportions of seating for fans and reducing corporate access at the stadium is also a good way to capitalise on the opportunity. But this could also generate a negative impact or publicity as the national stadium is for the people and employing such a strategy will limit public access and use. The factor of probability should be used to prioritise the immediate attention to opportunities or threats of the sports marketer.

Case study: Adidas SWOT & PESTLE analysis (White, 2017) and (swotandpestle.com, 2020)

Adidas, a Germany-based sports shoe, clothing and apparel company was founded by Adolf Hassler in 1949. The company also has Reebok, Taylor Made and Rockport. Adidas is known to be one of the largest sportswear companies in Europe and in the world.

SWOT analysis of Adidas

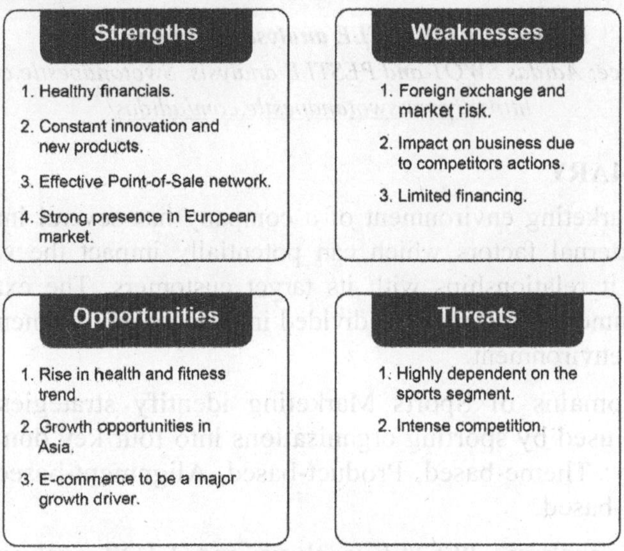

Figure 2.9 – SWOT analysis of Adidas (2020)

Source: *Adidas SWOT and PESTLE analysis. Swotandpestle.com* *https://www.swotandpestle.com/adidas/*

PESTLE analysis of Adidas

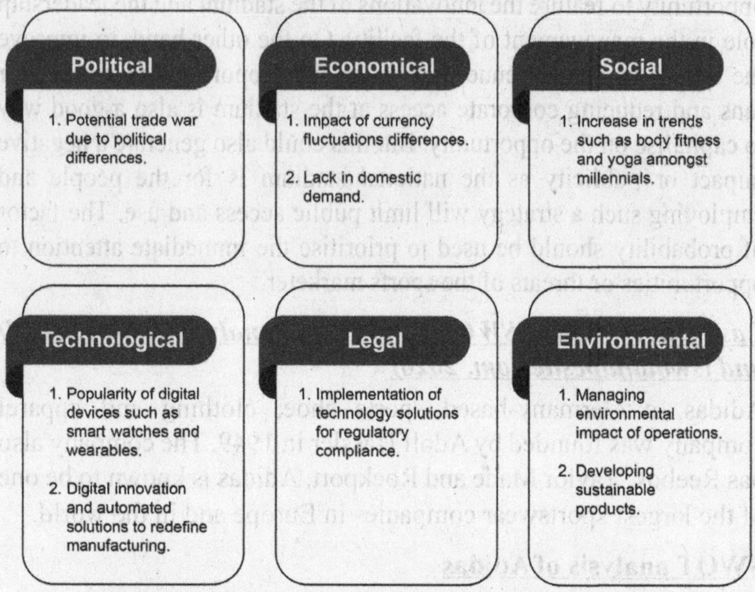

Figure 2.10 – PESTLE analysis of Adidas (2020)

Source: Adidas SWOT and PESTLE analysis. Swotandpestle.com https://www.swotandpestle.com/adidas/

SUMMARY

The marketing environment of a company has several internal and external factors which can potentially impact the way it builds it relationships with its target customers. The external environment can further be divided into micro environment and macro environment.

The domains of Sports Marketing identify strategies and tactics used by sporting organisations into four key domains, namely: Theme-based, Product-based, Alignment-based and Sports-based.

SWOT analysis, PESTLE analysis and ETOP analysis are prominent techniques used to gather environment information and assess the application of the same to a sports organisation.

Chapter **3**

Market Segmentation, Targeting and Positioning

INTRODUCTION OF SPORTS MARKETS

The sporting industry is a widespread business that covers the field of play and off-the-field components like food, collectible stands at the stadium, media rights and sponsorships. The amount of money spent every year in the sporting industry is catering to a passionate fan base. This business environment has many participants like rights owners, athletes, clubs, leagues, federations, sponsors, sports agencies and broadcasters, etc. The sports market comprises the sale of sports goods, services and related goods by various entities that offer different types of sports in the sporting industry. According to The Business Research Company report 2021, the value of the global sports industry has nearly reached $388.3 billion in 2020 at an increased compound annual growth rate (CAGR) of 3.4% ever since 2015. The sports market saw a decline from $458.8 billion in 2019 at a rate of – 15.4% mainly due to social distancing norms and lockdown imposed in various countries. The economic slowdown across countries contributed to the decline because of the COVID–19 pandemic. The sports market is expected to surge by 54.49% in 2025 and by 122.72% by 2030, from 2020, as per the report.

India's sports sponsorship report 2021 by GroupM Media India Private Limited states, "The size of the Indian Sports Industry in 2021 is estimated at INR 9,530 Cr ($ 1288 Mn). This takes into consideration Sports Sponsorship Spends, Media Spends on Sports Properties and Sports Celebrity Endorsement. The biggest share here goes to media, where advertisement expenses on TV, digital and print media were to tune of INR 3,657 Cr ($ 494 Mn); this accounts for 62% of the total." Sponsorship Spends include On Ground Sponsorships, Team Sponsorships and Franchise Fee which takes up 28% of the industry pie, which translates to an amount of INR 1,673 Cr ($ 226 Mn)." The report also states that approximately 10% of the expenditure comes from endorsement deals from the country's favourite sports heroes which amount to INR 564 Cr ($ 76 Mn). The 2020 lockdown also prompted growth in certain sectors like OTT platforms, a boom in ESports, social media influencers, etc. There was a significant week on week increase in the gamer base as well as viewership data during the lockdown.

PRODUCTS IN THE INDIAN SPORTS MARKET

A sports product does not only refer to a physical good that has been manufactured, i.e., apparel, shoes and equipment but also refers to services and ideas. Hence, in Sports Marketing, the term 'product' could indicate any of these –

- Goods – Physical items.
- A Service.
- An Idea.
- A combination of the above.

Sports products can further be characterised as a mix of tangible and intangible elements.

The principle advantage of buying a sports product is that the consumer receives the core benefits of the product from buying and using it. The consumer receives the benefits of the actual product as well as the additional features or add-ons of the product. A sports industry signifies a large number of sporting organisations which manufacture/ include a particular sports product or provide a specific sports service, whereas a sports market is the place where sports customers are present or exist.

The sports market contains the sale of sports products, services and related goods by entities that offer two types of sports, namely –

1. **Spectator Sports:** The sports that feature clubs or teams and independent athletes that play sporting events before a paying audience is spectator sports. For example, the team owners of a racing team enter their participants into racing events or other spectator sports events.

2. **Participatory Sports:** Sports that people participate in with or without spectators are participatory sports. For example, sports coaches, trainers who offer specialised support to participants in sporting events or competitions are part of participatory sports.

The sports market is seen as one that involves the sale of sports services and related goods. The organisations that are involved in these activities could either be engaged in bringing live sports to an audience, or in the running of clubs, teams and facilities related to sports.

Sports goods are apparel and equipment that will be required for participating in sports and prevent related injuries. Fitness goods are also a subset of sports goods that people use during fitness workouts. These goods help maintain overall fitness, improve muscle strength, flexibility, cardiovascular and pulmonary health of a person.

Indians have started focusing on their well-being. As a consequence, there is a rise in the number of fitness centres and gyms which is boosting the sales of goods in the sports market. Social media acts as another catalyst in pushing the growth of the sports market. Manufacturers are directly communicating with the audience through social media channels such as Instagram, Twitter, Facebook, Snapchat, etc. These platforms are used to promote and advertise the functionalities of sports goods to potential consumers. Innovations in domestic and international manufacturing technologies have led to the entry of a variety of advanced equipment and goods in the sports markets, like for instance, specialised training equipment, smart racquets, wearable devices, etc.

Sports product types prevailing in the sports market can be classified based on end usage as –

- **Balls used in the sports:** Balls are the most popular product type in the sports market due to the popularity of sports like cricket, hockey, tennis, football, basketball, bowling, handball, squash, etc. The usage of balls in international and domestic sports events in India like Hockey World League, World T20, IPL, PKL, Khelo India Games, gully cricket also boost growth for sports products.
- **Fitness related:** Fitness goods can further be categorised into Strength training goods and Cardiovascular training goods. Cardiovascular training goods help in the increase of muscular endurance and improvement in the performance of the heart and lungs. This further aids in the effective distribution of the blood and oxygen to the rest of the body. For example, treadmills, rowing machines, stationary bikes, ellipticals, etc. are some of the cardiovascular training goods that are popular in the sports market.
- **Service-oriented institutions:** End-use goods are further classified into health clubs/gyms, hotels, corporate offices, hospitals, medical centres and public institutions. Health clubs/gyms claim the leading sports market share because rising lifestyle diseases and high obesity rates have led to an increase in health consciousness amongst individuals.

  Any other goods that cannot be classified into the above categories but still contribute towards the growth of the sports market. For example, adventure sports goods, etc.

Being a diverse nation, sports market in India can be classified geographically as:

- West and Central India.
- North India.
- South India.
- East India.

West and Central India represent the largest market, because of the rising per capita income and rapid urbanisation in the region. Going ahead, the rise of ESports, increase in internet accessibility and rising sponsorships will drive the growth of the Indian sports market. An increase in regulation of sports and threats from home entertainment like OTT platforms, home game consoles and virtual reality headsets could deter the growth of sports market.

SPORTS PRODUCT TANGIBILITY SPECTRUM

Sports products can be viewed as having tangible as well as intangible elements; there are many products that tend to be mainly tangible or mainly intangible. The different kinds of products in the sports markets could be classified depending on where they appear on the tangibility spectrum.

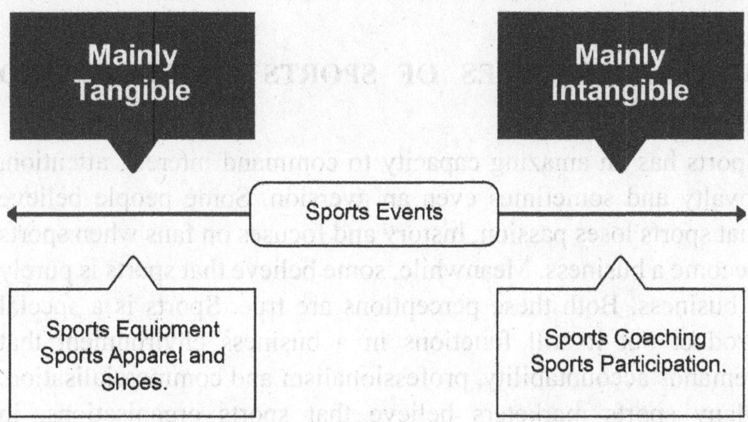

Figure 3.1 – Sports product tangibility spectrum continuum tool

Fig 3.1 indicates that some products like tennis balls, jerseys, equipment used in fitness centres, or different sports shoes and apparel are mainly tangible. Even though these products may offer intangible benefits the consumers want, these products are determined by their physical elements. If the physical aspect is taken away, the product is non-existent. On the other hand, participation in a tennis competition or taking swimming lessons are examples of sports products that are mainly intangible. There is a physical element part involved in this sports product like the tennis racquet or a swimsuit and swim goggles in this service, the sports product depends on its intangible service element. If such a service is removed, the product becomes invalid. Finally, sports events provide the perfect examples of a sports product that is a mixture of tangible and intangible elements. The intangible elements in any ISL game include the outcome of the match between Mumbai City FC and Goa FC on the field whereas the tangible elements include the merchandise, food and beverage offered as a part of the experience during the match. Fans usually look for a combination of these elements in any sporting event. The sports spectrum is a useful tool for sports marketers to develop a useful exercise to locate all their products on the spectrum scale.

SPECIAL FEATURES OF SPORTS PRODUCTS AND SPORTS MARKET

Sports has an amazing capacity to command interest, attention, loyalty and sometimes even an aversion. Some people believe that sports loses passion, history and focuses on fans when sports become a business. Meanwhile, some believe that sports is purely a business. Both these perceptions are true. Sports is a special product but it still functions in a business environment that demands accountability, professionalism and commercialisation. Many sports marketers believe that sports organisations, in whichever scope or size, can no longer be disconnected from the commercial world. Even non-profit sports clubs need to perform financially well to survive in the sporting environment despite high competition. Sports is a special form of business and needs to be put into a commercial framework just like any other enterprise. The key to formulating a good commercial framework is to understand the special features of sports products and sports markets along with their relevance to meet the needs and satisfaction of the sports consumers.

Following are some of the special features of sports products and market –

- **Emotion**

  Sports can stimulate emotional responses in fans which are rarely generated by other products. A bank customer or a consumer who identifies strongly with car insurance will not get a tattoo done of that bank or the logo of an insurance company. Sports fans are very passionate about teams, players and the game itself. This interest can become an obsession in some cases. This provides an emotional glue that helps retain a loyal fan even after an on-field failure. Many a times, emotions that are stimulated by sports can also have a negative effect. Sports organisations can have strong attachments to the past through the emotional intensity of nostalgia and club tradition, thus, ignoring efficiency, productivity and the need to adapt quickly to the changing market. For example, a change in the colours of a club or team to launch a more attractive look may not be adapted as it breaks the tradition.

- **On-field versus off-field success**

  Sports fans and clubs assess the performance of a sports team based on rankings, trophies, cups and championships won. However, on-field and off-field successes do not necessarily go together. A sports team may go bankrupt paying high salaries to the coaches and players to win the championship. On the contrary, the team may have a good standing financially but may not perform well on the field of play (FOP). Sports teams, clubs and organisations have to manage competing demands. They have to find a perfect balance where not only do they need to maximise profits to invest in their activities but also perform well on the FOP. Sports Marketing augments the possibility of an organisation to support the revenue without compromising on sporting performance.

- **It is competitive yet a level playing field**

  Generally, in business settings, an organisation has a desire to put competitors out of business. Less competition leads to more availability of customers. However, the sports market is different. Sports organisations competing in leagues count on the health of their competitors for their success. For example, fans are more attracted to a game where the winner is unknown and there is close competition. Domination in a league or competition can be defeating to that organisation as the fans' interest can decline. Sports leagues like IPL, PKL, ISL, etc. attract higher attendance and viewers when the prediction of the winner is difficult. For leagues and competitions to be successful, clubs need to be as competitive as possible. If the outcome of a match is predictable, it will not attract a large crowd which eventually will lead to a reduction in revenue collection from ticket sales, sponsorship and media.

- **Collaboration and rivalry**

  Sports clubs and teams must cooperate with their rival to render what the consumers want. They need their competitors to be successful and may cooperate with them to share revenues. They might trade players to uphold a competitive balance. In many industries, businesses will have an anti-competitive behaviour and will not be allowed to cooperate because of regulations in place that prohibit it. However, in sports markets, such arrangements are very common. For example, clubs and teams may share revenues, collectively fix prices, prevent other teams from entering the market to limit the amount of competition.

- **Variable quality**

  Businesses aim for certainty and predictability about product quality. However, certainty and predictability are not always valued in the sports markets. Sports events and experience is better when the game is unpredictable. Sports organisations depend upon the unpredictability factor to gain an advantage and be attractive to the fans. Attendance at sports games is higher when the result of the game is unpredictable leading to higher profits for the league, clubs and teams. Nonetheless, the absence of predictability leads to substantial variability in the quality of sports performances. Many factors like venue, weather, quality of opponents, injuries of players, close scores and size of the crowd can contribute to the variability of sports products. For example, a cricket match can be boring or frustrating sometimes, but fans still pay the same price. The sports marketers must try to improve the product in many effective ways like offering premium seats or including star athletes or providing entertainment or fashioning attractive facilities etc. The uncertain nature of sports games is just one of the important elements of a total experience for financial success.

- **Product and brand loyalty**

  Emotional attachments of sports consumers towards their favourite games, teams, players lead to strong product and brand loyalty. A test of sports product loyalty is when a consumer continues purchasing a product even though the price of a competing product reduces. A lifetime of bond is created between the fan and the sports product due to the massive amount of energy and time invested. Besides, the fan often considers their team as an extension of themselves and part of their self-identity.

Passionately supporting a particular sport or specific team or brand or specific competition leads to low cross elasticity of demand. Low cross elasticity of demand is an economic term that justifies the difficulty to replace or substitute one sports product for another. Many sports games or competitions have inelasticity of demand and a high degree of product loyalty. Although the fans might be unhappy with the result of the game or the refereeing or winning margin, etc. it is doubtful that they would change their sporting loyalty or preference. For example, if a fan's football team is playing a match and the match is not aired on television, it is highly unlikely that the fan would attend a hockey game or badminton game, irrespective of the attractiveness of the venue or free ticket. But the situation is different for other products. If a consumer bought a watch and she/he was not satisfied with the quality, she/he would likely consider changing outlets or brands the next time. In sports, it is not so simple to substitute products.

- **Supply schedule**

  A supply schedule indicates the ability of a business to modify its production rates to meet consumer demands. Some sports retail organisations can increase or decrease the production level of their products depending upon the demand. But sports clubs and teams have an inflexible production capability. Clubs and teams can play only a certain number of times during their season. If fans are unable to attend the game or reach the venue, that opportunity is lost forever. Even though sports leagues and teams may have a fixed schedule, it may be possible to increase the viewership by providing more seats, extending the playing season, changing the venue etc.

CONVERGENCE IN SPORTS MARKETS

Recent years have seen a convergence in the sports markets at different levels, such as –

1. **Media consumption:** This principle is based on the idea that new forms of media are more allowing and accepting of consumers' behaviour. Before the emergence of new media forms, sports fans used to just watch, listen or read about the game. But because of new media, fans can do more than just focus on the game. They can float effortlessly between watching a game, sharing a highlight, creating and sharing memes, buying merchandise and so on. Media convergence allows fans to take up more than one behaviour simultaneously.
2. **Fan participation:** This principle speaks about communities of fans who have a course of transitioning from consumers to active content producers. Fans are empowered to contribute and create fandom. Fans want to be a part of producing content in sports by providing analysis, sharing highlights, creating own insights and commentary over live matches, generating and sharing memes in the fan community.
3. **Collective intelligence:** This can be seen as a significant source of power in the connected world. This principle has more inclination towards being philosophical and is said to be quite tricky. This happens when very large groups of individuals come together, pool in their knowledge, skills and assets, thereby finding solutions to larger issues that affect the society.

These three principles have converged into sports business models and industries in the sports market. The table given below shows the convergence of sports market into different verticals based on the above three principles –

Sports — Leisure — Healthcare

Sports management	Leisure management	Healthcare management
Sports equipment	Tourism, travel, hoteling	Hospital management
Sports trading	Wellness (SPA)	Out-patient care
Sports facilities & infrastructures	Leisure facilities	Integrated care
Media & communications	Corporate leisure management	Health maintenance organisations
Sport consulting & coaching	Media & entertainment	Medical devices & equipment
Sports clubs & administrations	E-games	Pharma & nutrition industries
Sports associations	Sporty lifestyle products	Disease management
Sports communications	Leisurewear	Corporate fitness
Event management	Clerical services	Employee recreation programmes

Figure 3.2 – Convergence in Sports Markets

Source: *University of Potsdam. (2010). Cornerstones of Sports marketing. Uni-Potsdam.De.* ***https://www.uni-potsdam.de/fileadmin/projects/*** *professional-services/downloads/skripte ws/Wintersemester2018/SpM3_ Sports_Marketing 2018-19.pdf*

SEGMENTATION

To effectively market the product to the right consumer segment, the sports marketer must –

I) Identify the different profiles of customers and divide them into groups, based on clear parameters for the grouping (segmentation).

II) Select the segment or segments you want to market your product to (targeting).

III) Communicate, and deliver the benefits of the offering, to the chosen target segments (positioning).

In this section, let us discuss market segmentation.

Through market segmentation, we are dividing the market into different well-defined parts. The output of this is that each segment will be characterised by groups of customers who have certain similarities.

All organisations face difficulties in connecting with all the consumers in the broad and diverse market. They aim to focus on consumers within their capacity. Due to this, the marketers divide the market into groups of consumers or segments with well-defined needs. This strategy of dividing a market in a homogenous group is called as Segmentation. If the needs of the consumers in a segment match up very closely, then we are likely to have a smaller segment. However, in such cases, the consumers are likely to show willingness to pay higher premium on the products that will cater to their specific needs. Segmentation allows marketers to identify separate groups of consumers whose behaviour differs significantly from others. This allows the organisations to adjust the marketing mix to satisfy the needs of different market segments. The idea of segmentation is to concentrate all the marketing energy and force on creating sections to gain an advantage within the segment.

There are four commonly seen segmentation bases, which feature most often in marketing discourses –

1. **Geographic segmentation**

   Division of a market into different geographical groups, such as nations, states, regions, cities, neighbourhoods, climate, or population density is called geographic segmentation.

2. **Demographic segmentation**

   Division of a market into different groups based on variables such as age, gender, family size, income, occupation, education, religion, race, generation and nationality is called demographic segmentation.

   Demographic segmentation also includes –

   - **Age and life-cycle segmentation**: A market is divided into different age groups and life-cycle groups.

- **Gender segmentation:** A market is divided and based on gender.
- **Income segmentation:** A market divided and based on income levels.

3. **Psychographic segmentation**

   A market, when divided into different groups based on social class, lifestyle or personality characteristics, is called psychographic segmentation.

4. **Behavioural segmentation**

   A market, when divided into different groups based on consumer knowledge, attitudes, uses, or responses to a product, is called behavioural segmentation. Behavioural segmentation further includes –

   - **Occasion segmentation:** A market divided according to occasions when consumers get the idea to buy, actually make their purchase or use the purchased items.
   - **Benefit segmentation:** A market divided according to the benefits that consumers seek from the product.
   - Markets can also be segmented based on user states, usage rate and loyalty status.

Marketers use multiple segment bases to identify a well-defined target group. To effectively segment the market, the groups must be measurable, substantial, accessible, actionable and differentiable. Business markets can be segmented with similar variables along with additional ones like purchasing approaches, customer operating characteristics and situational factors. Organisations can also discover new segments by researching the hierarchy of attributes that the consumers will consider while choosing a brand.

Sports markets can be segmented on the basis of different criteria, like the nature of the sport in consideration, or where the revenue is coming from, or the part of the world where the market is located. Fig 3.3 shows the segmentation of the Sports Market; the different segments are discussed here along with their respective growth trends as per The Business Research Company Report 2021.

Segmentation by type of sports

- Spectator Sports.
- Participatory Sports.

The participatory sports market was the largest segment of the sports markets segmented by type of sports, accounting for 72.1% of the total in 2020. Spectator sports is projected to be the fastest-growing segment in the sports markets segmented by type of sports, moving ahead, at a Compound Annual Growth Rate (CAGR) of 11.1% during 2020-2025.

Spectator sports are further segmented into – 1) Sports teams and Clubs and 2) Racing and Individual Sports. The sports teams and clubs were the biggest segments of the spectator sports market, accounting for 75.5% of the total in 2020. Racing and individual sports are projected to be the fastest-growing segment in the spectator sports market segmented by type of sports, going forward, at a CAGR of 11.8% during 2020-2025.

The participatory sports market is further segmented into field sports, indigenous sports, Olympic sports, adventure sports, ESports, fitness and recreational sports along with other participatory sports like bowling and casual sports. The fitness and recreational sports centres market was the biggest segment of the participatory sports market segmented by type of sports, accounting for 39.9% of the total in 2020. The other participatory sports are expected to be the quickest growing segment in the participatory sports market segmented by type of sports, going forward, at a CAGR of 10.9% in the period from 2020-2025.

Segmentation by revenue source –

- Tickets.
- Media Rights.
- Sponsorship.
- Merchandising.

The media rights market was the biggest segment of the sports market segmented by revenue source, accounting for 38.3% of the total in 2020. Going ahead, merchandising segment is expected to be the quickest growing segment in the sports market segmented by revenue source at a CAGR of 12.7% in the period from 2019-2023.

Segmentation by geography –

- Countries.
- Regions.
- States.
- Cities.
- Areas.

North America was the biggest region in the global sports market, accounting for 35.0% of the total in 2020. It was trailed by Asia Pacific, Western Europe and then the other regions. Going ahead, the fastest-growing regions in the sports market will be South America and the Middle East, where growth will be at CAGRs of 12.1% and 11.3% respectively. Next to follow will be Eastern Europe and the Asia Pacific, where the markets are predicted to grow at CAGRs of 10.5% and 10.4% respectively.

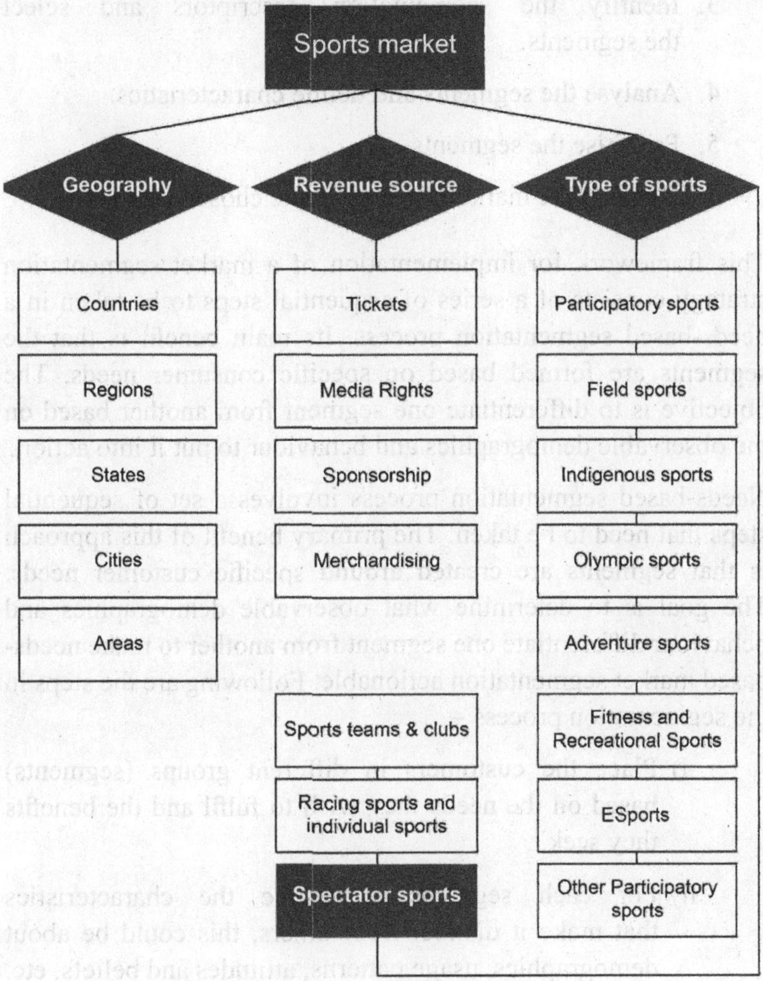

Fig 3.3 – Segmentation of Sports markets

Steps in Market Segmentation

Market Segmentation entails certain steps, such as –

1. Decide on the section of the sports market to be studied.
2. Select the basis on which we segment the market.

3. Identify the segmentation descriptors and select the segments.
4. Analyse the segments and define characteristics.
5. Prioritise the segments.
6. Develop the marketing mix for the chosen segments.

This framework for implementation of a market segmentation strategy consists of a series of sequential steps to be taken in a needs-based segmentation process. Its main benefit is that the segments are formed based on specific consumer needs. The objective is to differentiate one segment from another based on the observable demographics and behaviour to put it into action.

Needs-based segmentation process involves a set of sequential steps that need to be taken. The primary benefit of this approach is that segments are created around specific customer needs. The goal is to determine what observable demographics and behaviour differentiate one segment from another to make needs-based market segmentation actionable. Following are the steps in the segmentation process –

i) Place the customers in different groups (segments) based on the needs they wish to fulfil and the benefits they seek.

ii) For each segment, determine the characteristics that make it distinct from others, this could be about demographics, usage patterns, attitudes and beliefs, etc.

iii) Analyse the segments on the basis of how attractive they are, the criteria for which should be arrived at separately.

iv) Evaluate how profitable the respective segments will be.

v) Create a value proposition statement for each segment based on their distinctive characteristics.

vi) Test how well the positioning statements work with the respective segments.

vii) Build the marketing mix (the 4 Ps or otherwise as appropriate) based on the positioning strategy.

For example, in market segmentation for sports shoes, five consumer segments can be identified, namely: Sporty, Elite sports, Everyday wearers, Fashion sports and Budget-conscious consumers.

TARGETING MARKETS AND UNDERSTANDING TARGET AUDIENCE

The marketer will find many segments to be appealing. However, a choice needs to be made in terms of which segments are to be targeted. To make sharply defined target groups, the marketer might need to combine multiple variables.

What is a Target Audience?

A target audience is a group of people the organisation will aim to divert all its marketing activities to. The marketing strategies have to consider traits such as location, gender, age, interests and income. Consideration of a target market allows the marketer to determine the way to reach them and which consumers to target.

A target market is the group of sports consumers that a team, club or sports brand plan to sell to or reach with its marketing activities. A target audience is a group of people or segments within that target market that is being served with advertisements. In many cases, the target audience can be a specific subset of a target market.

For example, a shoe brand's target market is marathon runners. If the brand has a promotional deal in a particular city, the target audience for the ad promoting that deal will be for all prospective runners in that particular city, not all marathon runners. The target market is often used interchangeably with the target audience.

It is important to determine the target audience and consider the following characteristics –

- **Location:** Keeping in mind the local sports clubs, teams and athletes, the marketer needs to decide whether to target a regional or a local audience.
- **Interests:** The marketer needs to understand the sports the audience prefers. Whether it is cricket, football, kabaddi, badminton or hockey the marketing strategy needs to be **specific and build a connection with the fans based on** their sports preferences.
- **Lifestyle:** Considering the goals and way of living of the target audience is also very important. Analysing if the audience is trying to get in shape or enjoys sports as a spectator or is a serious athlete is a vital part of any marketing strategy.
- **Income**: Understanding the spending capacities of the target audience with respect to their money and time is important for a marketer.
- **Age**: **Marketing tactics need to be modified based on the** age of the target audience.
- **Level of athleticism:** The interest of the customer's level of athleticism or aspiration needs to be considered. A marathon runner may not be interested in the same products or services as a casual jogger.

Market Targeting

Market targeting is a method of evaluating each market segment's appeal and selecting one or more segments to enter. While evaluating the segments, a sports marketer should consider the segment's size, growth potential, structural attractiveness, company objectives and resources. There are various forms of market targeting –

- **Undifferentiated (mass) marketing:** In this strategy, the sports organisation decides to go after the whole market to target with one offer and ignores the market segment differences.

- **Differentiated or segmented marketing:** This is a market-coverage strategy where a sports organisation decides to target various market segments and proposes different offers to each.
- **Concentrated (niche) marketing:** This type of market-coverage strategy includes a sports organisation deciding to go after a large share of one or a few niche segments.

Organisations need to consider a lot of factors while deciding on a targeting strategy. Available resources, competitors' strategies, market variability, etc. are some of the factors that need to be considered.

DIFFERENTIATION AND POSITIONING

Differentiation involves separating the market offering to generate superior customer value. A sports marketer must understand the sports consumer's needs to build profitable relationships. When a team, club or sports brand is differentiated based on superior value, a competitive advantage is created. An advantage over competing teams or brands is gained by offering greater customer value. The team or brand can differentiate itself via –

- Product differentiation.
- Service differentiation.
- Channel differentiation.
- People differentiation.
- Image differentiation.

Positioning means arranging a market offering in a way to occupy a distinctive, clear and desirable place in the minds of the target consumers over competing products. A sports product is positioned in the mind of the consumer by how a product is defined or perceived by him/her on important attributes. It is the place a team or club occupies in the fan's mind over competing teams or clubs.

A positioning statement summarises the place or position of a team, league, club or sports brand. It is a brief description of a sports product or service and target market. It also includes how the sports product or service fulfils a particular need of the target market. It is intended to be used as an internal marketing tool to align marketing efforts with the team or sports brand and their value proposition. To construct a positioning statement, the sports marketer will need to get clarity on the following aspects –

- Who does the organisation serve?
- What does the organisation offer them?
- How the organisation offers their products and services?
- Why the organisation offers them?
- How does this offering compare to already existing ones?

The following is an example of a general template of a positioning statement –

1. (Company name) is targeted toward (core customers) who want (what they want). (Company name) offers (how you propose to give the customer what they want) and makes customers (how your company makes them feel).

The creation of a powerful positioning statement involves a few key principles; a few boxes to be ticked. A good statement should –

1. Be based on a structured thought process.
2. Specify the focus market.
3. Aim at fulfilling the needs of the target segment.
4. Be succinct and easy to articulate.
5. Be unique and compelling.
6. Align with the organisation's value systems.
7. Clearly communicate what the brand delivers.
8. Differentiate the brand offerings from other players.

A brand positioning statement benefits customers, but this benefit is brought about by adherence to the statement from internals.

For example, Nike's Positioning Statement –
"For athletes in need of high-quality, fashionable athletic wear, Nike provides customers with top-performing sports apparel and shoes made of the highest quality material. Its products are the most advanced in the athletic apparel industry because of Nike's commitment to innovation and investment in the latest technologies." (Hart, Hubspot.com)

Nike targets all types of athletes who want apparel that offers comfort during the performance apart from standing for something more. Nike ensures that its customers understand the edge they will be getting over their competitors with their apparel. Nike also makes the athletes feel like they are a part of something better and bigger.

Examples of Segmentation, Targeting and Positioning of a sports brand

Name	Segmentation	Target market	Positioning
Punjab Kings	Cricket lovers in different parts of the world	Male, Female, Age 15+, in India and abroad	Aggressive and courageous team with intent to win
Wimbledon Championship	Tennis enthusiasts all over the world	Male, Female Age 15-60	Most prestigious tournament with a rich grass court legacy
La Liga Football League	Football fans all over the world	Male, Age 15-60	Entertaining competition with high-scoring matches

SPORTS VALUE CHAIN

Sports organisations have to put many efforts into the development and implementation of value-creating strategies that will prevail in the sporting market. The onus for setting the terms of engagement, running the show and maximisation of revenue generation opportunities lies with the rights owners, viz. the clubs, leagues, federations and athletes. As sports organisations become more professional, value analysis is a helpful tool for them to increase their profits.

Following are the four key building blocks of a sports value chain –

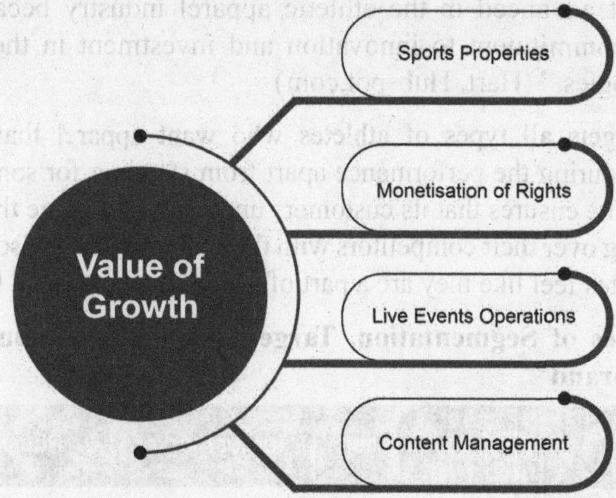

Figure 3.4 – Four building blocks of sports value chain

1. **Sports properties:** The rights owners manage the properties that are intangible assets that attract fans and draw money. These assets include a wide range of parties like leagues – Premier League, pro tours – Golf's PGA Tour, teams – Mumbai Indians and athletes – Virat Kohli, Roger Federer.

2. **Monetisation of rights:** Generally, monetisation of properties was based on the "take", i.e., revenues. However, professional sports now depend on marketing and media rights for more revenue generation sources. Sports agencies act on behalf of those sources. These agencies not only structure the deals but also trade marketing and media rights.

3. **Live event operations:** The effectiveness of rights management depends on operating live events. Additional

revenue opportunities can be created by providing an enjoyable experience for fans.

4. **Content management:** The stadiums can only seat a maximum capacity of fans. Packaging content for broadcasters and sponsors' also needs to be an important part of creating revenue in modern sports.

SUMMARY

The sporting industry is a widespread business that covers the field of play, from food, collectible stands at the stadium, media rights and sponsorships. The amount of money spent every year in the sporting industry caters to a passionate fan base. This business environment has many participants like rights owners, athletes, clubs, leagues, federations, sponsors, sports agencies and broadcasters, etc.

A sports product does not only refer to a physical good that has been manufactured, i.e., apparel, shoes or equipment but also refers to services and ideas. The principle advantage of buying a sports product is that the consumer receives the core benefits of the product from buying and using it. The consumer receives the benefits of the actual product as well as the additional features or its add-ons. Sports products are characterised as a mixture of tangible and intangible elements, but some products are mainly tangible or mainly intangible.

The sports market comprises the sale of sports goods, services and related goods by various entities that offer different types of sports in the sporting industry. Sports is a special form of business and needs to be put into a commercial framework just like any other enterprise. The key to formulating a good commercial framework is to understand the special features of sports products and sports markets along with their relevance to meet the needs and to satisfy the sports consumers.

Sports can provoke an emotional response in its consumers that is rarely found in other businesses. It not only stimulates loyalty but also develops strong attachments to nostalgia of club or team tradition. Sports organisations measure their success both on and off the field of play. On-field success denotes the achievement within sports competition. Off-field success denotes financial profitability and stability. Sports organisations that compete in leagues and competitions depend on the health of their competitors to support their success. Sports consumers are more attracted to attend games and matches where there is a balanced competition. Sports leagues and competitions put into effect policies to encourage competitive balance. Policies are related to salary caps for players, rules about sharing revenues and regulations about how players are to be exchanged between teams. Unpredictability can be beneficial in the competitive sports market because it makes sports more attractive. In competitive sports, there is low cross elasticity of demand because it is difficult to replace one sports league, team, brand or competition with another. The competitive sports product is confined by a fixed supply schedule making it difficult to modify the production rates to meet the demand of consumers but can be overcome through different distribution channels.

The marketers divide the market into groups of consumers or segments with well-defined needs. This strategy of dividing a market in a homogenous group is called as segmentation. A target market is the group of sports consumers that a team, club or sports brand plan to sell to or reach with its marketing activities. A target audience is a group of people or segments within that target market that is being served with advertisements. This makes the target audience a specific subset of a target market. Differentiation involves separating the market offering to generate superior customer value. A sports marketer must understand the sports consumer's needs to build profitable relationships. When a team, club, or sports brand is differentiated based on superior value, a competitive advantage is created. Positioning means arranging a market offering in a way to occupy a distinctive, clear and desirable place in the mind of the target consumers over competing products. As sports organisations become more professional, value analysis is a helpful tool for them to increase their profits.

Chapter 4

Strategic Planning, Concepts and Sporting Applications

INTRODUCTION AND OVERVIEW OF PLANNING

Strategic marketing is a technique used by an organisation to differentiate its products and services from its competitors. This method focuses on its strengths to provide better value and service to its customers. The goal of strategic marketing is to create a positive differentiation for an organisation over its competition from the customer's perspective. Strategic marketing revolves around three questions –

1. In which markets do we compete?
2. How to compete?
3. What is the right time to compete?

A marketing strategy will focus not only on clear objectives and targets to achieve the organisation's goals but also aims to create a sustainable competitive advantage that enables future profitable growth for the business. The process involves conducting research and establishing goals and objectives to maximise the success and effectiveness of the organisation's overall marketing strategy. The success of a strategic planning process includes:

- Setting measurable and achievable goals.
- Conducting thorough market and competitors' research.
- Preparing concise and easy-to-understand plans.
- Ensuring there is sync between the plans made and the needs of the consumers.

A few issues like lack of skilled workforce; wrong assumptions about the requirements of the consumers without conducting thorough research; changing demographic of the consumers, management issues, coordination problems, incorrect SWOT analysis, issues while conducting marketing research, confusing marketing feedback obtained, budgeting issues, etc. may arise while preparing a strategic marketing plan.

The marketing planning process of every strategy includes four stages –

1. **Analysis:** Analysis of the organisation's situation is the most critical step in the planning process. The organisation should analyse its internal and external environment, strengths and weaknesses, opportunities and threats as well as possible marketing actions to decide which opportunities can best be pursued. The analysis provides information and additional inputs for other stages in the process.
2. **Planning:** Marketing planning includes finalising marketing strategies that will help the organisation achieve its objectives.
3. **Implementation:** In this stage, strategic plans are put into action to achieve the organisation's objectives.
4. **Control:** In this stage, measurement and evaluation of the marketing activities planned is conducted. If needed, corrective measures are taken to ensure that objectives are

achieved. This evaluation provides information needed for other activities.

Fig 4.1 shows the planning process and the impact of each stage on the other.

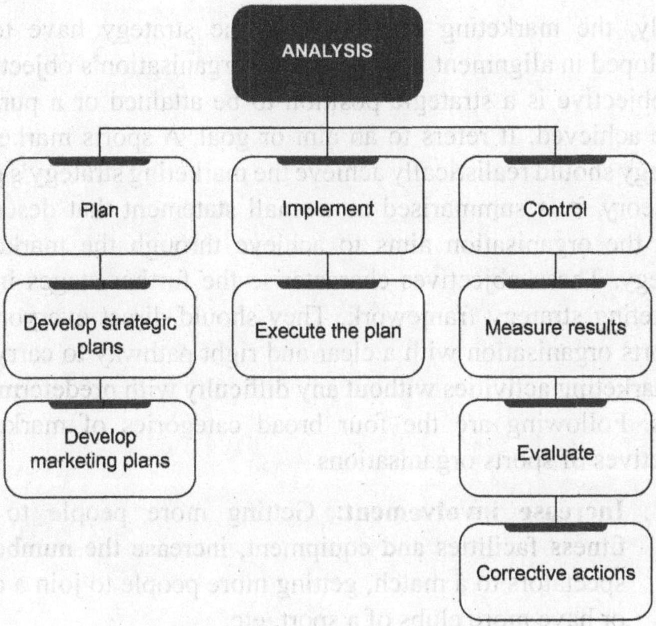

Figure 4.1: The stages of planning process

DEVELOPING A SPORTS MARKETING STRATEGY

There are two distinct stages in the development of a Sports Marketing Strategy –

1. **Decision to take the strategic direction:** This gives clarity on the marketing objectives and ways to measure success against these objectives.
2. **Decision about the position in the market:** This helps segment the market and develop a compelling and differentiated position for the organisation.

Phase 1: Develop a Strategic Marketing Direction

There are two steps involved in developing the direction of a sports organisation's marketing strategy, namely,

I. Marketing Objectives

Firstly, the marketing objectives of the strategy have to be developed in alignment with the sports organisation's objectives. An objective is a strategic position to be attained or a purpose to be achieved. It refers to an aim or goal. A sports marketer's strategy should realistically achieve the marketing strategy's goal. In theory, it is summarised as a small statement that describes what the organisation aims to achieve through the marketing strategy. These objectives characterise the further stages in the marketing strategy framework. They should direct everyone in a sports organisation with a clear and right pathway to carry out all marketing activities without any difficulty with predetermined goals. Following are the four broad categories of marketing objectives of sports organisations –

1. **Increase involvement:** Getting more people to use fitness facilities and equipment, increase the number of spectators to a match, getting more people to join a club, or have more clubs of a sport, etc.
2. **Influence customer satisfaction:** Improve gratification levels of fans in a stadium, meet varied customer needs through wider product range, etc.
3. **Manage perception:** Create the image of a socially responsible entity, drive awareness about your event and change your image in the eyes of the public.
4. **Drive growths and profits:** Increase sales revenue, improve profit margin percentage, get a new sponsor, etc.

The main objective for privately owned sports facilities like fitness centres, gyms and recreation centres will be to earn profits.

Many sports equipment, apparel and retail brands like Decathlon, Nike, Adidas, Shiv-Naresh, Cosco, etc. or professional sports leagues, teams like IPL, PKL are more commercially inclined. Any other objective that these organisations may develop will remain compliant or as a means to achieve a greater profit. Privately owned professional clubs or teams would want to sign up more club members to earn more profits.

On the other hand, many sporting organisations do not have profits as their main objective. Community-based clubs and sports clubs may have performance and participation objectives. National sports associations like the Indian Olympic Association, national sporting federations of each sport and governing bodies like the Sports Authority of India have an interest in promoting athletes, sports and healthy lifestyles (participation, performance and promotion objectives). It is still important for such organisations to earn money to cover their costs and spend on developing new schemes or investing in facilities, equipment, etc. Profit for them is a means to an end, not a primary objective.

II. Performance Measures

Once the objectives have been finalised, performance measures should be added to these objectives. Performance measures are the way to collect, analyse, estimate and assess whether an objective of a marketing strategy has been fulfilled. It generally involves finding a way to quantify an objective. For example, if a fitness centre's objective is to increase profits, a performance measure is added to indicate its increase in the number of memberships within a period which eventually might lead to an increase in profits. '20 more members than the previous year'. This performance measure – 'Sell 20 more fitness memberships than the previous year in the centre', has added quantity to the profit-increasing objective and has also created a benchmark to determine if the objective is achieved or not. Following are a few examples of possible performance measures –

Common Examples of Marketing Objectives
To increase club/ gym memberships
To increase the number of people who use our sports product or service
To increase customer satisfaction levels
To improve spectator levels at a game
To increase profits
To increase awareness of our sports product

Possible Performance Measures
To increase membership from 70 to 100 members by January 2022
To increase the number of people who use our sports products or service
To increase spectator levels to an average of 15,000 spectators per game, by December 2022, as measured by ticket sales
To increase customer satisfaction levels to 7/10 as rated by them on an annual customer satisfaction survey
To increase the profit to INR 25 lakh, calculated at the end of the 2022 financial year
To increase the number of people who heard of our product in India to 1,00,000 as measured by market research

Phase 2: Develop a Sports Marketing Position

There are two steps involved in the development of a marketing position for a sports organisation, namely –

I. Market positioning and differentiation.

II. Market segmentation.

The development of sports marketing positions involves market segmentation, market positioning and differentiation leading to the development of a Sports Marketing mix (5Ps).

Step 1: Divide the market into different groups based on certain similar characteristics.

Step 2: Select one segment, or more as the focus or target.

Step 3: Arrive at a positioning plan for the chosen segment or segments.

Step 4: Develop the marketing mix for the chosen segment or segments.

STRATEGIC MARKETING PLANNING PROCESS FOR THE SPORTS SECTOR

Sports Marketing involves all activities related to the planning and execution of marketing initiatives aimed at driving the sports organisation towards its goals. Understanding the sports consumers is a crucial aspect of the planning process. When it comes to planning, it requires that there is a clear concept of the mission statement, objectives and goals of the sports organisation. Planning requires thinking of future, forecasting and a clear goal as to what needs to be done in the sports organisation. Planning affects the influences within the organisation and must make practical conclusions that concern the future of the organisation and its challenges.

In simple terms, marketing actions that are connected to sports are sports marketing actions. When these approaches are taken together within a marketing plan, these actions contribute to converting a marketing plan into a strategic Sports Marketing Plan. The following areas are included in a strategic Sports Marketing Plan which will further give a sports organisation an edge over its competitors –

- Study of market and competition.
- Understanding fan psychology and preferences.
- Correlation between marketing activities and their objectives.

These areas are strategic elements that highlight the path to be taken, supported by market analysis and those of the competitors.

An organisation can include sports events and their extended products into their strategic marketing plan to catch the attention of the consumers by touching their hearts. They can try and communicate with their target market using very popular sporting events which have a large viewership impact. The strategic approach is very important and deserves a great deal of attention and competence. Approaches can include the use of sports, linking up to a single event or series, sponsoring an athlete, financing grassroots activities, etc. Sports and their simple rules need no explanation, and are an easy way to communicate with everyone, providing good opportunities to organisations to use sports in their strategic marketing plans.

A brilliant example of a strategic sports marketing campaign is Procter & Gamble's "Thank You, Mom" campaign during the Olympic Games, London 2012 that showed the world the key role that moms play in the growth of a champion. The campaign included a short film, "Best Job" that celebrates the role mothers play in nurturing Indigenous sports and ESports, athletes and Olympians all over the world. This campaign was promoted through various media channels. An in-store worldwide retailer programme was endorsed five months before the London 2012 Games which involved four million retailers all over the world. There were also videos of the mothers of some of the 150 athletes that were sponsored by P&G brands. The campaign also was tied to the effort of raising over 25 million dollars to support youth sports programmes aiding the Olympics and moms all over. Promotions involved around 34 P&G brands including Pantene, Tide, Ariel, Pampers, Gillette etc. A "Thank You Mom" app was introduced that allowed everyone to thank their moms with personalised videos of themselves. P&G successively implemented tactics aimed to promote the purchase of specific products. These tactics were related to the supply of sports materials needed in local schools located close to supermarkets. This was undertaken to contribute to the growth of the region where its customers live and their children go to school. These direct tactics were also implemented in schools. P&G-sponsored athletes met the students and their mothers intending to inspire the champions of the future and supporting the pillars of their success.

This marketing strategy scaled over dozens of brands in many countries and generated an estimated $500 million in global incremental P&G sales, 76 billion global media impressions, over 74,000,000 global views and over 370,000,000 Twitter interactions (Wieden Kennedy+, 2010). The campaign provided the energy of being involved in the Olympics and support to youth sports. The videos of real moms who fed babies, provided lunch, supported during games and events, bandaged injuries, and shared the joy of winning medals at the Olympics connected with everyone emotionally. P&G's strategic approach included a synergy between its multiple brands which spread across their various products in different countries. The strategy chosen by any organisation can be based on its sensitivity, target market and many other factors including those connected to the region and budget.

Based on the studies of Shilbury, Lancaster, and Massingham (1996); Kotler (1997); Quick and Westerbeek (1998); McDonald (2000); the following are 8 steps in the strategic marketing planning process for the sports sector –

Step 1: Determine the sports organisation's mission statement.

Step 2: Set corporate objectives of the sports organisation.

Step 3: Analyse the sports market environment.

- Analyse the external environment in which the sports organisation competes – external forces, competition, market, etc.
- Analyse the internal environment of the sports organisation – the capabilities of the sports organisation's financial strength, employees, operations, etc.

Step 4: Conduct the SWOT analysis

Step 5: Set marketing objectives.

Step 6: Determine marketing strategy, using marketing mix variables (Sports Product, Sports Price, Sports Place and Sports Promotion Mix).

Step 7: Formulate detailed action plans – these plans incorporate decisions about actions, timetables, budgets and personnel.

Step 8: Plan review and control.

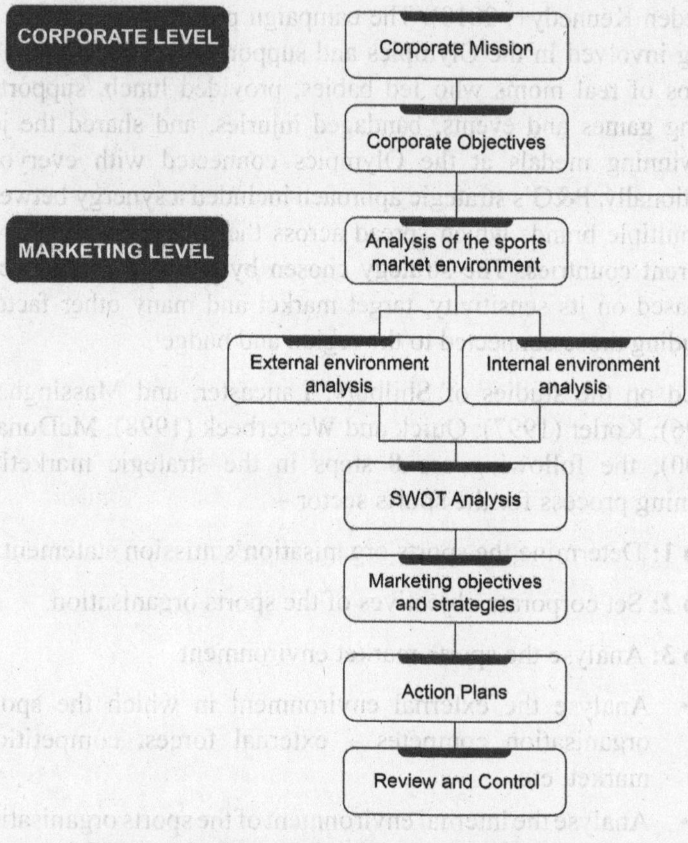

Figure 4.2: Steps to develop a marketing position

Source: Kriemadis, T., & Terzoudis, C. (2007). Strategic marketing planning in the sports sector. Sports Management International Journal, 3(1)

The planning of a Sports Marketing strategy begins with defining the mission statement and corporate objectives of a sports organisation. The elements in the planning framework represent the culture and operations of the whole business hence making it vital for the organisation to understand the components of these elements clearly. Various departments operate in different strategic directions in a sports organisation. This may cause disastrous results if the boundaries and the way forward have not been defined. All the elements at both, the corporate level as well as marketing level are fundamental while formulating the marketing planning process. Sports marketers need to understand corporate planning to align and integrate the same within the marketing planning towards a strategic direction of the sports organisation.

Corporate Mission

A mission statement is a formal summary of the aims and values of a company, organisation or individual. It includes a clear declaration of what the organisation wants to achieve, seeks to do and what kind of organisation it wants to become. The mission is the summarisation of the assignments and purposes that supports the vision, values, profitability and overall growth of the sports organisation. The main element in the mission of a sports organisation is supported by the belief that the sports results and the provided sports services respond to the needs of the consumers of the sports events, auditorium and fans, employees, owners and managers, media and the sporting community as a whole. Defining the mission of sports and the sports organisation aids to confirm the main area of interest of the sports operating system, the attainability of the planned activities and their previous values. After defining the mission, a strategy is developed and followed by the operating policies/ processes of the sports organisation.

For example, below is the mission and vision statement of Sportskeeda, a global sports and ESports news website established in 2009. The website has news, features, commentary and videos on sports like cricket, football, tennis, WWE, NBA, NFL, along with news on video games such as Minecraft, PUBG, GTA, Fortnite, Valorant and CS:GO etc.

Sportskeeda's mission is as follows –

"To revolutionise the way sports are followed all over the world. Our team of sports fanatics strive to give sports fans the best experience in following their favourite sports, teams, tournaments and players"

Another example of a mission statement is that of the National Sports University (NSU) established by the Department of Sports, Ministry of Youth Affairs & Sports (MYAS) in 2018 to promote sports education in the areas of sports sciences, sports technology, sports management and sports coaching.

NSU's mission statement is as follows –

- *"To produce top athletes, sports scientists, competent physical educationists by offering programmes that cultivate learning through competition, recreation, physical activity in addition to classroom learning.*
- *To mentor students by inculcating values and leadership skills in them by providing diverse opportunities that develop character to succeed in all facets of their lives.*
- *To study human potential holistically by conducting pioneering research in the field of sports science and use its findings to boost public health and enhance international performance of Indian athletes.*
- *To develop the entire sports eco-system including sports management, sports journalism, sports architecture, sports equipment manufacturing, etc.*
- *To contribute towards promoting international peace with the power of sports by helping build a society and country healthy in mind and body." (Source: NSU website)*

Corporate Objectives

A corporate objective is a targeted goal that an organisation strives for, one that its regular operations need to be aligned with. For sports organisations, corporate objectives may include an increase in viewership of the game, financial viability, increase in participation, return on investment, brand awareness, increase in the number of members, quality of sports products, etc. Management authors in the past have stated that corporate objectives or goals should be SMART – Specific, Measurable, Achievable, Realistic and Timely.

Below is the objective of Olympic Gold Quest (OGQ) – a programme of the Foundation for Promotion of Sports and Games, a Not for Profit (Section 25) Company:

"OGQ aims to create a level playing field for our athletes to enable them to be competitive at the highest level of sport" (Source: OGQ website).

The objective of NSU –

"The National Sports University has distinctive approaches to academics, research, athletic performance and extension services, which sets it apart from other universities or institutions of higher education.

***Academics:** The university shall impart undergraduate, postgraduate and doctoral programmes in sports coaching, sports sciences and physical education in various disciplines. Specialised degree programmes in various disciplines of sports education and coaching are also envisaged for the future.*

***Research**: NSU shall focus on collaborating with leading researchers within and outside the country to undertake pioneering research programmes and exchange information in various research areas, particularly in the field of sports coaching and performance enhancement of athletes.*

***Performance:** One of the significant functions of the university shall be to conduct sports training programmes to enable athletes to enhance their performance and attain excellence in sports.*

Serving the Community: *Providing extension services to the local community with the objectives of improving their health and lifestyle as well as giving impetus to sports of local origin like Sagol Kangjei (polo), Thang-Ta (Manipuri martial art), Yubi Lakpi (rugby), Mukna, Kang, etc. shall also be one of the key functions of NSU." (Source: NSU website).*

Analysis of the Sports Market Environment – Internal Environment and External Environment

The purpose of the analysis of the market environment is to study the conditions and factors that exist in the internal and external environment of a sports organisation. The sports marketer has to ascertain whether these factors will affect the operations positively or negatively.

In this step, important external factors of the macro environment like political, economic, socio-cultural, technological, legal and environmental forces are studied. This analysis is called the PESTLE analysis (ref Unit 2) of the sports organisation's environment. Sports marketers should also examine the factors of the micro environment such as the customers, consumers, competitors, sports market, etc. The favourable legislation of the current government or the technological advancements can work in favour of the sports organisation's marketing strategy. Whereas, external situations and factors that prevent the sports organisation from achieving its objectives like intensive competition of sports clubs and teams, the economic recession and unfavourable government legislation are some of the situations that may not work in favour of the sports organisation's marketing strategy.

SWOT Analysis

After identifying, estimating and assessing the key factors of the internal and external environment that will affect the organisation, the sports marketers then begin developing effective marketing strategies based on the analysis of SWOT – Strength, Weaknesses, Opportunities, Threats (ref Unit 2).

SWOT analysis of sports organisations comprises the following:

- **Strengths:** Skills, resources, competencies and other advantages relative to competitors.
- **Weaknesses:** Deficiencies in the skills, resources and capabilities that confine the sports organisation's effectiveness to competitors.
- **Opportunities:** Favourable situations in a sports organisation's environment.
- **Threats:** Unfavourable situations in a sports organisation's environment.

SWOT analysis shows the strengths and weaknesses of a sports organisation to its competitors, as well as the opportunities and threats that arise from the external environment.

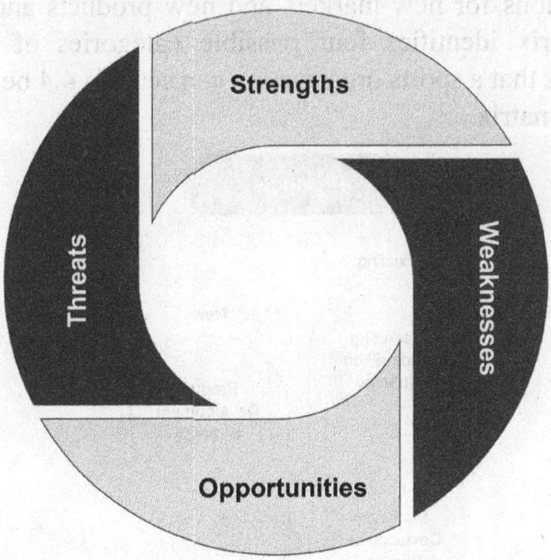

Figure 4.3 – SWOT analysis framework

Marketing Objectives and Strategies

The next step after SWOT analysis is to focus on creating the marketing objectives and strategies. Marketing objectives are stated and measurable goals in terms of the quantification of what a sports organisation sells (its products or services) and to whom it sells (its target market). Sports marketers can use Ansoff's matrix as a useful tool to define marketing objectives and develop strategies based on the objectives set.

The Ansoff model was developed by H. Igor Ansoff and published in the Harvard Business Review in 1957, in an article titled "Strategies for Diversification." The Ansoff model, due to its grid format, also referred to as the Ansoff matrix, helps marketers identify opportunities for revenue growth and business by tapping into new markets or developing new products and services.

The Ansoff Matrix is used to evaluate opportunities for organisation to improve their growth through alternative combinations for new markets and new products and services. This matrix identifies four possible categories of marketing objectives that a sports organisation can set. Fig 4.4 below shows Ansoff's matrix.

Figure 4.4 – Ansoff's matrix

Based on markets (new or existing) and products (new or existing), below are the four growth strategies in the Ansoff Matrix. We will look at T20 Cricket as an example to be taken into consideration with each strategy of the matrix related to an event.

1. **Market penetration strategy:** This strategy focuses on the increase in sales of existing sports products to an existing sports market. The market penetration strategy may be implemented by sports marketer in several ways like –

    - Decreasing prices of the sports products and services to attract new customers.
    - Increasing promotion and distribution efforts.
    - Acquiring a competitor in the same marketplace.

    For example, the introduction of IPL is the best example of a Market Penetration strategy where an already existing cricket product, the T20 Cricket format was developed as a league in its biggest existing market in India. IPL included the country's two biggest passions — Cricket and Bollywood.

2. **Product development strategy:** This strategy focuses on the introduction of new products to an existing market. The product development strategy may be implemented by a sports marketer in several ways –

    - Investing in R&D to develop new sports products and services to cater to the existing sports market.
    - Acquiring a competitor's product and merging resources to create a new sports product that better meets the need of the existing sports market.
    - Forming strategic partnerships with other sports organisations to gain access to each partner's distribution channels or brand.

    For example, after the year 2006 - 07, T20 Cricket had attracted immense crowd attendance in domestic matches in England and South Africa. The then ICC chairman, Ehsaan Mani recognised the potential of the T20 format and saw it as a great way of promoting cricket in countries such as China, the USA, Canada with a view to potentially turn Cricket into an Olympic sport in the long run. ICC introduced the T20 World Cup in 2007 in South Africa with a sense of urgency. This product of T20 proved to be a first-mover advantage leading to the grand acceptance of this format by fans all over the world. Entrepreneurs and media welcomed the popularity of this format and began capitalising from it. The existing cricket market was used to Test cricket and ODIs. The new T20 format, in the existing market, was introduced using two key strategies –

I. Cheap tickets were priced at one-tenth of the ticket prices of the Cricket World Cup in the Caribbean earlier that year. The tickets were priced at R20 (South African Rand) for the group stage and R40 for the super eight stages.

II. Scheduling of the matches resembled the fixtures of the FIFA World Cup. The timings of the matches are also suited to the TV audience of the biggest market for cricket in the world – the Indian Subcontinent.

3. **Market development strategy:** This strategy focuses on entry into a new market with existing products. This strategy is most successful in new sports markets when the sports organisation can leverage their proprietary technology, potential customer base possessing high disposable income and consumer behaviour that does not deviate much from the consumers in existing sports markets. The market development strategy may include one of the following ways –

   - Catering to a different sports customer segment.

- Entering into a new domestic sports market (expanding regionally).
- Entering into a foreign market (expanding internationally).

For example, The Big Bash League (BBL), Australian professional franchise of Twenty20 cricket league, similar to IPL which was established in 2011 by Cricket Australia. Around 2010, research conducted by Cricket Australia (CA) showed that cricket was losing out on its youth market in Australia. According to the research, cricket was the 7th Favourite sport for boys and 14th Favourite sport for girls, both groups aged 15 years old. The BBL then went on to develop a completely new market focusing on Australian families for their existing product of T20 Cricket. BBL targeted the younger fans who dragged their parents along to the matches. The tournament was then packaged not just for traditional cricket fans but also for children and their moms who were new to this game. Similar to IPL, the result of this strategy was a 3-hour cricket entertainment. Cricket remained the core product of the strategy along with few value-added services to keep the children interested and families to return for the BBL games. In 2016, the stadium at Adelaide Oval witnessed a record attendance of 52,637 people for the BBL game between the Adelaide Strikers and Sydney Sixers.

4. **Diversification strategy:** This strategy focuses on entry into a new market with the introduction of new products. This strategy has high risk as both the market and product need to be developed. This risk may be mitigated to some degree through related diversification. This strategy may offer the greatest potential for increased revenues, as it will open up an entirely new revenue stream for the organisation as they will have access to consumers that

the organisation did not have access to previously. There are two types of diversification an organisation can use –

- **Related diversification:** Potential synergies need to be realised between the existing business and the new sports product/market.
- **Unrelated diversification:** Potential synergies need not be realised between the existing business and the new sports product/market.

Thus, marketing objectives need to be aligned to the strategic direction of the sports organisation to serve its mission, needs and purpose. It is important that the marketing objectives contain these three aspects –

1. The criteria on which we measure success, like sales growth, market share, etc.
2. The value selected; for example, 40 percent market share.
3. The operating period, for example, by December 2023.

Once the marketing objectives are determined, the sports marketer should decide the way to achieve these objectives by designing their marketing strategy. The route to achieving the marketing objectives and the way these objectives are achieved are termed as marketing strategies. As discussed in Unit 1, marketing strategies revolve around the elements of the marketing mix.

As a rule, in marketing, the marketing mix is always viewed as the 4 Ps of marketing – product, price, place, promotion. However, in sports marketing, there is a need for an expanded role that publicity/ PR plays.

Hence, the sports marketing mix has evolved into the 5 Ps of Sports Marketing –

1. Sports Product.
2. Sports Price.
3. Sports Place (Sports Distribution).

4. Sports Promotion.
5. Publicity.

Action plans

An action plan is a comprehensive plan which outlines the actions required to reach one or more goals/ objectives of the organisation. It can be also be defined as a series of steps that must be undertaken, or activities that must be performed, for a marketing strategy to succeed. Sports that determine the Sports Marketing mix around which the strategy needs to focus on, sports marketers need to create a detailed action plan to execute the strategy and achieve the desired results. The action plan is generally prepared for a time period, say one year or until the end of the league season, and is described qualitatively, quantitatively and in a timely manner. The action plan will entail details of what is to be achieved, how to achieve it, who is responsible to achieve the results and the resources required.

The following are the characteristics of every action plan that a sports marketing strategy should have –

- **Fragmentation:** Fragmenting the action plan into individual sub-projects and determining appropriate tactics to achieve the goals of these sub-projects is a very vital characteristic of the action plan. Each sub-project is required to define the description of the work, the process to be executed, requirements for the execution, specific resources and capabilities of the personnel working on the sub-project.
- **Roles & Responsibilities:** Determining the roles and responsibilities of every individual who will be involved in the action plan is a prerequisite for the success of the strategy.
- **Timeline:** The total processes and sub-processes need to be given a timeframe. This timeline will help determine

the accuracy of the implementation of each action plan in a timely manner.

- **Budget**: An action plan should include a tentative and analytical budget to estimate the cost of sub-projects, individuals working on the total projects and other operational expenses.
- **Control and monitoring:** A mechanism should be developed to identify problems that may occur or have occurred to take corrective measures.

Plan Review and Control

Review and control of a strategic marketing plan involves goal-setting, reviewing the performance against the goals and then taking necessary corrective steps. The review control process is continuous and relates to all levels of the organisation. The evaluation of the strategic marketing planning process is carried out at different levels.

1. **Annual plan:** The function of this control is to make sure that the organisation achieves the objectives that are described in the action plan. In sports organisations, measures of attendances or participation, on-field success, ticket sales, financial performance, etc. are the tools used to measure success and to achieve control. The discrepancy between the output of the sports organisation and their objectives will lead to the determination of the real cause for such a gap. It also helps in regulating corrective measures to bridge the gap between the objectives and output. These corrective measures can also lead to modification of the sports marketing objectives and strategies.
2. **Profitability:** This function measures the profitability of the sports products and services that the organisation offers to the target markets.

3. **Efficiency:** This function focuses on determining ways to increase the efficiency of the components of the Sports Marketing mix such as publicity, promotion, advertising, distribution, sponsorship, endorsement, television rights, merchandising, sales force, service quality, etc.

4. **Strategy:** This function focuses on the periodical reassessment of the organisation's strategic approach and mission.

SPORTS MARKETING RESEARCH

Just like every organisation, a sports organisation also needs to engage in the research of its market before defining a marketing strategy. Research is conducted when there is a lack of information about the target market, and the organisations cannot make informed decisions about their marketing activities. Research is also utilised to study the perceptions of sports consumers about numerous areas ranging from attendance at events to brand awareness and sponsorship. Sports Marketing Research is also needed when there is existing information but the application of that information is unknown.

The purpose of Sports Marketing Research can be seen as two-fold –

1. **Determining market opportunities:** This could involve a segment of the market that is underserved, a particular niche in the market that is emerging, or an opportunity to enhance the experience of the customer through a superior offering.

2. **Determination of threats:** This could involve emerging trends that the sports organisation is not geared up for, an entry of a new player or other

changes that can detrimentally affect the sports organisation.

Researching the sports market will significantly decrease the uncertainty in making marketing decisions. Unfortunately, many organisations are not willing to spend the resources and time necessary to conduct appropriate sports marketing research. This may be due to a lack of funding, resources or time. But a major reason to not conduct research is that they do not know how to conduct research effectively and efficiently.

Another key problem is not being able to separate being a marketing manager and a marketing researcher. In larger organisations, these may be two different positions –

- The marketing manager regulates the marketing resources, activities and efforts of the sports organisation.
- Marketing researcher studies the needs of the sports organisation and creates plans for meeting those needs.

However, many sports organisations are start-ups or small organisations where there will be only one position of a marketing manager. This manager must not only regulate the marketing resources and activities but also conduct research for the organisation by generating answers to questions and developing techniques to accomplish the objectives at hand. The research should be free of bias or emotional involvement. The data might be invalid and unreliable if bias enters the equation, during the process of research, further hampering the determination of the most suitable method for solving the problem.

Just like every other organisation, sports organisations should also follow the general steps to conduct research (Schwarz & Hunter 2008).

1. Defining the problem.

2. Establishing research goals and objectives.

3. Choosing the appropriate research methodology –

    a. **Exploratory research:** refers to initial research undertaken to investigate a problem which is not clearly defined.

    b. **Descriptive research:** refers to a research method that explains the characteristics of the population or situation being studied. This focuses more on the "what" than the "why" of the research subject.

    c. **Causal research:** refers to a research method that determines the cause-and-effect relationship between two variables.

4. Identifying sources of information –

    a. **Primary sources of information:** Raw data, original research, letters, photographs, artefacts, audio or video broadcasts, eyewitness accounts, interviews, legal documents, government documents, public records or other documents created by organisations.

    b. **Secondary sources of information:** Books, journals, articles, newspapers, etc.

5. Designing data collection forms –

    a. **Open-ended questions:** Questions that get elaborate and brief answers from the respondent.

    b. **Close-ended questions:** Questions that can only be answered by selecting the limited options of answers given like 'yes' or 'no' answers on a rating scale – 1 to 5 or strongly disagree to strongly agree.

c. **Scaled-response questions:** Questions that have a predefined list of answer options that are related to each other to measure the intensity of each respondent and their feeling toward something.

6. Determining sample size –

   a. **Probability sampling:** A sampling method where samples from a larger population are chosen using a method based on random selection aligning with the theory of probability.

   b. **Non-probability sampling:** A sampling method where samples are chosen based on the subjective judgment of the researcher instead of random selection.

7. Examining data and drawing conclusions.

Sports marketing managers also conduct a cost-benefit analysis to determine the loss to the organisation if the problem identified is not addressed. A cost-benefit analysis is an organised process to analyse which decisions to take and which ones to omit. The cost-benefit analysis determines potential rewards estimated from a situation or action and then deducts the total costs related to the execution of that action.

Thus, Sports Marketing Research should be conducted when changes or problems arise in the sports market or new marketing objectives are established which would lead to changes in the marketing strategy or opportunity to gain competitive advantage.

SUMMARY

Strategic marketing is a technique used by an organisation to differentiate its products and services from its competitors. This method focuses on its strengths to provide better value and service to its customers. The marketing planning process of every strategy includes four stages – Analysis, Planning, Implementation and Control. There are two stages to develop a sports marketing strategy – 1) Deciding on a strategic direction and 2) Deciding on a position to take. Sports Marketing involves all activities related to the planning and execution of marketing initiatives aimed at driving the sports organisation towards its goals. Understanding the sports consumers is a crucial aspect of the planning process. The planning phase begins with understanding of the consumers' sports habits through marketing research and identifying consumers' wants and needs.

Strategic Marketing planning process for the sports sector involves a series of steps –

Step 1: Understand the Corporate Mission of the Sports Organisation.

Step 2: Articulate the core objectives of the organisation that flows from the mission.

Step 3: Understand the Sports Market Environment.

Step 4: SWOT analysis.

Step 5: Clearly define the marketing objectives.

Step 6: Develop the marketing strategy inclusive of positioning, marketing mix.

Step 7: Create a detailed execution plan inclusive of timelines, budgets, organisational issues and other key aspects.

Step 8: Review and Control.

Sports Marketing Research should be conducted when changes or problems arise in the sports market or new marketing objectives are established which would lead to changes in the marketing strategy or opportunity to gain competitive advantage.

Chapter **5**

The Marketing Plan – Development and Implementation

INTRODUCTION

A marketing plan is a well-written document that defines the organisation's strategy and course of action required to implement that strategy. This marketing plan is invaluable, irrespective of whether the organisation is small or large, professional or amateur. Sports organisations generally develop marketing plans on an annual or seasonal basis, depending upon their nature of work, to support their ongoing sporting programmes.

Following elements are key to most marketing plans –

- Having clarity of objectives.
- Gaining insights through research.
- Segmentation of market to clearly define the target.
- Formulation of the marketing strategy.
- Implementation and review of the strategy.

As discussed in the previous Unit, the process of developing the plan is extremely important. Organisations need to evaluate their current situation, analyse the internal and external environment, study potential strategies and evaluate the logistics of implementation of the plan to ensure good decision making.

The following considerations are key to a good marketing plan –

- Introduction
  - What is the organisation's mission?
  - What are the existing products and who are its current customers?
  - What were the results of previous marketing efforts?
  - What is the nature of business – is it a club or team or league or governing body or a consultancy?
- Research - Data collection and analysis of the environment.
  - What are internal and external factors to be considered?
  - How can we assess our strengths, weaknesses, opportunities and threats (SWOT)?
  - PESTLE analysis
- Goals and objectives of the marketing strategy.
  - What are the overall marketing goals?
  - What specific objectives need to be set related to those goals?
- Segmentation and defining Target Markets
  - How to describe the current market?
  - What is the basis of segmentation of the market?
  - What is the Target Market and how is it described?
  - How will the product be positioned in the minds of the Target Market?
- Designing the tactics in the Marketing Strategy.
  - What is the long-term marketing strategy?

  - What tactics are necessary to accomplish the marketing strategy?
  - **Defining the marketing mix – Sports Product, Sports Price, Sports Promotion, Sports Place.**
- Implementation of the strategy
  - What tasks are necessary to implement the tactic?
  - Who is responsible for executing each task?
  - What is the timeline for each task?
- Evaluation of a strategy
  - What are the steps to evaluate the effectiveness of the plan?

THREE KEY PRINCIPLES IN DEVELOPING A MARKETING PLAN

A highly effective marketing plan should adhere to these three key principles –

- **Course of action:** The marketing plan should describe the course of action to be taken to achieve the objectives of the organisation. The course of action that is proposed must develop or modify one or more characteristics of the organisation's offerings with respect to the product, service, brand, price, communication, incentives and distribution. This plan must also include the timeline to implement the course of action and entities responsible for implementing them.
- **Clarity of purpose:** One of the key principles of a marketing plan is to inform the appropriate stakeholders about the organisation's action plan and persuade them about its viability. Due to this, the marketing plan should very clearly state the goals the organisation aims to achieve and describe the course of action. The information in the marketing plan regarding the objectives, strategy, tactics,

implementation, evaluation, etc. must be presented systematically to highlight the logic of the proposed course of action.

- **Crisp articulation:** Many marketing plans are unnecessarily long and filled with irrelevant information. The length of the marketing plan cannot be used as a reliable indicator of a broader and deeper analysis of the course of action. That is the most common mistake made by marketing managers. The marketer needs to include relevant information which is crisp, clear and not filled with unnecessary information just to make it seem longer and therefore better.

G-STIC FRAMEWORK FOR MARKETING PLAN

The marketing plan of the organisation should be in alignment with its value creation objectives. An organisation's offering in marketing terms is what the organisation offers to its customers. An offering includes not only the product itself but also includes elements that represent extra value to the customers, such as easy accessibility, availability, quick delivery, technical support, or quality of service. A sports organisation's offering can include the event or game, merchandise, food and beverage during the game, team or club apparel, athletes, etc.

To promote these offerings, they are further included in a marketing plan framework that outlines the strategies and tactics. The marketing plan framework can be defined by 5 key activities –

1. Setting a ***Goal.***
2. Developing a ***Strategy.***
3. Designing the ***Tactics.***
4. Defining the ***Implementation*** plan.
5. Identifying a set of ***Control*** metrics to measure the success of a proposed action.

These 5 activities comprise the G-STIC framework. The Goal-Strategy-Tactics-Implementation-Control framework is the foundation of market planning and analysis. The key components of the marketing plan and main decisions underlying each individual component are shown below. (Fig 5.1)

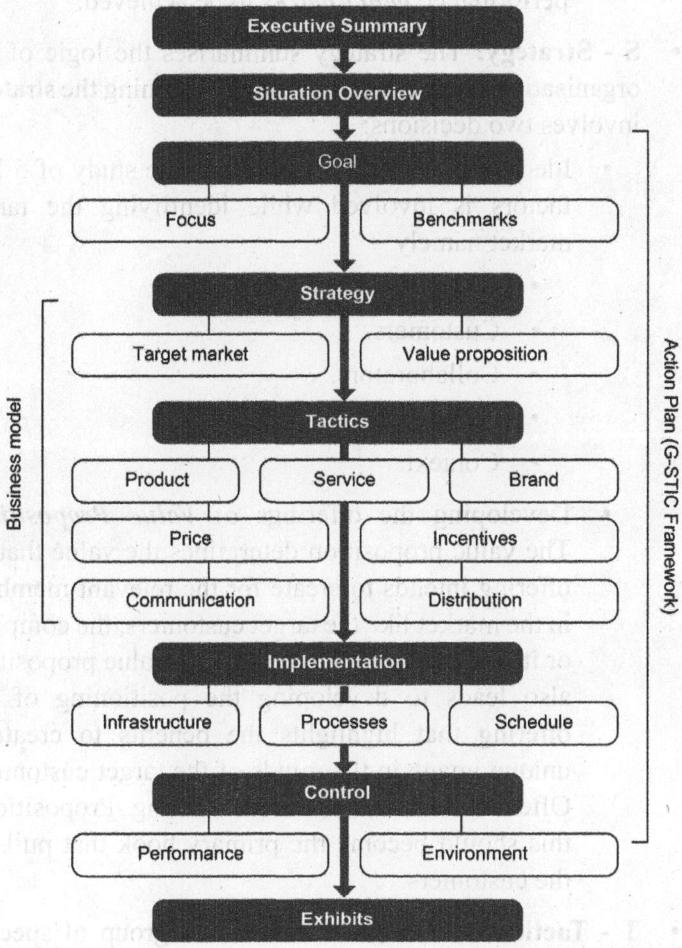

Figure 5.1: G-STIC Model – Marketing Plan as a Business Document
Source: *Chernav, A. (2020). The Marketing Plan Handbook (6th ed.). Cerebellum Press.*

- **G - Goal:** The goal identifies the ultimate standard for success that guides the organisation's marketing activities. Setting a goal further involves two decisions:
    - Identifying the ***focus*** of the organisation's actions.
    - Defining the specific quantitative and sequential performance ***benchmarks*** to be achieved.
- **S - Strategy:** The strategy summarises the logic of the organisation's value-creation model. Defining the strategy involves two decisions:
    - Identifying the ***Target Market***: The study of 5 key factors is involved while identifying the target market namely –
        - Company.
        - Customers.
        - Collaborators.
        - Competitors.
        - Context.
    - Developing the offerings of ***Value Proposition***: The value proposition determines the value that an offering intends to create for the relevant members in the market like the target customers, the company or its collaborators. Developing a value proposition also leads to developing the positioning of the offering that highlights the benefits to create a unique image in the minds of the target customers. Often called USP (Unique Selling Proposition), this should become the primary hook that pulls in the customers.
- **T - Tactics:** The tactics summarise a group of specific activities that will be undertaken to execute the planned strategy. These tactics are the ways to execute an organisation's marketing strategy and create an optimal

value proposition for the target market. The tactics include the key aspects of an organisation's offering commonly referred to as the marketing mix –

- Product.
- Service.
- Brand.
- Price.
- Incentives.
- Communication.
- Distribution.

- **I – Implementation**: The implementation describes the logistics and course of action of executing the organisation's strategy and tactics. Implementation has 3 key components –
    - Defining the business ***infrastructure***: This refers to the organisational structure. It includes the identification of the group in charge of the plan and key personnel and collaborators.
    - Designing the business ***process:*** This portrays the activities involved in designing and managing the offering like the flow of information, goods and money.
    - Setting the implementation ***schedule***: This includes the sequence and timelines for the strategy and tactics.
- **C – Control:** The control activity determines criteria for evaluating the progress of the organisation's goal and objectives. Control involves two key processes –
    - Evaluation of the ***performance*** towards the goals defined.
    - Analysis of the changes in the ***environment*** in which the organisation operates.

DEVELOPING A SPORTS MARKETING PLAN

A sports marketing plan needs to be developed to address the needs and wants of the sports consumers. Sport marketing plans are comprehensive frameworks to identify and achieve a sports organisation's marketing goals and objectives. Below is a 10 – step process identified in developing a sports marketing plan.

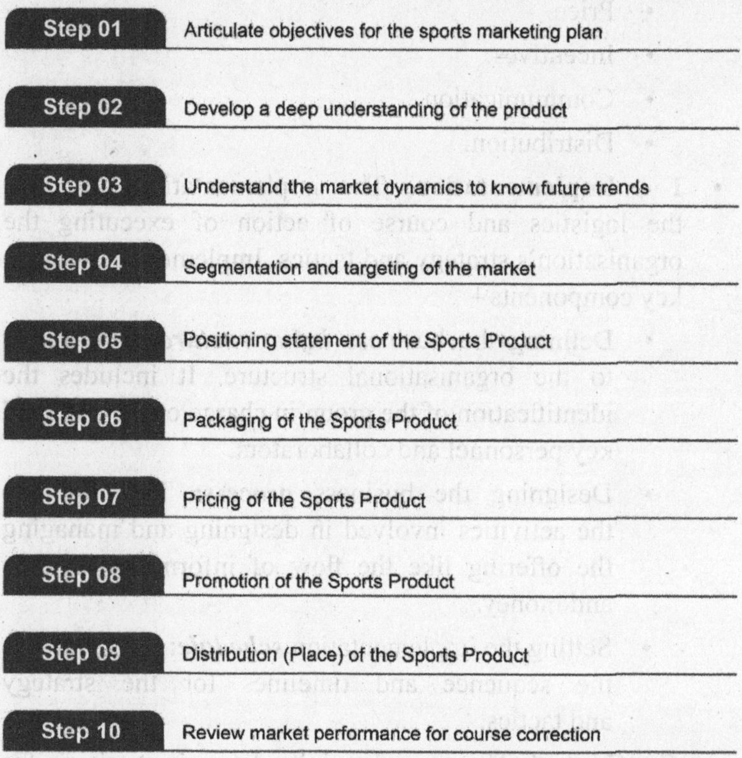

Figure 5.2: 10-step Process to Develop a Sports Marketing Plan

Step 1: Articulate Objectives for the Marketing Plan

The purpose or reason for creating a marketing plan is to provide a direction to the individuals who will be working on the sports marketing strategy. All these individuals should be involved in the course of defining the mission and vision statement along with developing the objectives of the sports marketing plan. This also ensures that the sports marketer, his team and the organisation are committed to carrying out the plan in alignment with the organisation's philosophy.

Step 2: Develop a Deep Understanding of the Product

As discussed in the previous Units, the sports product consists of tangible goods, intangible services and the event or game itself.

- Goods comprise tangible items such as sports apparel like shoes, jerseys and equipment like shuttles, racquets, bats, balls etc.
- Intangible services include activities or programmes that are additional to sports but necessary for its operation like game officials, operations staff, office support etc.
- The game or event itself includes two parts – the core product and the related product or additional enhancements:
    - The core product of the event is the actual competition taking place. For example, a football match.
    - The related product is the add-ons during the event, such as the music, mascots, entertainment, food and beverages and cheerleaders. These enhance the overall experience for sports consumers or fans.

In any case, analysing the type of sports product is important during the development of a marketing plan.

Step 3: Understand the Market Dynamics to know Future Trends

Examination of the internal and external factors of the sports organisation that affect the success of the marketing strategy is crucial during forecasting of the sports market situation. SWOT analysis and PESTLE analysis assist in determining the factors that will lead to the success or failure of a strategy.

Step 4: Segmentation and Targeting of the Market

Segmentation and targeting help to identify smaller groups to be targeted and aid the sports marketer to develop an effective and efficient strategy in the marketing plan to reach the target market.

Step 5: Positioning Statement of the Sports Product

Sports marketers should take into account the diverse primary and secondary markets of sports to position a sports product. The primary and secondary sports markets are –

- Primary sports markets
  - Participants: **Athletes, coaches and games officials.**
  - Spectators: Stadium attendees, television viewers, newspapers, OTT platform viewers or magazine readers.
  - Volunteers: Social hosts at sports events and team managers.
- Secondary sports markets
  - Advertisers: They use sports to target and communicate their products to large groups of audiences.
  - Corporate sponsors: They use sports to target and communicate positive and unique images about their products to large groups of audiences.
  - Athletes' endorsements of sports, non-sports products, and licensed products: Personalities and celebrities, unique symbols, logos or trademarks are used to encourage consumers to perceive products as popular, trendy and prestigious.

Step 6: Packaging of the Sports Product

Packaging of a sports product is the way the target audience will view the product. Considering that each targeted consumer segment views the sports product in different ways, it is important to present it in as many ways. Packaging tangible sports products include explaining the benefits of these products. For example, mentioning the strength and longevity of certain bats, the comfort and safety of cricket helmets, or the importance of oversized tennis racquets. Packaging the core product of sports, i.e., the game or event itself includes communicating the expectations of the product and presenting information before the point of purchase. Another aspect of packaging the related product is how product add-on (discussed above in Step 2) is included in the overall sports experience. The packaging of sports products is also associated with merchandising. Sports teams and events offer t-shirts, caps, jackets, apparel, mugs and other novelty items. Sponsorship is another sports product that can be packaged. Sponsorship involves an agreement between a brand and a sports organisation, team or athlete where the brand pays a fee to acquire certain rights for the team, athlete or event. Sponsorships help brands increase their sales, increase awareness, change consumer perceptions and maintain a positive relationship with the audience. Hero Motorcorp is the title sponsor for the Indian Super League (ISL) and is known as Hero ISL.

Step 7: Pricing of the Sports Product

Designing a pricing strategy is an integral part of any marketing plan because it not only has a significant impact on the revenues but also determines the success of a sports organisation. Pricing is the most flexible component in the Sports Marketing mix. It is mainly affected by the spending capacity of the sports consumer. In addition, it is also affected by external factors like the economy, politics and government regulation.

Step 8: Promotion of the Sports Product

The promotion of sports products, teams, athletes and brands involves the implementation of activities that communicate the image of the said product to the target market. These promotional activities should aim to educate the target market about the sports product and persuade the sports consumer to purchase it. The following are the elements that are included in a promotion mix –

- Advertising.
- Community relations.
- Media relations.
- Personal selling.
- Promotions.
- Public relations.
- Sponsorship.
- Endorsements.

Step 9: Distribution (Place) of the Sports Product

As discussed in the previous Units, place refers to

- The location of the sports product: The stadium or arena.
- The point of origin for distribution of the product: Ticket sales at the stadium, sales by a toll-free telephone number.
- The geographic location of the target markets: Global, national, regional, state, communities and cities.
- Other channels and media outlets like online websites, apps, social media sites, etc. ensure accessibility of products to target audiences at any time, day, season, month or year.

These factors that are related to the physical or virtual location of the sports may have a favourable or unfavourable impact on the marketing plan.

Step 10: Review Market Performance for Course Correction

The sports marketer needs to obtain feedback from the inside as well as the outside of the organisation to ensure the viability of the sports marketing plan. The analysis of this feedback needs to be evaluated and incorporated into the plan. The evaluation of the feedback further determines the extent to which the plan has helped the organisation achieve its objectives. The plan should also be modified based on the feedback received.

INNOVATION TO BREAK THE CLUTTER

The evolution of sports as an industry comes with the increasing recognition of it as a brand-building platform by non-sporting brands. Advertising was the principle route to take the brands to their consumers for many decades in the 20th century. Gradually, it got supplemented by initiatives in PR, Customer Relations and other such efforts. Sponsorships, especially in the sports arena, grew in prominence much later. As the sports industry went on an upsurge, avenues for brands to associate with marquee events started manifesting in different ways, aided by the advancements in technology. Sports events became ideal opportunities for brands to connect with their target consumers. Consequently, over time, with growing brand clutter in the sports event space, regular brand presence that came as a part of the sponsorship package became par for the course. To make sure that the brands get firmly entrenched in the minds of the consumers, it became imperative that they needed to do more than simple visibility initiatives. Today brands can gain a lot by innovating to stand out in a clutter.

To illustrate an example, let us consider the association between DHL and ISL. 2020 marked the sixth consecutive year in which the logistics major partnered with the event as Associate Sponsor. It is an association that kept getting stronger each year and the way the brand leveraged the event, is a testimony to how brands can get the perfect fit with the sporting occasion. Known for perfect on-time delivery of goods, DHL Express delivered the match ball 'on time' at the sporting spectacle, among other activation ideas that highlight this promise from the brand. Also conspicuous at the event was the DHL delivery person, in the signature uniform and parcel packaging from DHL which has high recall value. In 2020, with greater emphasis on remote activation caused by the COVID pandemic, drones and remote-controlled miniature DHL delivery cars were engaged as part of the activation.

Moving onto cricket, India's most commercialised sport, here's another example that brings out the beauty of a well-curated association between a sport property and an event partner. In 2018 Star India became the media partner for the IPL, an association they leveraged well by creating a property that brings out the essence of a channel from the Star Network. Their General Entertainment Channel, Star Plus, had the campaign "Rishta Wahi Soch Nayi" (Same old relations, new thinking) which highlighted the changing dynamics of relations in Indian households as depicted in their TV shows, something which they wanted to portray as progressive thinking in Indian joint-families. At the IPL, in the post-match presentation show, there was a "Nayi Soch" (new thinking) award given for the player who demonstrated innovative thinking during the match, possibly impacting the outcome of the match. This was an activation that helped further strengthen the positioning of Star Plus, on a platform as big as the IPL.

Media Innovations Accelerated by COVID Threat

Necessity is the mother of invention! With social distancing being the need of the hour at IPL 2020, the stadia were closed to fans, and the broadcast had to be designed in a way that fans viewing the games on media feel they are a part of the community, which is a vital aspect in any sport. The IPL broadcast on the Star Network was welcomed with joy by the Indian cricket fans who were deprived of cricketing action from their favourite stars. BARC India viewership data indicates that the tournament had a cumulative reach of 405 mn viewers, which is almost half of the total TV universe of 836 mn. No other broadcasting property in India ever had as much viewing time as the 13th edition of India's top sporting league. With the acceleration of the digital shift in the direction of fan engagement, considerable value has been unlocked by tech-oriented businesses operating in that space.

Among the many firsts at IPL 2020, were the digital fan walls that were put up in every game. This helped in enabling a large number of fans to connect with the game and to get a community viewing feel that you experience in a stadium. Augmented

Reality (AR) graphics that give impactful visuals, LED Walls, pre-recorded fan cheer score, pre-recorded cheerleader videos and other such effects created a seamless experience and a sense of continuity for the fans viewing the games from the safety of their homes. Deployment of AR technology helped in taking the attention away from the empty stands, providing a true spectacle to fans watching the game through their gadgets. Star India, the official broadcaster, had partnered with bookmyshow.com to provide virtual match tickets through which selected fans became part of live streaming of the match. To engage the young fans on Disney+Hotstar, the platform had a feature by which fans could join a virtual community where they could use interactive emoji streams and be a part of the action.

This IPL also saw the teams using virtual meet and greet with players and other video conferencing techniques to keep the fans engaged. For instance, Mumbai Indians had launched 'MI Live' which streams the team's live shows on their official channels and shared on their official pages on platforms like YouTube, Facebook and Twitter as well as on Jio TV. Star India had a virtual studio with an immersive mixed reality LED stage that allowed presenters to be teleported to the ground for face-to-face conversations with players via a graphics engine, while adhering to all social distancing norms.

TYPES OF MARKETING STRATEGIES IN THE INDIAN SPORTS INDUSTRY

Promotional Marketing

Promotional marketing is a marketing strategy intended to encourage a customer to purchase a particular product or service. The technique of marketing comprises several incentives to buy, such as –

- **Contests:** Contests provide an attractive marketing way for small businesses to acquire new customers and create awareness. Many interesting online contest formats can be applied for a sports organisation –

- Motivational contest: Before/ after contest.
- Creative photo contest: For example, the most unusual place for a training practice.
- Sports goals for couples.
- Professional awards for sport coaches.
- Video contest: The best set of fitness moves/ exercise.
- Hashtag contest.
- Voting contest.
- Sports diet ideas.

- **Coupons:** Coupons work as an affordable marketing strategy for businesses. For example, many sports retail brands like Nike, Adidas, Shiv-Naresh, Cosco, etc. can pull customers to buy their products by providing discount coupons. Similarly, sports events like cricket or football matches can also have coupons for free food or beverage along with the tickets for a game/ season.
- **Sampling:** This method of giving the product might appear profit-limiting, but this gives the customers a small taste of the product which can lead to a big purchase. Trying before buying strategy can potentially tap into customers who do not know about the product and can be converted to loyal customers.

Traditional Marketing

Traditional marketing refers to print, broadcast, direct mail, phone and outdoor advertising like billboards. This technique includes advertising through mediums like newspapers, radio, magazines, telephone, mail, billboards, pamphlets, etc. to reach targeted audiences. These ads can be kept for a long period.

Traditional marketing technique includes any type of marketing that is not online. Sports organisations, teams, athletes, clubs, etc. use traditional methods of marketing regularly.

Digital Marketing and Social Media Marketing

Digital marketing refers to marketing efforts that are primarily enabled through internet connectivity. Businesses leverage digital channels such as search engines, social media, email and other websites to connect with current and prospective customers. Any marketing that is conducted online is called digital marketing. Paid social media ads, email marketing, websites, social media marketing, Pay - Per - Click (PPC) advertising, etc. are examples of digital marketing methods. Digital marketing is very popular due to the cultural, technological, social and societal shifts in the environment.

Social media marketing refers to the use of social media platforms to connect with the target audience to build the organisation's brand, increase sales and drive website traffic/ engagement. This includes creating and posting great content on the organisation's social media profiles. It also involves listening to and engaging followers, analysing results and administering social media advertisements. Social media platforms like Instagram, Facebook, Twitter, LinkedIn, Snapchat, YouTube, Pinterest, Quora, etc. provide a unique opportunity for organisations to invest in customer engagement.

For example, let us look at the digital marketing strategy of Kolkata Knight Riders (KKR). KKR, a franchise in the Indian Premier League is owned by Shah Rukh Khan, Juhi Chawla and Jay Mehta. The main objectives of the KKR's digital marketing strategy are –

- To increase brand awareness of KKR.
- To stay connected with the fans.
- To ensure fans and users are updated with IPL news, images and scores.

KKR is the IPL team that has the most engagement with their fans and followers as of 2020 (Kreedon 2020). The following are the highlights of the digital strategy implemented by KKR since 2014:

- KKR has an exclusive YouTube Videoblog "Inside KKR" to ensure fans are easily updated with its news and their favourite players.
- KKR team has a website blog and an official mobile app that keeps fans engaged and updated with the latest news about the team.
- KKR has also organised a live screening on Facebook chat at Facebook HQ in Hyderabad.
- KKR players had Q&A sessions on Twitter with their fans.
- They also ran a special "Cheer for KKR campaign" on all social media platforms. This is the first for any sports team in the world.
- KKR introduced a new member on the social media front. Tutul Da, a typical Bengali gentleman from Kolkata, India, who is an ardent fan of KKR shared trivia about the players. The character has been designed keeping in mind the supporters and audience of KKR on Facebook. The snippets portray Tutul Da in various situations giving information about the matches, team and players.
- KKR fans were also given a chance to receive a customised, personalised and acknowledgment video.
- A special Google widget was also created for KKR which is a first for any sports team in the world.

Results of the Campaign – As of August 2021

- The Facebook page of KKR has 16 mn likes.
- On Twitter, KKR is the one of the most engaging IPL team.
- KKR became one of the most followed IPL team on Instagram with more than 2.6 mn followers.

- KKR also gained traffic and presence on its Pinterest page and Google Plus profile.
- Personalised video activity reached 10 mn cricket followers to conclude having made an impact both on and off the field.

Offline Marketing

Many companies are finding new and innovative ways of strategies that are not digital or online. These offline strategies integrate ideas already around with new technology to create a more engaging experience for customers.

For example, the launch of RCB Bar and Cafe right in the heart of the Bengaluru city, less than a kilometre away from the stadium of Royal Challengers Bangalore, i.e., the M Chinnaswamy Stadium. The RCB Bar and café consists of –

- A 40 - feet curvy linear bar.
- Sensory experiences intended to provide the combination of a bar and cafe in an experiential setting.
- An assorted culinary journey designed with passion and panache, artisanal cocktails, etc.
- Eclectically programmed music.
- Indoor and outdoor seating facilities, sports, live events and more.

This place serves as the perfect go-to destination for its night and pub culture.

Cause Marketing

Cause marketing is a marketing strategy that has the dual purpose of increasing profitability while bettering society. Cause marketing occurs when a company does well by doing good. This includes the planning and execution of marketing efforts that involve a contribution of a certain amount to a cause even as the organisation pursues its stated business objectives. In other words: "You buy. We'll give." One of the important aspects of this strategy is to find a cause that both the organisation and its customers care about.

An example of cause marketing is the "IndusInd Bank Para Champions Programme" in association with GoSports Foundation, a non-profit organisation, working towards securing funds and professional expertise for some of India's junior Olympic and Paralympic athletes. The programme supports the development of 32 Para-athletes as of 2021. The bank is very committed to the cause of sports and has a dedicated non-banking vertical called "IndusInd for Sports". The vertical has even supported the shooting stars of our country by offering jobs at their branches through the M.P Shooting Academy Programme. The vertical is also used as a client and employee engagement tool through constant use of marketing.

Another example is of one of the greatest football clubs in the world, Manchester United, which has one of the biggest fan bases globally not limited only to their presence on the field but have also impacted lives. Manchester United Foundation uses football to engage and inspire young people to build a better life for themselves and the community they live in. In 2020, Manchester United Foundation teamed up with Supporters' Clubs worldwide, to form a fundraising initiative 'United for the Children' involving 247 Supporters' Clubs both across the UK and overseas. Youth-focused charities will be offered up to £1,000 from the Foundation, to aid children who were affected by the COVID-19 crisis. An initial £500 donation from the Foundation was offered to the nominated charity of each Supporters' Club. This was then supposed to be topped up with a further £500, to match local fundraising efforts by each club. Fundraising activities included bike rides, virtual quizzes and organised runs for fans from across the world. Until September 2020, branches have raised over £41,000, with the Lancaster branch raising over £5,000 and the Norway branch over £7,000 for their chosen charities (inyourarea.co.uk, 2020).

Relationship/ Customer Relationship Marketing

Relationship marketing refers to an approach that is built around networks and symbiotic relationships. Relationship marketing focuses on customer relationship that centres around customer loyalty and aims to build long-term customer engagement rather than shorter-term goals like customer acquisition and individual sales. The goal of relationship marketing is to create a strong and emotional connection to a brand that further supports the ongoing business, free word-of-mouth information from customers that can generate more potential customers.

There are five levels of relationship marketing namely –

1. Basic marketing.
2. Reactive marketing.
3. Proactive marketing.
4. Accountable marketing.
5. Partnership marketing.

For example, the homepage of Nike states that "it's not about transactions, it's about connections" (Nikeinc.com). This statement emphasises Nike's relationship marketing orientation. At a global level, Nike's relationship marketing activities are based on two theoretical frameworks (Grin.com, 2012) –

1. **Four partnership approaches to relationship marketing**

   These four partnerships are –

   a. External partnerships with alliances, competitors and governments.

   b. Internal partnerships with functional departments, employees and internal business units.

   c. Supplier partnerships with goods suppliers and service suppliers.

d. Customer partnerships with intermediate customers and final customers.

In each of the four partnerships, an exchange affecting the effectiveness of Nike takes place. Instead of taking a simple buyer and seller approach, this model meets the requirement of relationship marketing by taking a constellation approach (Godson, 2011).

2. **The 30Rs of Relationship Marketing**

The 30Rs of relationship marketing are 30 identifiable relationships that incorporate a mixture of relationships between Nike and other parties. The 30 relationships are further sub-divided into four broad categories –

- Classic market relationships.
- Special market relationships.
- Mega relationships.
- Nano relationships.

The classic market relationships and the special market relationships represent Nike's market relationships mainly with its customers, suppliers and competitors. The mega relationships and nano relationships comprise non-market relationships that have an indirect effect on the efficiency of Nike's market relationships. The mega relationships are concerned with the environment and society at large. They apply their influence on a higher level than the market relationships and set the conditions under which market relationships operate. Nano relationships or internal relationships exercise their influence on a lower level than the market and represent relationships within Nike.

Word-of-Mouth (WOM) Marketing

Word-of-mouth marketing (WOM marketing) is when consumers endorse or talk about a company's product or service organically with their friends, family and other close relationships. WOM includes the passing of information from person to person by oral communication. According to Investopdia.com, WOM marketing is said to be one of the most powerful forms of advertising as 92% of consumers trust their friends over traditional media. Companies drive WOM marketing by providing good customer service, exceeding expectations on a product and giving exclusive information to consumers.

For example, Under Armour's Word-Of-Mouth Strategy aimed to create an innovative product with little to no competition. Under Armour (UA) initiated word-of-mouth marketing by setting itself apart from its potential competition. Instead of throwing itself into a crowded athletic wear market, UA created athletic apparel focused on athletes' performance and comfort, "built from microfibers that wicked moisture and kept athletes cool, dry and light." (Underarmour.com). Founder Kevin Plank played football throughout high school and college. His experience of wearing cotton shirts under his football gear, where they would become heavy and uncomfortable with all the sweat they were drenched in, led to the creation of a product and niche that no one else had dreamt of before. He gave the first samples to his friends who also played football and who had gone on to play for prestigious college and professional teams in the US. His friends spread the word about his product to their respective professional teams aiding him to competitively position UA to sell to collegiate and professional football teams in the USA. Soon, athletes of all levels and sports, their families and friends were constantly speaking about Under Armour which is now a premium athletic apparel giant all on its own.

Diversity Marketing

Customers from different cultures have different experiences, values, expectations and ways of interacting, etc. Even within a culture, different subgroups are prevalent not just based on ethnicity but also age, gender, religion, marital status, profession, education, occupation, family size, physical environment, etc. It is vital to develop a customised marketing plan by analysing all customer segments based on cultural differences including beliefs, tastes, expectations, world views and specific needs. It is also known as inclusive marketing, inclusion marketing or in-culture marketing. Multicultural marketing refers to a marketing strategy that recognises the differences in culture and ethnicities of a target market.

For example, Puma, one of the largest brands in the sports and lifestyle space has designed campaigns and strategies that are inclusive of culture and ethnicities at a global level as well as in India. Puma entered the Indian market in the 2006. The brand is very popular among millennials (born between the years 1981 and 1996) and generation Z (those born between the years 1997 and 2015). Puma ensures that all their strategies are relevant to their consumers and help them stay connected with the brand. They also ensure that their products are high on style and performance as per the demands of the target market. To promote inclusivity, expand and connect with the target market, Puma sponsored or collaborated with athletes from different sports, ethnicities and genders. Campaigns like 'Propah Lady' was highly creative and successful featuring some strong female ambassadors like Mary Kom - boxing, Dutee Chand – Gay athlete and others. This campaign tries to reconceptualise the traditional and stereotype of a woman. Puma also invited a number of sporting legends to engage with sports enthusiasts of India. This provided fans of these athletes and sport with an unforgettable experience that money cannot buy. Fans got to interact with sporting legends like Usain Bolt – Jamaican athlete and sprinter, Asafa Powell – Jamaican athlete, Boris Becker – German tennis player, Robert Pires – French football player and Thierry Henry – French football coach. Puma has also collaborated with Virat Kohli to launch his athleisure brand One8 which reflects Kohli's personal beliefs.

Co-Branding

A co-branding strategy employs multiple brand names on goods or service in the form of a strategic alliance. Co-branding is also known as a brand partnership. It incorporates different types of branding collaborations, generally at least involving the brands of two companies.

Co-branding can help boost the reputation of these two or more brands involved, conditional to the strategy employed. Co-branding includes four distinct strategies –

- Market penetration.
- Global brand.
- Brand reinforcement.
- Brand extension strategy.

Co-branding strategy will aim to combine brand awareness, market strength, positive associations and subtly push consumers to pay a greater premium for them. Co-branding is beneficial for any brand that aims to broaden its audience, increase brand awareness and offer a new type of content to its audience.

For example, the brands GoPro and Red Bull.

Both GoPro and Red Bull have established themselves as lifestyle brands. They not only sell portable cameras and energy drinks respectively but also sell a lifestyle. They promote a lifestyle that is adventurous, action-packed, fearless and very extreme. Their shared values make them a perfect combination for co-branding campaigns, especially those surrounding extreme and action sports.

In this partnership, GoPro provides athletes and adventurers of the world with the equipment and funding to capture stunts, races and action sports events on video from the athlete's perspective first-hand. At the same time, Red Bull uses its reputation and experience to sponsor and conduct these events.

Another example of co-branding is Nike and Apple. They have been working together since the first line of iPods was released, i.e., since the early 2000s. The partnership has since advanced to become Apple Watch Nike+ in 2016 which uses activity tracking technology built into athletic clothing and gear to sync with Apple iPhone apps to track and record the workout data of the consumer. Pairing exclusive Nike Sport Bands with Apple Watch Series2, featuring GPS, a two-times-brighter display, water resistance and powerful dual-core processor. Tracking transmitters were installed into shoes, armbands and even basketballs to measure distance, time, heart rate and the calories burned.

The co-branding partnership initially aimed to bring music from Apple to Nike customers' during their workouts using the power of technology. Nike+iPod produced fitness trackers, sneakers and clothing that tracked activity while connecting people with their music tunes.

Event Marketing/ Experiential Marketing

Event marketing defines the development of a themed display, exhibit, or presentation to promote an organisation's product, service or cause. Events can be online or offline and can be hosted, participated in, or sponsored as a type of engagement. The use of events as a marketing channel provides potential customers a first-hand interaction and unique position of the organisation and gives an understanding of the organisation's perspective, focus and personality. Event marketing can benefit by helping build brand presence before, during and after the event. The organisation can generate leads and new opportunities. Event marketing can aid in promoting a specific product feature and increase overall customer satisfaction, engagement and retention.

Experiential marketing includes direct engagement with consumers and interacting creatively with them in a memorable way. It's also known as live marketing, engagement marketing or participation marketing and is often clubbed into event marketing.

For example, to celebrate and support FIFA World Cup 2018, Coca-Cola placed a Virtual Reality (VR) experience in front of a train station in Zurich that gave football fans the chance to play alongside Switzerland star Xherdan Shaqiri. In this experience, fans could stand in front of a screen and see Shaqiri play next to them. Footage of Shaqiri was taken in front of a green screen before being adapted to allow participants to play alongside him. Participants viewed a show of skill from Shaqiri before he gestured the fans to play a few shots against him. At the end of the experience, the fans were prompted to take a photograph, they could then enter their details to receive a copy of the photograph and a chance to win a FIFA World Cup Official Match Ball.

Another example is American Express (AmEx), financial services corporation that fashioned a complete digital experience at the 2014 US Open that allowed tennis fans to engage in multiple ways. The US Open American Express Fan Experience was covered with various activities that kept the fans entertained in more ways than one.

Attendees who arrived at the AmEx experience were all given RFID-enabled wristbands that obtained on-site information and personalised emails of experiences were sent to fans. One section of the onsite experience included a 180-degree rally cam which highlighted a video camera and backdrop of Arthur Ashe stadium, the biggest tennis stadium in the world (tenniscreative.com) allowing fans to take photographs and upload them on their social media platforms. Additionally, there was a life-size hologram of tennis champion Sloane Stephen. Fans who had AmEx cards/ were members could pose for pictures with the hologram. The on-site setup also included a text cafe that served the purpose of a digital hub, allowing fans to charge their phones while watching a live newsfeed of US Open fan buzz from all over the world.

Guerrilla Marketing

Guerrilla marketing is a tactic used by an organisation to promote a product or service by an unconventional method.

Guerrilla marketing is very different from traditional marketing. It often includes personal interaction, has a smaller budget and concentrates on smaller groups of loyal customers who will assist in getting the word out in a particular location than through widespread media campaigns. This technique is untraditional, includes low-budget methods, involves creativity and the element of surprise to market or promote a product, service, brand, event or new launch.

For example, the Austria-based energy drink manufacturer Red Bull GmbH was launched in 1987, has sold 7.9 billion cans as of 2020 with a presence in more than 171 countries. Red Bull's main product category is energy drinks and adapts a unique marketing concept. Since its inception, the company has applied guerrilla marketing tactics to popularise Red Bull. In 1998, it launched the Red Bull Dolomite Man, an extreme endurance event in kayaking and paragliding. This was followed by events like 'Flugtag' where participants could fly the machines they had built. Red Bull associated itself with extreme sports like biking, skating, free-running, etc. They also venture into traditional and unconventional sports depending on the country in which the strategy will be implemented.

The Red Bull Stratos jump campaign is a great example of guerrilla marketing. The Stratos campaign in 2012 took this to new heights when it partnered with Felix Baumgartner the skydiver to jump from the edge of space and set a world record skydive of 39km (24 miles) above the earth. This record was subsequently bettered by another skydiver a few years later. Felix became the first skydiver to break this barrier. The hype and the publicity were extraordinary, social media and networks amplified the excitement. People all over the world were able to watch and engage with this heart-stopping attempt by Felix live via a dedicated website, through YouTube, Twitter and Facebook. As Felix dived into the earth, there were 8-million live views on YouTube (meltwater.com, 2021). Subsequently, the YouTube video has notched up 46.8 million views as of June 2021. This guerrilla marketing campaign caught the eye and got a lot of people talking. Red Bull's deep connection with the sporting world inevitably made this a great fit for their brand.

There are many different types of guerrilla marketing, namely –

- Ambient marketing.
- Viral marketing.
- Undercover marketing.
- Presence marketing.
- Wild-posting marketing.
- Presume marketing.
- Pop-up marketing.
- Stealth marketing.
- Experiential marketing.
- Ambush marketing.

Ambush marketing is one of the most widely used guerrilla tactics in the Sports Marketing industry.

Ambush Marketing

Ambush marketing is a unique marketing tactic in which organisations and brands advertise their product or service in the place where the same product is being advertised by another organisation or by their competitors. Ambush marketing generally takes place in some big sporting events like Olympics, football, cricket, etc. or concerts where advertisers do not pay a sponsorship fee to the event organisers but try to grab people's attention in the same event by promoting their product against their competitors.

The best example of ambush marketing in India was during the 1996 Cricket World Cup. Coke was an official sponsor for the event, but Pepsi's brilliant counter-ad, "Nothing official about it", clearly occupied more of the consumer's mind space. While PepsiCo did not hijack a brand, it almost hijacked the entire event. Consider the Olympic Games held in Atlanta 1996. Reebok was the official sponsor for the games. Nike did not pay for Olympic sponsorship but chose to advertise its product and brand by lining the street of the city of Atlanta with Olympic-themed advertisements. Michael Johnson, the athlete sponsored by Nike, posed for pictures by wearing his gold medal and his gold Nike shoe that also created a buzz around the city. Due to this, everyone remembers the presence of Nike at these Olympics over Reebok.

Another example is of how Puma ambushed International Olympic Committee (IOC) with a pair of gold shoes. Usain Bolt is the most important athlete in Puma's portfolio. At the 2016 Rio Olympics, Bolt won the gold medal in the 100m sprint. As soon as he finished the race, he took off his gold shoes and flashed them at media. Shortly afterward this incident, Puma's social media team posted pictures on the brand's Instagram and Twitter accounts that read: "When you are @Usain Bolt, you are #ForeverFastest", which was an alteration of the Puma slogan "Forever Faster". There was no reference to the Olympics in that post, thereby avoiding any legal problems with IOC. There was no mention of Rio 2016 or the Olympics.

Emotional Marketing

Emotional marketing technique includes telling a story that connects audiences with the brand in a personal and humane way. Emotion is such a powerful force because it can create relatability to further influence a decision and urge people to act. Emotional marketing, thus, has been an effective marketing technique to inspire people to take specific actions and reach business milestones.

Emotional marketing is a measured use of persuasive messages that strike into human emotion to form a deep connection with the audience to achieve the desired result. It often appeals to a single emotion only. It can be joy, fear, anger or any other human emotion that is strong enough to influence and persuade the consumer's decision-making. According to a 2016 Nielsen study, human emotions, notably negative emotions, linger in the minds of people leading to uneasiness because of their emotions being unaddressed. This leads to the need to free oneself from it and act on it. More often, this action gives better sales figures — ads with an above-average emotional response from consumers caused a 23% sales increase as opposed to average ads (2016 Nielsen study).

Tamil Nadu Cricket Association (TNCA) organises Tamil Nadu Premier League (TNPL), a month-long professional Twenty20 cricket league since the year 2016 broadcasted on Star Sports. The campaign theme during the first two seasons of TNPL was "TNPL – Namma Ooru Namma Gethu" which means "Our land our pride." These anthem-based promos were showcased everywhere showing Tamil fans celebrating TNPL as the pride of Tamil Nadu.

Niche Marketing

Niche marketing focuses on a unique new target market. This strategy focuses exclusively on one group or demographic of potential customers instead of marketing to everyone who could benefit from the organisation's offerings.

A niche market is unique from others because of –

- Lifestyle.
- Geographic area.
- Profession.
- Occasion.
- Culture.
- Style.
- Behaviour.

- Activity or habits.
- Demographic.
- Feature addition or reduction.
- Need.

For example, gaming is a niche market that has traditionally been dominated mainly by a younger male population. But due to the pandemic, changes with the real customer persona have taken place and sub-niches have shown potential. Women gamers, middle-aged gamers, mom gamers, etc. also exist creating a new niche for the gaming industry to target.

For example, Mobile Premier League (MPL), the real money gaming service, was established in 2018. MPL was shaped by multiple strategic sponsorships and marketing partnerships to create a niche in the growing Fantasy Sports market in India. MPL partnered up team sponsorship of two Indian Premier League (IPL) teams in 2020, Royal Challengers Bangalore and Kolkata Knight Riders. Cricketer Virat Kohli was the brand ambassador of MPL.

Community Marketing

Community marketing is a brand growth technique focusing on bringing customers together over a particular topic that is directly related to or aligned with a brand in an engaging and non-intrusive way. Community marketing stimulates greater loyalty and higher levels of engagement within an existing brand community. Community marketing is also a great way to induce word-of-mouth marketing.

There are two types of community marketing –

- **Organic community marketing:** In this type, the customers interact with each other without the assistance of the organisation. They might begin to interact through social media platforms like Twitter, Instagram, etc. Customers get in touch with each other, ask questions, share feedback and create assumptions all on their own. This can be very encouraging but it can also be a matter of concern as the product or brand might suffer if the customer is unhappy about it. Organisations need to monitor discussions of their brand to understand when a product is not meeting the expectations of the public.

- **Sponsored community marketing:** In this type, the organisation develops a strategy that involves managing social media platforms and allows customers to interact with the brand as well as other customers. This interaction is monitored and all the questions, concerns regarding the product or service are answered by the brand. This provides first-hand information to customers directly from the brand which can help create a loyal base and ensure control over the kind of discussion the customers are having.

Both these strategies together will connect existing customers with the brand to foster an interaction built on satisfaction.

A great example of community marketing is Bharat Army. Bharat Army is an official Indian cricket supporters' group, which provides a unique, innovative voice and is committed passionately to support cricket teams in India. They aim to create a community of the most passionate cricket fans in the world and provide an electrifying atmosphere for fans in stadiums across the world. Bharat Army also provides many services for fans to feel included and to increase their loyalty. They constantly strive to engage the Indian cricket community.

Another example of community strategy is the establishment of IPL Fan Parks which aim to bring a social change through community viewing. These were initiated in the year 2015 as VIVO IPL Fan Parks to get fans closer to the action and replicate a stadium type experience. As of 2019, IPL Fan Parks were spread across in 21 states and covered 36 cities with a motive to defy boundaries of limited entertainment for thousands of fans.

This strategy focused on building a culture of community among cricket fans from the northernmost part to the southernmost part of the country while also extending its wings towards the east and the west. Each venue broadcasted all the LIVE matches of IPL on giant TV screens, creating a stadium-type feel and experience for fans. Entry for fans was free and included music and multiple stalls for food, beverage, merchandise and other activations by IPL's official sponsors to the atmosphere.

Cloud Marketing

Cloud marketing covers all of an organisation's online marketing efforts. It also includes the process of an organisation's efforts to market their goods and services online through an integrated digital portal and experiences specialised for every single end-user. Online portals allow organisations to present products, engage with customers and push brand messages in a new way. To market the products online, organisations use online applications such as apps, websites, web portals, social media platforms like Instagram, Facebook, Twitter, Snapchat, etc.

Personalised Marketing

Personalised marketing is the implementation of a strategy by which an organisation aims to deliver individualised content to customers through data collection, analysis and the use of automation technology. Personalised marketing aims to personally engage customers or prospective customers by communicating with a personal touch to make them feel valued. Personalised marketing is also called personalisation or one-to-one marketing. It can also be very close to an extreme form of a product differentiation strategy. Differentiation tries to differentiate a product or service from the competition whereas personalisation tries to make a unique product offering for each customer. For example, brands like Nike, Adidas, Shiv-Naresh, Cosco, Decathlon, etc. undertake a personalisation strategy by developing a unique product for each sport based on the requirements and also develop unique products for the athletes that they are sponsoring or endorsing.

Moment Marketing

Moment marketing is an opportunity for brands to take advantage of situations and events by creating marketing collateral around these events. This strategy is used by brands when they want to take advantage of ongoing conversations and insert themselves to be relevant in the market. Due to the advent of social media, people are always finding and forwarding the latest content like a viral video, a tweet, a meme or a social media post with just a few clicks.

For example, Cristiano Ronaldo – the football star moved aside two Coca-Cola bottles that were kept in front of him on the table and displayed a water bottle during a pre-match press conference before the Euro 2020 match between Portugal and Hungary. Few hours after Ronaldo's episode, Coca-Cola, who was also one of the official sponsors of Euro 2020, observed a drop in market value of its brand by around $4 billion. Fevicol, a brand of adhesives by the Indian company Pidilite Industries Limited, used this episode to create a humorous ad-based picture meme that went viral on social media. Fevicol, recreated the scene from the press conference, with a few exceptions like the chair was left empty and two bottles of Fevicol were kept on the table instead of Coca-Cola with the caption – "Na bottle hategi, na valuation ghategi" which means "Neither the bottles will move, nor will the valuation drop".

Amul India, an Indian dairy cooperative society, is way ahead in Moment Marketing for a long time now. The Amul girl has always been portrayed speaking about current sporting, political and non-political scenarios happening around the world. Amul has always been posting and extending their support to all of India's sporting wins. The recent post by Amul when Neeraj Chopra won the gold medal at the Tokyo 2021 Olympic Games has a cartoon of him and the Amul girl sitting together with the caption 'Neeraj on the thrown!'. The picture depicts Chopra showing his gold medal to the Amul girl and she is saluting the medal. The picture also contains Amul's association as the official sponsor of the Indian Team for the Tokyo 2021 Olympics to depict their support and pride towards the medal.

KEY TAKEAWAYS FOR SPORTS MARKETERS IN INDIA

Sports organisations, brands, consultancies, etc. are directly affected by the massive shifts in the sporting environment. But these brands that associate themselves with major sports events or sub-products of sports can stay ahead by investing in digital components of marketing. The key takeaways centre around these trends –

- Capturing sports fans' interest is a big opportunity for brands who take the proactive approach because fans spend more time online to get information about their favourite team. This is true for sports like kabaddi or badminton as the interest levels are growing from a nascent stage. Brands have the opportunity to claim the ground and steer potential viewers to become fans.
- Fans of every sport have a player that they follow or look up to. They are interested in everything these sports stars do. From where they eat to their workout regime to their clothing style, etc. the fans wants to know everything. Sports marketers should capitalise on the massive social media following of sports stars or keep an eye on a potential sports star to their advantage which will give their brand a new playing field. This will help ensure interest and drive engagement with different sports.
- Different sports attract different audiences. The sports marketer should map the brand's target market for

different sports and key people in all demographics who search for sport-related content. For example, the sport women are mostly inclined to or fan following of football in different regions.

- Sporting activities provide a great opportunity for brands to consolidate their marketing activities every year. Tournaments in India are often multi-day events, so brands can stand out with pre-and post-match campaigns to increase the buzz and brand association. The strategy should include tactics that find ways to take advantage of big moments in sports and engage with India's passionate fan bases.

SUMMARY

A marketing plan is a well-written document that defines the organisation's strategy and course of action required to implement that strategy. This marketing plan is invaluable, irrespective of whether the organisation is small or large, professional or amateur. Sports organisations generally develop marketing plans on an annual or seasonal basis, depending upon their nature of work, to support their ongoing sporting programmes. With rising levels of clutter in the area of brand associations with sports, it is increasingly becoming important to innovate to bring out the brand story in an impactful manner.

The G-STIC marketing plan framework can be defined by 5 key activities –

1. Setting a ***Goal.***
2. Developing a ***Strategy.***
3. Designing the ***Tactics.***
4. Defining the ***Implementation*** plan.
5. Identifying a set of ***Control*** metrics to measure the success of a proposed action.

The following is a 10 – step process identified in developing a sports marketing plan. This process is a combination of the G-STIC model by Alexander Chernav (2020) and a 10-step process to develop a marketing plan by Schwarz & Hunter (2008) –

Step 1 - Articulate Objectives for the Marketing Plan.

Step 2 - Develop a Deep Understanding of the Product.

Step 3 - Understand the Market Dynamics to know Future Trends.

Step 4 - Segmentation and Targeting of the market.

Step 5 – Positioning Statement of a Sports Product.

Step 6 - Packaging of the Sports Product.

Step 7 - Pricing of the Sports Product.

Step 8 – Promotion of the Sports Product.

Step 9 - Distribution (Place) of the Sports Product.

Step 10 – Review market performance for course of action.

Chapter 6

Sports Consumer Behaviour

INTRODUCTION

As discussed in Unit 1, often, "customer" and "consumers" are used interchangeably and are easily confused with one another. A customer is a person who purchases the goods or services of a certain producer or a business by paying a price in exchange. However, the customer is not always the consumer. The customer might pay the price and buy the products but those products may be consumed by a different person. A consumer is a person who consumes or utilises goods or services. The customer can be the consumer, but not in all cases. The consumer will know the nature and genuine quality of the product or the service. The sports customer expresses their personality and values to others through their choice of a particular team/product and its distinguishing attributes and brand personality.

One situation critical to a sports marketer is to attract and retain consumers. The core sports product is variable and subjective; hence consumer insight is central to decision-making in this domain. The idea is that consumer associations, whether based on marketing or personal experience, contribute to the equity of the brand, specifically to brand loyalty. Sports managers aim to understand the development of fan loyalty towards the brand, team or club.

SPORTS CONSUMERS

Sports consumers exhibit a range of values and behaviour that are quite unique. Not every sports consumer is equally passionate or uses their favourite brand, club or team to identify himself/herself. Neither are they interested in history, completely loyal and resistant to change their preference. Some attend games on special occasions while some attend games regularly. Some sports consumers spend their time engaging with their favourite brand or other fans online whereas some showcase their fandom by watching the sport on television or OTT platforms.

In general, there are two types of sports consumers –

1. **Personal consumer**: An individual who purchases goods and services for their use. This personal use can often extend to household use, use by a family member or by a friend. For example, a family buying a set of tickets to a game.
2. **Organisational consumer:** A business entity, profit or non-profit entity that purchases goods, services and/or equipment for the operations of the organisation. For example, a cricket team purchasing equipment, balls and a bat for practice.

Sponsors are also considered as consumers for a sports organisation or team. Similar to a B2B marketing strategy, sports organisations or teams try to attract other organisations or brands to get sponsors on board for a particular period. The sponsor as a consumer will help in revenue generation and help the sports organisation or team reach the consumers in the network of the sponsor brand. For example, VIVO, who is the title sponsor of IPL is a sports consumer for IPL brand.

The personal consumer can further be split into two groups of sports consumers –

- **Spectators:** Spectators are described as individuals who witness a game or performance at a sporting event. There are many factors that the sports marketer considers to attract as many spectators as possible to a sports event. An important factor is motivation. Motivation encourages an individual to work toward accomplishing the desired goal giving purpose and direction to an individual's behaviour. In sports, many motivational factors encourage spectators to attend an event. Intrinsic motivation is the desire to satisfy natural needs and interests, including accomplishment, knowledge and experiences. Extrinsic motivation involves incentives or rewards used by an individual to bring about desired behaviour in another person. Amotivation is where there is no desire intrinsically or extrinsically. Sports marketers should have a clear understanding of these motivational factors to persuade the sports consumer to consume the sports product. Some of these factors include economic value, self-esteem enhancement, affiliation, diversion from everyday life, entertainment value, eustress, aesthetic value and family ties.
- **Participants:** Participants are individuals who take part in an activity. However, the manner in which the participant takes part in the activity varies greatly. The participation of the individual is determined by the actions performed while searching for, participating in, or evaluating the sports activities the consumer thinks will satisfy their needs. As with the spectator, the participant also has internal and external influences that shape their level of involvement in sports. The decision of the participant,

internally, is affected by their motivation, personality, perceptions, ability to learn and personal attitudes. Externally, decisions are driven by social class, culture, family, reference groups, friends, peers, colleagues, etc.

Although there are many similarities between a general consumer and a sports consumer, the two are different in many ways. Sports consumers are more passionate, show high loyalty towards their favourite team or players and tend to display irrational consumer behaviour. For example, let us consider Indian cricket fans – they are usually very passionate and partisan than general consumers are about their preferred brand. Cricket fans show a high level of loyalty to their heroes. They discover something they do not get from any other activity – the adrenaline rush, the escape from routine, the thrill of a game and the feeling of being part of a community. These are elements that attract the sports consumer. Therefore, fans vow allegiances to their favourite teams, leading to irrational behaviour, even in acts like purchase of fan merchandise and other such products. General consumers may have their preferences or choice between several products. But sports fans would rarely shift their support to another team just because the ticket price of the competitor is more economical. They can, therefore, be called captive consumers.

SPORTS CONSUMER BEHAVIOUR

Sports consumer behaviour refers to the process by which consumers come to know about sports-related products, purchase and use them, to satisfy their needs. It refers to the conduct displayed by the sports consumers while seeking out, buying, ordering, using and assessing sports products and services that would potentially satisfy their needs and wants. The sports marketer must recognise the internal and external factors that affect sports consumers. The internal factors include the – personality of the sports consumer, the learning process of sports consumers, their motivating process, formation and change in attitudes of the sports consumer and the perceptions about a sports product. External factors that result from environmental influences include demographics, culture, social setting, international and global interaction.

Why Do People Consume Sports?

Consumer behaviour is affected by many individual and environmental factors. For a sports consumer, three sub-factors have the most influence, namely –

- **Socialisation:** Socialisation is described as a process where individuals attain values, attitudes and actions appropriate to the members of a particular culture. In the sporting culture, sports marketers study the process in which fans develop and incorporate knowledge, skills, attitudes and equipment necessary for that particular sport. Socialisation in sport mandates some type of involvement which creates a close connection between the sports consumer and the sport.
- **Involvement:** Involvement in sports is simple and easy. Sports activity involves attitudes, feelings and emotions such as happiness or sadness of the sports consumer when their favourite team wins or loses. Behavioural actions or reactions in fans are directly related to internal and external motivations that sports provide. For example, giving a 'high-five' or cheering along with other people during a match when the team is playing well. Cognitive actions are the process of obtaining knowledge about the sporting activity like researching online about the players or games, listening to expert podcasts, asking questions about any activity to someone who understands the brand or sport.
- **Commitment:** Commitment is a process where a consumer is intellectually and emotionally bound to the course of action. In sports, commitment describes the

duration, frequency and involvement of a sports consumer in a sports product or service. Study of the commitment levels of sports consumers relates to concepts such as willingness to spend time, money and energy on their favourite sport and team.

The understanding of these three factors, especially commitment directly relates to the escalator concept discussed in the sections below.

PARETO PRINCIPLE – 80/20 RULE

The Pareto Principle, also known as the 80/20 rule, is accredited to Vilfredo Pareto, an Italian economist. In simple words, the Pareto Principle infers that there's an 80-to-20 relationship between effects and their causes. In sports, for example, at least 20% of athletes win 80% of the time or that about 20% of training and exercise impacts 80% of an athlete's performance. In a business application, the 80/20 rule suggests that 80% of an organisation's growth (profits, sales, brand value, etc.) come from 20% of the organisation's customers. Alternatively, according to this principle, 20% of what any organisation does, represents 80% of that particular activity's outcome. The utilisation of the 80/20 rule by marketers is fundamental to the development of segments to target for a particular product or service. The concept that is important to this development process is the escalator concept.

ESCALATOR CONCEPT

Sports marketers strive to ascertain new customers while engaging current sports consumers to become more involved in the sports product. This helps the sports brand, team or club to provide value to the sports consumer. With the help of the Pareto Principle – 80/20 rule mentioned above, the Escalator Concept is utilised to characterise the movement of sports consumers to higher levels of involvement into a specified product or service (Schwarz & Hunter, 2008). Figure 6.1 shows the Escalator Concept model –

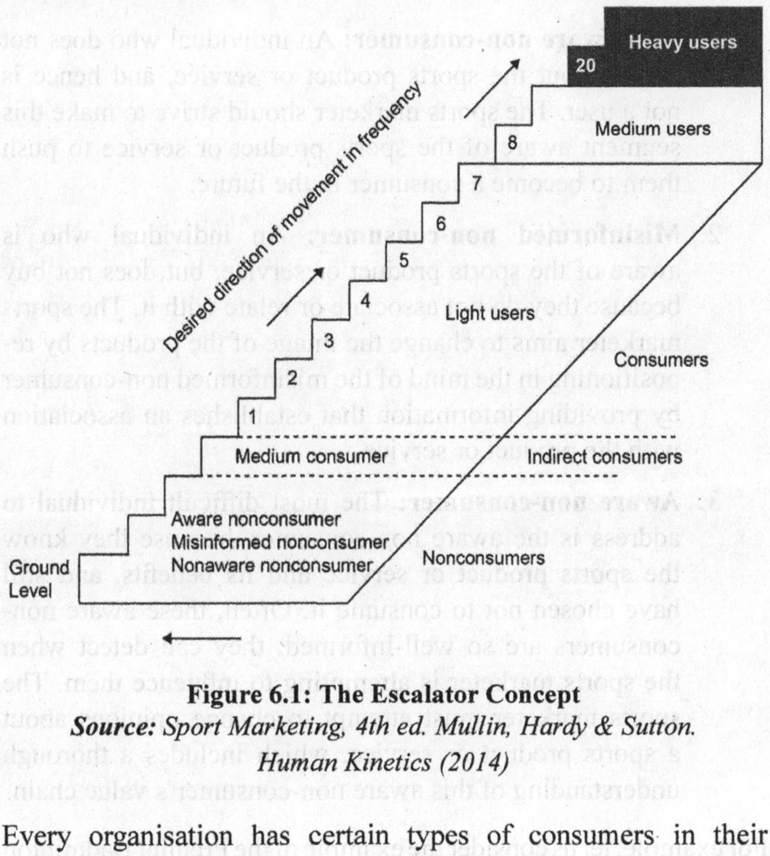

Figure 6.1: The Escalator Concept
Source: *Sport Marketing, 4th ed. Mullin, Hardy & Sutton. Human Kinetics (2014)*

Every organisation has certain types of consumers in their environment and market –

- Non-consumers.
- Indirect consumers.
- Light users.
- Medium users.
- Heavy users.

Non-consumers

A non-consumer is a person who does not use the organisation's product or service. In Sports Marketing, there are three levels of non-consumers, namely –

1. **Non-aware non-consumer:** An individual who does not know about the sports product or service, and hence is not a user. The sports marketer should strive to make this segment aware of the sports product or service to push them to become a consumer in the future.

2. **Misinformed non-consumer:** An individual who is aware of the sports product or service, but does not buy because they do not associate or relate with it. The sports marketer aims to change the image of the products by re-positioning in the mind of the misinformed non-consumer by providing information that establishes an association with the product or service.

3. **Aware non-consumer:** The most difficult individual to address is the aware non-consumer, because they know the sports product or service and its benefits, and still have chosen not to consume it. Often, these aware non-consumers are so well-informed, they can detect when the sports marketer is attempting to influence them. The sports marketer must attempt to change opinions about a sports product or service, which includes a thorough understanding of this aware non-consumer's value chain.

For example, let us consider the example of the Premier Badminton League (PBL). Premier Badminton League is a badminton league held in India since 2016. Sportz & Live Private Limited has the management and execution rights to manage PBL. The *non-consumers* for PBL are people who do not watch, follow or actively engage in PBL. *Non-aware non-consumers* have no knowledge of the existence of such a league or badminton as a sport. The individuals who do not watch or follow PBL even after knowing of the existence of the league are *misinformed non- consumers*. Individuals, even after being well-informed about the game of badminton and the details of PBL, still do not watch, follow or engage in PBL are called *aware non-consumers*. The sports marketers need to identify with each non-consumer and include tactics to change the perceptions in their minds regarding PBL.

Indirect Consumers

Indirect consumers are those who utilise the sports product or service from a distance via intermediate or intervening opportunities in the sports market. This might include causally watching sports on television, or only being a part of a fantasy league, or only purchasing non-essential products such as hats, keychains, etc. For example, indirect consumers for PBL might watch PBL on television or OTT because there is no other interesting content to watch or be a part of the fantasy league because of their friends or buy keychains of any team of PBL because they like its colour and design. The goal of the sports marketer is to persuade such indirect consumers to increase their level of involvement by purchasing more sports products, or more realistically, attending events in person.

Light Users

The light users are those individuals who not only get actively involved as indirect consumers but also attend at least one or two events in a year. For example, light consumers for PBL will attend one or two games during the season, depending upon their schedule. They know the rules of badminton. They will also have a superficial knowledge of the players and the league in general. They might follow the teams and players on social media but will not engage. The goal of the sports marketer is to persuade them to get more involved and attend more events. Strategies like ticket packages and group plans can help accomplish this.

Medium Users

The medium users are more involved with the sports brand. They are most likely to attend atleast half of the events related to the sports product. For example, medium users for PBL will watch every match on television or on OTT platforms and attend at least half the games of the season. They also engage with the brand on social media and show interest in discussions regarding badminton. The sports marketers should aim to steer this sport type of consumer to move higher to the top of the "escalator" (as shown in fig 6.1) by designing strategies and presenting the benefits of having season tickets, discount coupons, etc.

Heavy Users

Heavy users are individuals who fully engage in the culture of the sports organisation at the highest consumer level. For example, heavy users of PBL will be individuals who attend all the games of every season, know the detailed stats of all the games, engage with the brand and other consumers on social media, create organic content by posting on their social media handles, holding discussion groups, podcasts, etc. They also spread word-of-mouth information about PBL, the players and the game in general. The sports marketer must aim to maintain the level of expectation of these consumers. These heavy users should continuously be appraised about their importance and should be given maximum benefit.

It is essential to make every effort to increase the level of involvement in the sports product or service over a period while limiting the fall or descent of any consumers down the escalator. It is important to remember and understand the consumers who reduce engagement levels with the sport. This will help the sports marketers design and improve their tactics toward preventing more dips in the escalator and involvement. Another challenge faced by the sports marketer is the placement of the same individual on different levels of the escalator depending on the sports product. For example, Mr X is a heavy user of football but a light user of cricket and an aware non-consumer for kabaddi. Marketing efforts and strategies must not only be different based on the type of consumer or non-consumer but also be established on different sports.

As the sport consumer becomes more committed to the sports product, they move up the escalator. Many products and services have a maximum limit of frequency. Household products, clothing, vehicles and other non-sports products or services reach a point where even the top 20% (Pareto Principle) of brand users will arrive at a limit in consumption. Sports products and services, particularly team-related, continue to be of interest to sports consumers and have relatively no ceiling or limit. For example, a casual fan of the sport of kabaddi can become a PKL season ticket holder. She/he can then move into premium seats, buy team apparel, new merchandise of his favourite team, watch playoffs and move on to having a collection of championship merchandise from year to year. VIP events can be also added as a special incentive for heavy use fans. Each new change is another opportunity to market to the sports consumer.

Customer service is also a way to move the consumers up the escalator passage. In addition, digital media can be used to help encourage this upward move in consumption. The more knowledge a consumer has, the greater the feeling of belongingness. People invest more time in learning about a sports product or team leading them to feel a part of the collective experience. They begin self-identifying with the team or product. For example, "I am a Mumbai Indians Fan" or "I only wear Nike" or "I only watch Badminton games". This understanding can help escalate the sports consumer from a light user or medium user to a heavy user as they more fully engage and understand the brand.

3F FANDOM CONTINUUM

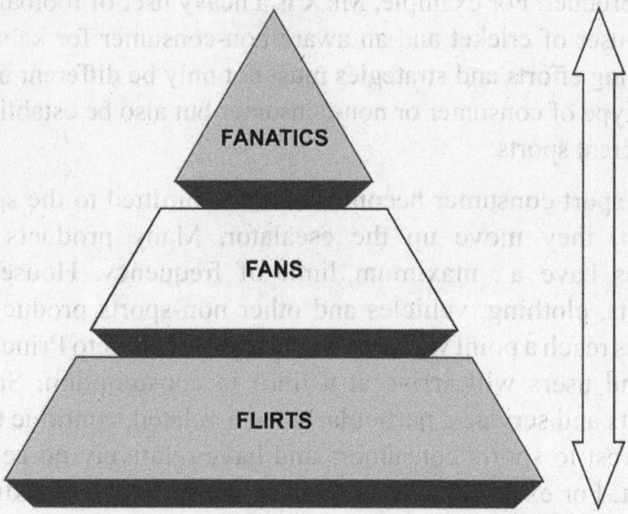

Figure 6.2: The different levels of fandom

Sports fans are the pillars of the industry. The business of sports is built around a strong sense of affiliation the fans have with the teams and athletes they adore. In the case with consumers across non-sporting product categories, the level of involvement with the offerings will be different for different people and they can be grouped into different levels of intensity of usage – like high, medium and low. Likewise, in the case of sports, they vary in the level of intensity they display in their affiliation with the sports entity they love. This behaviour can be explained by the 3F Fandom Continuum model.

At the top of the pyramid are the "Fanatics" who can be considered as die-hard fans. For them the team is a huge part of their individuality; they are elated when their favourite team wins and dejected when it loses on the field, almost as if they are encountering wins and losses personally. Even though they may not be too many in numbers, they represent strong marketing opportunities for the sports team they support. The fanatics are the ones who are most likely to buy fan merchandise, with least sensitivity to price increases. Owing to the fact that they represent strong monetising potential, they are a high priority group to engage, as they identify most with the heritage and other cultural assets of the team.

One level below the fanatics are the "Fans" who demonstrate medium levels of fandom. Their affinity to the team might be high, often reaching levels similar to the fanatics, but in terms of behaviour, they are more reclusive. Marketing initiatives targeted at them could be aimed at elevating their fandom to that of the fanatics. The band at the bottom represents the "Flirts" who can be classified as casual fans. They are well-wishers and supporters, but they demonstrate lower propensity to watch the matches of their favourite teams and are even less likely to wear their fandom on their sleeves. They would be most conscious about the costs they incur while they support the team on the ground, through online activities and at other such opportunities. They are at the bottom of the pyramid since they demonstrate least levels of passion as fans; however they make for the largest base in terms of numbers. They represent huge opportunities for the teams as they look at expanding their base of loyal fans. The levels of fandom demonstrated by an individual fan can change from time to time depending on external factors and hence the same person can move up and down the continuum from one band to the other.

SPORTS FAN AS A CONSUMER

A sports fan is a person who shows a huge orientation towards sports in such a way that even when they are not watching live sports, their minds are occupied by related thoughts. It reflects in the general discussions they have and in how they plan their days. According to Stewart, Smith & Nicholson, (2003); Johnston (2004), a sports fan shows consistency, loyalty and dedication in three forms –

1. **Cognitive form:** The sports consumer builds up knowledge about the sport and team.
2. **Attitudinal form:** The sports consumer believes strongly in the team and the sport.
3. **Behavioural form:** The sports consumer shows her/his commitment through tangible acts such as purchasing tickets or merchandise.

Thus, sports fans are individuals who are genuinely committed to a sport, team, club, athlete or brand. This commitment attests itself to the long-term affiliation with a club or team, significant time and money expenditure and loyalty, despite the performance of the team. They tend to be –

- Passionate, sometimes fanatic.
- Highly committed.
- Vested.
- Loyal.

As a result, a distinction between a mere spectator and a sports fan has to be established. Spectators are individuals who observe a sport and then forget about it whereas sports fans will intensely observe the sport and devote a part of every day to the sport or the team. Spectators will only witness a sports event in person or through various mediums like television, OTT platforms, radio, podcasts, websites, etc. But sports fans will not only witness the sports event but will also follow the sport, team and athlete to gather more information to engage with the sport.

Cricket has dominated the sporting culture in India over the last few decades. However, the emergence of domestic leagues of other sports has changed the structure of Indian sports and how people view them. Franchise leagues like Indian Super League (ISL), Premier Badminton League (PBL), Pro-Kabaddi League (PKL), etc. have been successful in generating a massive fan following and ensure good level of attendance at stadium, match after match. Every season, thousands of fans gather to consume sports, either at home on television, OTT platforms, etc. or the stadiums wearing their favourite team/player's jersey.

Characteristics of Sports Fans

Following characteristics are typical of a sports fan –

1. The involvement and identification of sports fans with teams may often reach points where the fans' moods and emotions are influenced by team results.
2. Some sports fans may particularly be intolerant to other supporters who are not as committed to the sport or team as they are.
3. Sports fanatics display behaviour where, based on their love for a sport or team, they choose their friends, in the type of media content they consume and the things they collect.
4. Sports fans also tend to collect various sport, teams and match related objects. This is also known as "capital collecting" (European Centre for Research Training and Development UK, 2017). Capital can include anything that can be bought or collected which represents the team or the sport. For example, posters, clothes, books, records, articles, autographs, videos of old performances, photos, newspaper clippings, match schedules, etc. Sports fans preserve these precious relics of their attendance.

Loyalty and Motivating Drivers of Attendance for Sports Fans

Fans are one of the most significant stakeholders when it comes to teams, clubs or leagues as they are an essential source of revenue for every club or team. However, not all fans are equally motivated and team/marketing managers need to understand the factors that encourage one to be a die-hard fan. Fan loyalty is a form of sports spectatorship depicted by a strong sense of attachment and affiliation to a particular sport or team. For a loyal fan, winning the game is only one of the several factors that influence their loyalty to the team. Many fans are extremely devoted to their teams or favourite athlete, often for their entire lives. They invest an ample amount of money, time and energy in their teams.

A sports fan's behaviour is effectively related to team identification. Team identification is the psychological connection and the fan's involvement with the sports team which determines the attachment to a group and develops social identity for the fan. Fan loyalty can be attributed to some factors like the history of the team, love for the sport, authenticity, entertainment value, fan bonding, etc. To design meaningful associations with sports fans, successful sports brands generally consider going beyond on-field involvement to keep them engaged. According to Bee & Havitz (2010), engaged and committed fans show high levels of behavioural loyalty by displaying psychological commitment and involvement in the sport.

The brand image of an IPL franchise mainly depends on effective player management, the legends in the team, the jersey, the iconic home venue, and other such factors that enable loyalty development. Loyalty programmes also shape fan attachment and help in promoting attendance at the games, viewership on media and other fandom aspects.

Team loyalty has a considerable positive impact on the fan's consumption attitude and behaviour. This suggests that generating maximum team loyalty or fan base is a crucial goal of every sports team. Therefore, team loyalty includes fan loyalty, fan allegiance, fan support, team attachment, fandom and sports customer loyalty. The greater the loyalty, the more likely the fan is to engage in commercial transactions.

Mentioned below are five different motives of a sports fan –

- **Socialising:** A desire to interact with other spectators and connect with new people in a certain context that appeals to all present.

- **Visual spectacle**: A desire to experience the visual appeal of the high-quality performance of the athletes — the grace and skill levels.
- **Stimulation:** A desire for psychological stimulation in a sports area by experiencing the thrills and uncertainties that make sports what it is.
- **Self-esteem:** A desire to get a sense of self-achievement by identifying with a winning team, thereby heightening self-esteem.
- **Escape**: A desire to be diverted from daily routine, albeit temporarily.
- **Economic gain**: A desire for monetary gains using the fan's knowledge and expertise of sports through Fantasy Sports.

Let us consider Royal Challengers of Bangalore (RCB) as an example to understand fan loyalty and the drivers of this loyalty better. RCB is one of the Indian Premier League (IPL) teams, who are yet to win the trophy. The first season of IPL was played in 2008 with a lot of fanfare and glamour. Bengaluru has always been a cricket-loving city that appreciates and understands the quality of the game, irrespective of the team. But the IPL has highlighted another aspect of their love for the game. Probably no other team in the league can claim the kind of fan base and love that RCB has in Bengaluru city. Good form, bad form, sunshine, rain, or whatever the situation, fans have always stood by their franchise. Karnataka State Cricket Association (KSCA) increased the stadium's seating capacity to about 42,000 in 2017 but RCB fans have never given any reason for the association to worry about empty seats, be it weekends or weekdays.

It is noted that the following are the reasons fans are so loyal to RCB –

- **Bengaluru city:** These fans are loyal to RCB because they hail from Bengaluru city or the state of Karnataka or have migrated to and from Bengaluru.

- **Sense of pride:** A feeling of pride and healthy competition with other states due to various other situations is also one of the reasons for a fan to be loyal. Fans, who know about conflicts of Karnataka with other states, say Maharashtra or Tamil Nadu, will attach their loyalty to RCB instead of Mumbai Indians (MI) or Chennai Super Kings (CSK).
- **Appreciation and emotional attachment for the game:** Different states and regions have a specific sport culture. Just like the northeast region of India is more football driven, people in Karnataka, in general, are cricket-loving. They genuinely appreciate and understand the beauty of the game, irrespective of the team. The Karnataka Ranji team has traditionally been one of the strongest teams in the domestic circuit and has produced many of the Indian cricket team's iconic players. This kind of history and culture of the game in Karnataka leads to a sense of pride and appreciation driving fans to be loyal to RCB.
- **Excitement:** Fans have been following the journey of RCB since 2008. The longing for RCB to win the IPL trophy has created excitement in the fans. Just like Indian fans were waiting for the Indian team to win the World Cup in 2011 for Sachin Tendulkar, similarly, RCB fans are eagerly waiting for the team to lift the IPL trophy since 2008.
- **Identification of culture:** RCB's engagement strategies focus on creating a culture among the fans where they identify with the brand. For example, a social media trend "Ee Sala Cup Namde" (The cup is ours this year) was started by the Kannada fans of RCB. The slogan was later adopted by RCB's official social media handles too. This strategy of RCB created a sense of belongingness for the fan as well as establish a connection with Kannada language. This drive facilitated the identification of the brand with the existing fans and connect with potential fans from Karnataka.
- **Impact of players:** Love and respect for a particular player can also drive the loyalty of fans. Cricketers like

Virat Kohli, AB De Villiers have massive fan followings and fans who are loyal to these players are loyal to RCB. Fans of players, who are from Karnataka like KL Rahul or Mayank Agarwal, might support Punjab Kings because of their loyalty towards the players.

The loyalty of a player towards their team also plays a vital role in retaining the loyalty of a fan. Kohli is the only player to have played for the same franchise from 2008 until 2021 at IPL. Kohli was drafted by RCB shortly after leading India to win the U-19 World Cup title in March 2008. Since then, neither Kohli nor RCB have parted ways. At RCB, Kohli has not only performed and led the team but also done more than enough as a brand ambassador. RCB brand has also treated Kohli with affection, respect and care. The following is a quote of Kohli's from an interview in March 2019 — "The thing that we have been able to do in the last ten years is creating a fan base which is impossible to create if you are striving for things that are not real. That has happened purely because of the spirit with which we played our cricket. We are not going to be here after a few years, none of us can be here forever. But, RCB will remain for a long, long time. To me, it has been a most special experience. I do not see myself leaving or playing for any other franchise" (firstpost.com, 2019) – This shows the dedication Kohli has towards RCB and it is this dedication that leads his loyal fans to be loyal to RCB as a brand.

A combination of all these factors drives the loyalty of RCB fans.

Sports Fans – Revenue Generation

Revenue flows in many directions from sports fans in the sports market. Fans are an important revenue generation element for sports leagues and teams. The sports ecosystem is characterised by a flow of money that is based on the attendance of sports fans in the stadium and at home on TV. Availability of seats in the stadium and greater travelling distances to watch the games are factors affecting sports viewership of fans. Sports viewership includes those fans that consume their favourite sport or team games by attending the games or via electronic media like websites and OTT platforms. The more loyal the fans, the more they are willing to engage in media consumption related to their favourite sport or team, including watching games.

Collignon & Sultan (2014) recommend the analysis of five crucial elements for generating revenues for sports teams or clubs –

1. **Fans:** Fans are excited to spend their money to buy subscription packages of OTT platforms for matches, become a member of the club and buy products related to their favourite sport, athlete, team or clubs.
2. **Media:** Media channels buy rights to broadcast and stream matches for an audience of fans, who can watch these games on different platforms, like TV, websites and apps.
3. **Brands:** Brands should choose the right partner clubs, leagues and athletes along with choosing the right types of partnerships, such as official partners, naming rights for arenas, suppliers or advertising inside arenas.
4. **Leagues:** Leagues organise championships and seasons, even though, in many cases, they also play an intermediary role supporting the flow of revenues to teams and clubs, especially, the money from media rights and sponsorships.
5. **Team or club (itself):** Teams or club generates revenues by selling game tickets, sponsorships, licensed products and media rights. These revenues may be increased if the team or club achieves these three indicators,
    a. Performance, i.e., winning generates interest in fans, which in turn generates media revenue through more viewership.
    b. Presence of star players, who activate sponsorships, ticketing and merchandise which are all a part of commercial revenues.
    c. Loyalty by keeping the fans excited, engaged. Providing membership to fans can also get more revenues.

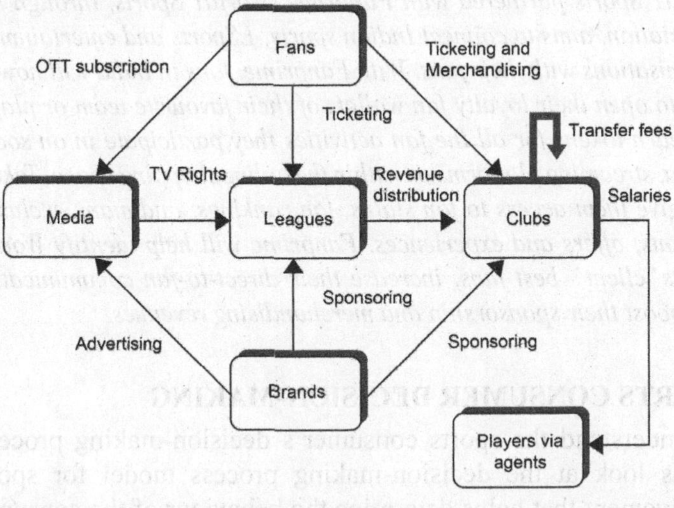

Figure 6.3: How Sports Fan Help in Revenue Generation

Source: Collignon & Sultan (2014, p. 6).

Example: World 1 Sports and Fanprime partnership

World1 Sports is one of the sports consulting companies in India. They operate out of Delhi, Chennai and London. Their clients consist of a varied set of organisations that range from professional football academies and clubs to business corporations. Their services include advising their clients on their market entry strategy, the conceptualisation of programmes, grassroots development, ground activations and brand development across various verticals.

Fanprime is a French start-up that aims to connect sports and celebrities with their fans, everywhere in the world. Using a fan wallet, Fanprime has created a unique tool to reward fans for their commitment, especially on social media networks and streaming platforms in a fun integrated way. Fanprime allows fans to become ambassadors of their favourite sports teams and allows the teams to connect directly with their fans. Fanprime brings an innovative solution to the recognition, loyalty and monetisation of digital communities in sports, ESports and entertainment.

World1 Sports partnered with Fanprime. World1 Sports, through this association, aims to connect Indian sports, ESports and entertainment organisations with their fans. With Fanprime, fans in India will now be able to open their loyalty fan wallets of their favourite team or player and earn tokens for all the fan activities they participate in on social media, streaming platforms or within the online shopping space. Tokens will give them access to fan status, fan rankings, and many exclusive contents, offers and experiences. Fanprime will help identify World1 Sports' client's best fans, increase their direct-to-fan communication and boost their sponsorship and merchandising revenues.

SPORTS CONSUMER DECISION-MAKING

To understand the sports consumer's decision-making process, let us look at the decision-making process model for sports involvement that helps determine the behaviour of the consumer while making up his/her mind about a sports product or service.

Decision-Making Process Model for Sports Involvement

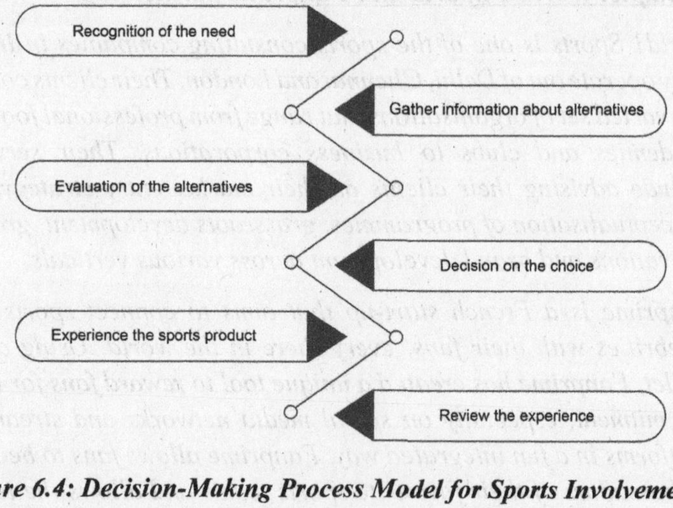

Figure 6.4: Decision-Making Process Model for Sports Involvement

Recognition of the need: The sports consumer recognises their need for the particular sports product or service. Often, needs are stirred when a consumer recognises a discrepancy between desire and ability to fulfil that desire. The consumer then takes an action when such discrepancy is recognised. For example, Mr X may want to go watch an ISL match at the stadium because he may never have been to the stadium and enjoyed the match experience.

Gather information about the alternatives: Search for information is driven by need recognition. Information search takes place when the sports consumer seeks information from various sources. For example, Mr X, after recognising his need to attend an ISL match because he has never had a football match experience at the stadium, may research about the teams in the league, rankings of the team, schedule and location of the game, ticket prices, etc. There are two ways to search for information – internal search which relies on the consumer's experience and external search which is undertaken when the internal search information is inadequate or inaccurate.

Evaluation of the alternatives: Once the consumer gains some information, she/he will evaluate the alternatives available to satisfy his need. The important component for the sports consumer here is the valuation of service quality. Sports marketers should aim to provide favourable choices for consumers to evaluate. For example, the alternatives in the case of Mr X would be – 'which game to attend', 'which seats should he buy', 'effective way to purchase tickets', 'additional benefit with each ticket package, if any' etc.

Decision on the choice: After evaluation of choices, based on various factors like spending capacity, probability of a good experience, time taken, etc. the consumer takes a decision. For example, Mr X, after evaluating the choices, decides to attend the Kerala Blasters v/s Chennaiyin FC match based on the previous rankings of the teams, the price of the tickets and the proximity of the stadium.

Experience of the sports product: This step encapsulates the experience of the consumer after deciding to purchase the sports product. Mr X attends the Kerala Blasters v/s Chennaiyin FC match and finally gets the stadium experiences which he never had before.

Review the experience: It is crucial that the consumer feels satisfied after experiencing the game because this will lead the consumer to repeat the action. Generally, spectators will attend another game when they are satisfied and are less likely to attend the game again, if they are dissatisfied. Nonetheless, if a consumer/spectator's team identification is compelling, it does not matter whether they were satisfied or not; they are not going to attend another game. For example, after watching the game and engaging in other activities at the stadium, Mr X will evaluate his entire experience and determine whether his decision to attend this game was satisfying or not. He will also evaluate whether attending a different match at a different location seated at a different angle would have enhanced his experience. If Mr X enjoyed the match, he will repeat the whole process and start going to the stadiums to watch the games.

Consumers have three options during this evaluation. Continuing our example –

1. If Mr X is satisfied with his stadium experience, he is more likely to re-purchase the tickets for Kerala Blasters v/s Chennaiyin FC match again.
2. If he is dissatisfied with his stadium experience, he may never return.
3. If he is slightly satisfied or slightly dissatisfied, he may search for more information or re-evaluate his process and options. He may choose to watch a different match at a different location with a different view.

The above process suggests that to increase the chances of consumers/spectators repeatedly attending their games, a team must strengthen customer identification, improve customer satisfaction and loyalty towards the team.

Decision Variables that Affect the Decision Process

Apart from the influence of marketing, the following factors influence a consumer's decision-making process.

1. **Individual uniqueness:** Includes demographics, psychographics and personal values or personality.
2. **External environment:** Includes influence exerted by culture, social stratum, family, relatives and other individuals.
3. **Prejudice:** Includes pre-existing information, learning from experience and attitude and behaviour modification.

In the decision-making process, many decision variables have a direct effect on the process. These decision variables are those individual behavioural factors that make sports customers unique. The qualities are –

- Personality of the sports consumer.
- Learning process of the sports consumer.
- Process of motivating sports consumer.
- Formation and change in the attitude of the sports consumer.
- Perceptions formed by sports consumers about a sports product or service.

SUMMARY

Sports consumers exhibit a range of values and behaviour that are quite unique. Not every sports consumer is equally passionate or uses their favourite brand, club or team to identify themselves. Sports consumer behaviour refers to the process by which consumers come to know about sports-related products, purchase them and use them, to satisfy their needs. It refers to the conduct displayed by the sports consumers while seeking out, buying, ordering, using and assessing sports products and services that would potentially satisfy their needs and wants. The Pareto Principle infers that there's an 80-to-20 relationship between effects and their causes.

Fans are one of the most important stakeholders when it comes to franchises/clubs/teams as they are an essential source of revenue for every club or team. However, not all fans are equally motivated and team/marketing managers need to understand the factors that encourage one to be a die-hard fan. Fan loyalty is a form of sports spectatorship depicted by a strong sense of attachment and affiliation to a particular sport or team. For a loyal fan, winning the game is only one of several factors that influence their loyalty to the team. Many fans are extremely devoted to their teams or favourite athlete, often for their entire lives. They invest an ample amount of money, time and energy in their teams.

Consumer behaviour is affected by many individual and environmental factors. For a sports consumer, three sub-factors have the most influence, namely, socialisation, involvement and commitment.

The decision making process model contains the following steps —Recognition of the need, Gather information about alternatives, Evaluation of the alternatives, Decision on the choice, Experience the sports product, Review the experience.

Chapter 7

Promotion in Sports Marketing

INTRODUCTION

Promotion is a part of the 5Ps of Sports Marketing. In a traditional sense, promotions include strategies and techniques that assist in communicating a product or service to the target audience. The objective of promotional activity is to present the product or service, increase demand and distinguish it from other products. The idea behind promotional activities is to initiate awareness, increase attraction and induce the audience to buy an organisation's product or service over others. Promotions may have many objectives including –

- Acceptance of a new product.
- Increase in sales.
- Creation of brand equity.
- Positioning.
- Competitive advantage.

The above objectives are not only taken into account while planning promotional activity in the sports industry, but also considered while developing strategies to improve the fans' experience, engagement or relationship. Sports organisations tend to undertake a promotional activity through online advertisements, events, endorsed gift giveaways, discounts and contests. In sports marketing, promotion covers a variety of inter-related activities. All these activities are intended to attract attention, stimulate interest and awareness of sports consumers/fans and encourage them to purchase a sports product or service.

The main purpose of a sports promotional strategy is to build brand loyalty, brand credibility, develop brand image and to position the brand. A promotional strategy is like a general marketing strategy, but the promotional strategy trails direct and indirect short-term goals. Promotional objectives normally contain increased sales, stimulate spontaneous buying, improve customer traffic and reinforce brand image. It also offers information about sports products and services, publicises new stores or websites and enhances customer satisfaction. Promotional objectives normally contain increased sales, stimulate spontaneous buying, improve customer traffic and reinforce brand image. It also offers information about sports products and services, publicises new stores or websites and enhances customer satisfaction. In the sports marketing domain, promotions involve communication of the sports organisation's products and services to people and thereby influencing their actions. It also includes community involvement and image. The sports organisation ensures that various segments of people like end consumer (fans), the business consumer (suppliers, retailers), the general community, the business community (collaborators) and the media become significant factors while developing promotion strategies.

COMMUNICATION MANAGEMENT IN SPORTS

The communication aspect in Sports Marketing facilitates the attraction of participants and spectators to the sports event or venue. The importance of communication is weighed in at many levels including school level, college level, professional sports level and public sports/ recreation level.

The following are the benefits every brand or sports organisation obtains by using promotion tools for communicating –

- Brand value.
- Public relations.
- Coordination.
- Revenues.

The sports organisation must use communication as a tool towards –

- **Teams:** Sports teams need to attract good players to compete at a high level and attract more spectators. Teams also aim to attract sponsors. Communicating a team's ambitions and success through various media platforms helps build a team's profile. This further helps attract players/athletes who have personal ambitions to compete at a professional level and enjoy the rewards of success.
- **Facility members:** Sporting facilities like gyms, fitness centres or swimming pools need to recruit customers and members to meet revenue targets. Communication about these facilities in the press through articles, social media posts, etc. about healthy lifestyles, costs and schemes will help increase the memberships. Direct communication to potential customers like schools, colleges and sports teams of the benefits and costs of using these sports facilities is also another way of ensuring memberships. Communication aids in attracting new members, retain existing members and replace people who drop their memberships.
- **Spectators:** Sports organisations promote sporting events by communicating with the public to generate/increase revenue from spectators and supporters. The organisers promote tournaments, games and events through

television, social media, press, radio, etc. Organisations intend to build anticipation and excitement through pre-meet communication to increase the number of television viewers and spectators for the event.

- **Sponsors:** Sports organisations can generate or increase revenue by appealing to sponsors for a team or a sporting event. Communication increases awareness of the organisation and determines the importance of sponsorship. Constant communication about the sports organisation's achievements, significant changes like the signing of a star player, maintaining the sponsor's interest and commitment are beneficial.
- **Fans:** Sports organisations promote their regular events to build loyalty among supporters and encourage them to purchase season tickets or join fan clubs. Fans provide a revenue stream that is recurring for sports organisations. Communication is used to increase or strengthen loyalty among fans by offering schemes like discounts, special merchandise deals, an invitation to the team's social events, reduced season ticket prices etc.

BRANDING IN SPORTS

Over the years, sports stakeholders and each person involved in sporting activities have understood the need to promote sports as a social phenomenon. Recent decades have seen significant progress in the coming together of sports and entertainment.

Branding determines the establishment of an image of an organisation, club, team or athlete in a way the customers need to perceive it. Organisations want customers to have a good positive image about them and their products. For a sports team, branding focuses more on their fans, members, athletes, sponsors, personalities and the sporting performances. Sports teams also want to position the brand image in a way to lead their sports consumers to cheer, support and respect a team. Branding, thus, influences the following elements of every sports team –

- Website design.
- Team colours.
- Team logo.
- Design of their social media account.
- Player uniforms – type and colours.
- Sponsors and partnerships.

Branding portrays representation of the sports organisation. It includes the thoughts and feelings the sports consumers experience when they think of a sports club or team or an organisation. Branding is not about constructing an image and forcing it on the customers. It is about portraying the core values of a sports organisation or a team. It also extends to small things like how the team or athletes present themselves at events or what people think about them.

Branding of sports teams gives numerous benefits –

- Provides a unique identity and personality.
- Increases trust and loyalty of fans who identify with a team and feel a sense of belongingness.
- Increases perception value to appear more professional.
- Increases credibility.
- Beneficial over the long-term.

Essentials of Sports Branding

Branding influences the perception of people about a sports organisation or a team. It assists in building connections with the target audience and increases recognition through various essential elements. The right elements in place ensure the desired image of the sports organisation. The following are seven essentials that all sports organisations should focus on to create a successful brand –

1. **Sports logos:** Sports is a very visual industry. It is vital to create impressive logos which leave a lasting impact on the viewer. Some sports franchises or teams may also have mascots.

2. **Endorsements:** Celebrity endorsements and increased purchase intent have a positive connection. Having a well–known person become a spokesperson for a brand is beneficial to reach the target audience. The celebrity endorser can be –

    - A star player – Virat Kohli for Puma.
    - A well-known coach – Zinedine Zidane for Kanakia Spaces.
    - A retired player affiliated to the target market – Sachin Tendulkar for Pepsi.
    - A sports announcer – Jatin Sapru and Mayanti Langer for MyTeam11.
    - A celebrity from a different stream – Shah Rukh Khan for Kolkata Knight Riders (KKR).

3. **Creation of a personality:** Logos, endorsers, colours and other visual elements are important aspects of an organisation's branding but the audience will also remember the brand persona. A brand persona is an attitude or personality a sports organisation or a team portrays. It should be reflected in all content produced including web content, blog posts, social media posts and advertising material.

4. **Study the target market:** The IPL franchise, ISL franchise, Olympic sports, ESports, fitness centres, etc. are all sports organisations. But despite the similarity, they attract different type of audiences as compared to one another. Analysing what one audience finds relatable in a brand from another is very crucial before making decisions regarding the look, attitude and feel of the brand.

5. **Identification of the most attractive aspect of the sports organisation or team:** Determining which part of the sports organisation or team is appealing or attractive to the sports consumers is crucial. Is it the products or the sport or the athletes, unique experience? Including this in the branding strategy adds more value to an organisation or team.

6. **Consistency and control:** Sports organisations, be it a franchise league, team, apparel company, etc. attract a lot of media and attention from influencers. People are bound to write and talk about the brand. It is absolutely important to take proper steps to ensure that the brand is represented accurately and consistently. Actions like –

    - Leveraging own media like blogs, social media platforms, websites to reach out to the audience with controlled branded content.
    - Creating a media kit that is readily available for journalists, bloggers, media or anyone interested in doing a story on the brand.
    - Creating a good media outreach strategy of the brand to ensure the right stories reach the public.
    - Creating digital assets library which consists of all the brand visual elements like logos, templates, images, colour schemes, etc. to ensure a consistent look and feel content reaches the public. This can be used by marketing team members, content creators or anyone who wishes to create a memorable look and feel.

7. **Reality trumps intentions:** It does not matter what the sports organisation or team wants the brand to be. It matters what the audience thinks the brand is. Direct and indirect feedback from the audience is very crucial for the brand. Polls and surveys can be used to get direct feedback from customers, collaborators and visitors. Reading

online reviews, visiting community forums, engagement on social media platforms and screening brand mentions are also ways to understand what is being spoken about the brand. This information will aid in understanding the differences between how the brand is perceived v/s how the sports organisation wants the brand to be perceived.

Stages of the Branding Process

Branding strategies include mandatory stages in the process. There are six main stages of branding –

Stage 1: Research and analysis within and outside the organisation.

Stage 2: Development of brand idea, image, values and spirit.

Stage 3: Finalisation of a brand name.

Stage 4: Finalisation of brand elements –

- Brand name, colours, music, catchphrase or slogan and all communication related to the marketing process.
- Brand design and product functionality.
- Brand outlets and online experiences.
- The services provided to establish a connection with the brand.

Stage 5: Release and presentation.

- Communication of the brand's vision within and outside the organisation.

Stage 6: Implementation.

Sports Branding Concepts

Different branding concepts have been undertaken in connection with sports. The following branding concepts can be applied to sports –

1. **Product branding in sports:** Product branding is a strategy that describes a unique series of marketing elements to distinguish any given product. It is an activity

that defines the interaction of a product and its customers through its logo, design and message. Branding a sports product can sustain over a period of time if it creates a powerful link between the consumer and the product throughout their lives. The branding strategy of sports products should aim to position and capture the main benefits, attributes, and values of the brand. In terms of sports and product branding, a sport is generally referred to as being a product. For example, football, badminton, cricket, swimming, wrestling, kho-kho, cycling, etc. are all considered as a product in sports marketing terms. It is important to understand the difference between –

a. **Branding of sports products:** Branding of sports products is a way through which sports organisations communicate about the brand by positioning them with different products. It can represent an alliance or partnership between a sports organisation and a manufactured sports product to develop and promote the brand. For example, the broadcasting alliance between Tokyo Olympics 2021 and NBC Universal is a case in point.

b. **Product branding of sports:** Product branding of sports focuses on the organisational support of sporting federations. Both the affiliated members of a sporting federation and the central governing body of sports must be mindful of the fact that their actions can increase or decrease the popularity of sports. For example, the popularity of the traditional sport of wrestling in India is supported and affected by the actions of the Sports Authority of India (SAI), the Indian Olympic Association (IOA) and the Wrestling Federation of India. These sports leadership associations are the decision factors affecting the branding of the sport in question. They must choose their target audience, competition and ensure that their sport is perceived positively. The positioning of the benefits of practicing a certain sport is the main way to grab the attention of sports consumers. This would significantly increase the growth of a certain sport in the market eventually leading to its commercial growth in professional events too.

2. **Personal branding in sports:** Personal branding in sports is built on the interactions the sports consumers have with an athlete. The athlete's *conduct* plays a big part in the way a sports consumer perceives the athlete. The actions of athletes can lead to positive or negative personal branding perceptions.

   Another important part of personal branding is the athlete's *performance*. Many athletes like Sachin Tendulkar, Sania Mirza, Mahendra Singh Dhoni, Virat Kohli, Mary Kom, etc. are perceived as brands due to their excellent performance in their respective sports. Many athletes have proved that even if they are not the top performers in their sport, they still have built their own personal brand and can have a huge financial impact on themselves as well as the team they are playing for.

   The engagement of fans is another important part of an athlete's personal brand. Many athletes engage with their fans to give them a full experience by conveying the branding idea to further develop a fan base. There are also cases where an athlete's success has also helped create their own individual brand through different sports organisation. Example –

   - Michael Jordan and Nike Jordan brand.
   - Virat Kohli and One8 brand.
   - Cristiano Ronaldo and CR7 brand.

The communication of an athlete's personal brand combines sports and entertainment. Athletes can be featured in promotional materials like –

- Displaying the athlete in their natural environment while performing or training.
- Posting the athlete's opinions, history, values, by directly interviewing him or indirectly presenting him through interviews of her/his entourage, i.e., family, team members, friends or coaches, etc.
- Provide inside access to the athlete's lifestyle, fashion choices, food habits, likes and dislikes.

Many times, intense promotion of an athlete can also lead to their entourage becoming famous and building their own brand. It generally is the case with the athlete's coaches. Coaches tend to create their own brand while associating with an Olympian or world champion to further train and develop other champions or simply benefit from their own personal brand. For example, swimming coach Nihar Ameen trained the first Indian swimmer to qualify for two events at a single Olympics, Shikha Tandon at Athens 2004. Ameen also trained Virdhawal Khade, the youngest Indian swimmer to qualify for the Olympics back in 2008, and many other swimmers who have represented India at the Olympics to date. Training Olympians led him to win the Dronacharya award and open up his own academy called Dolphin Academy which is known to be the most prestigious training centre for swimming in India.

There are also times when an athlete chooses to leverage her/his personal brand to further build upon it. For example, Pullela Gopichand, an Indian badminton player won the All-England Open Badminton Championships in 2001 to become the second Indian to achieve this feat after Prakash Padukone. He is now a well-known coach and runs the Gopichand Badminton Academy training world champions and Olympians.

3. **Corporate branding in sports:** Corporate branding refers to the method of developing and promoting the brand of a corporate entity as opposed to promoting the individual entity's products or services. This broad concept supports product branding, has an impact on its stakeholders, the products, the services, the identity to further get the organisational culture designed, promoted and evaluated.

   First, branding should focus on building a positive image of the brand itself within the consumer range through advertising and only then offer a positive experience. The development of a corporate brand in sports may be the most complex process. If the Olympics display the most intense international business, then corporate branding in sports might be one of the major challenges in terms of development. This would involve strategic planning regarding social responsibility, developing worthy commercial connections with sponsors where both parties involved have the need of a strategic common objective and lastly, creating a brand capital. This means that corporate branding in sports goes beyond the simple understanding that branding is the development of a "name, design, term, logo, symbol, or any other element that would identify one seller's good or service as distinct from those of competition."

   A series of variables must be taken into consideration for corporate sports branding that would surpass the interpretation of their logo, symbol, etc. Logos and symbols matter but they also constitute a very small part of the process. Sports organisations, clubs, teams might change their logos but the brand experience, the atmosphere that is offered to the public, whether at a game or a sports club, is what matters. Many elements aid in creating a unique brand experience for a sports club or sports team like social media engagement, fan clubs, merchandise, own media channels, books, podcasts, restaurants, club shops, foundations, and charity. All these platforms offer and create their own brand experience for the fans. Sports clubs or teams try to keep their branding identity within reach of the local communities for whom they were formed, thus making the corporate branding process very closely related to the place branding process. For example – all the teams of IPL have their brand elements centred around the city the team is connected to. Place branding also helps in the growth of sports organisations, sports arenas and sporting events are often promoted as tourism destinations. Due to the focus on communities, a sports club or team develops competitive rivalries with other local communities. There are many examples of such rivalries in the sports world such as:

- Promotion of local independence desires of the local community.
- Promotion of a deep local origin that is opposed to the capital cities of certain countries.
- Promotion of local rivalries that globally identify both clubs.
- Promotion of local identity of a community recognised worldwide (Liverpool FC as 'scouses', FC Bayern Munchen fans as 'bavarians' etc.)
- Promotion of different rivalries between different ethnicities.

4. **Re-branding in sports:** If the branding process has already been executed, sports organisations, clubs, teams may have to undertake the re-branding process. Re-branding is described as a method where a different position or identity of an existing brand is created to be distinct from the competitors in the eyes of a consumer.

Sports organisations, clubs, or teams need re-branding when –

- The target audience has a confused or non-existent perception of the sports brand.
- Sports organisations, clubs or teams want a change in the way they approach the promotion of products and services.
- The sports organisations, clubs or teams want to change their identity through various changes at the shareholder level.
- The sports organisations, clubs or teams' image is distorted due to management errors.
- The sports organisations go into a new business and their current position in the sports market is no longer adequate.
- A new, possibly strong competitor enters the same market.
- The competition has interfered with the sports organisation's current brand and turned it into an inefficient mechanism.
- The organisational culture is reintroduced.
- The sports organisations, clubs or teams want to expand the scope of their current brand depending on the rigidity of the market.

Re-branding also depends on several internal and external factors. It is undertaken in seven phases mentioned below –

Phase 1: Execute the existing plan and identify the strength of the need to change it.

Phase 2: Analysis of the market, current situation, competitors and decision-making about possible alternatives.

Phase 3: Develop plans to create a new brand.

Phase 4: Preparation for testing and launching the brand.

Phase 5: Launch the new brand to the stakeholders, employees and then the general public.

Phase 6: Evaluation of success or failure of the re-branding process.

Phase 7: Continuation of necessary measures for final assessment to accomplish the initial goals of the brand.

The above phases, when applied to sports organisations, depict those organisations periodically choosing to revive their existing brands through numerous changes in the elements of the brand and ways they communicate about it to the sports consumers. Sports teams might –

- Annually change their logo, equipment kit, etc.
- Announce new promotional products.
- Consider new destinations for promotional tournaments.
- Establish foundations and charity actions etc.

The re-branding process helps sports clubs or teams expand their fan base and aid in the promotion of the product brand of their sport. Here are three decisive factors in the sports re-branding process –

1. Communication to various stakeholders.
2. The conduct of athletes, support staff and all people concerned.
3. Monetary and non-monetary support that the organisation gets.

For example, IPL franchise Kolkata Knight Riders (KKR) undertook re-branding in 2012 and entered Season 5 of IPL with a new brand identity. The following were the tactics employed by KKR –

- *i. KKR maintained the original team colours of purple and gold but introduced a new logo which was the centrepiece of all their marketing campaigns.*
- *ii. Their marketing campaign "New Dawn, New Knights" had strategies to grow their fan base, add value to their sponsors and build a more profitable business.*

iii. The re-branding was also reflected on screen, in stadia, social media platforms, merchandise, etc.

iv. They also used this platform to help IPL maintain their positive image after the IPL scandal in 2010.

Building Powerful Brands out of Sports Properties

Over the course of the 20th century and in the past two decades, we saw sports getting increasingly commercialised. The rate at which this happened varied from sport to sport, and from country to country. This unlocking of the commercial value of sports has got to do a lot with the increasing role of media in bringing fans closer to their sport. As a result, owners of famous sports clubs tend to demonstrate an inclination to run the teams as if they are commercial businesses. As is the case with assets that are owned by business houses, the franchise and club owners of popular teams in sports like football and cricket look at their teams as brands. The adulation these teams receive from the fans mean a lot to these clubs and this fandom is the main driver behind the business-oriented outlooks of these sports properties. The sports industry in India took a steep growth curve after 2008 when the IPL created a host of exciting investment opportunities for some of the biggest corporations and businessmen in the country. Since then, this annual sporting spectacle has caught the imagination of cricket lovers in the country with the atmosphere and excitement it creates season after season. To put it from the perspective of brand building, the IPL teams are brands that have grown in stature since 2008. This is evident from the increased valuations as seen in deals involving transfer of stakes within the franchises in recent years.

Team sponsorship represents a great source of revenue for these franchises. In the Indian sports industry, sponsorship of teams saw a jump from INR 494 crore to INR 934 crore from 2014 to 2019 (India Sports Sponsorship Report. Group M). Some of the biggest brands in their respective categories are present in the sponsors list for the IPL teams. While team owners keep an eye on maximising the revenue streams, they are also looking at building the strength of the sports properties they own by pushing up their valuations by driving growth in respective fan bases. Hence, we can look at these teams having agenda around two aspects –

i. Driving growth by building the team into a powerful brand that can be valued basis the potential to monetise it.

ii. Driving profitability by continuously working on optimising cash flows by unlocking revenue potential.

Performing well on the field is a critical aspect of building team loyalty in the minds of the fans; at the same time it is important to be authentic to the values that are seen as integral to the club. In this context, it is important to build on the unique experiences the club can deliver, to make sure that the key players, coaches and other popular faces in the club embody the characteristics that the club believes in, and to ensure that the club fits well into the greater community in an appropriate manner. It is vital that the team leverages its assets well to maximise its revenue possibilities like gate collection, sale of fan merchandise, licensing, advertising and sponsorship.

Popular sports teams have significant levels of fan following on major social media platforms. These pages are direct opportunities for teams to connect with fans, communicate with them, engage them, give them opportunities to express their fandom, and thereby build a strong relationship with the fans. The La Liga Club Real Madrid, in July 2021, became the first sports club to reach 100 mn followers on Instagram, and as of September 2021, the count has reached 103 mn followers. Major sporting teams have presence on leading social platforms which can be leveraged for possible monetisation opportunities. For example, in September 2020, FC Barcelona decided to offer Facebook's fan subscription services. These services lend well to access of premium content against a subscription amount, as well as in pay per view models for chosen matches.

Digital marketers have relied on data by means of cookies that are stored on the browsers, which enable targeted activities at the digital consumer. However, with increasing data security concerns in recent years, we are moving in the direction of a world devoid of cookies, and hence, it is important to have digital assets that you own. Sports teams have made significant progress in this regard. Take the case of the IPL team Delhi Capitals. The franchise owns a content platform called DC TV which is an asset that can be leveraged to connect with large number of supporters of the team. Among the features on the platform is a property called "DC All Access", which offers behind the scene fun content from the team. In addition to this, they have "DC On The Pitch", offering content from the team's training sessions as well as "DC Unplugged" which covers interviews and other match-day content. As a part of the community initiatives of the franchise, the platform had a section called "Salaam Dilli", which pays tributes to real life heroes from the capital city who contribute to the society at large. These programmes enjoy good reach among the fans and are great opportunities to sponsors of the team; at a small additional cost the brands that are already in the sponsor list can get incremental reach and attention among loyal DC fans.

SPORTS PROMOTIONAL MIX

Based on Lucian (2013) theory, the Sports Promotional mix includes the following important elements like –

- Sports Advertising.
- Sports Sponsorship.
- Athlete Endorsements.
- Sports Public Relations.

- Sports Licensing.
- Sports Personal Selling.

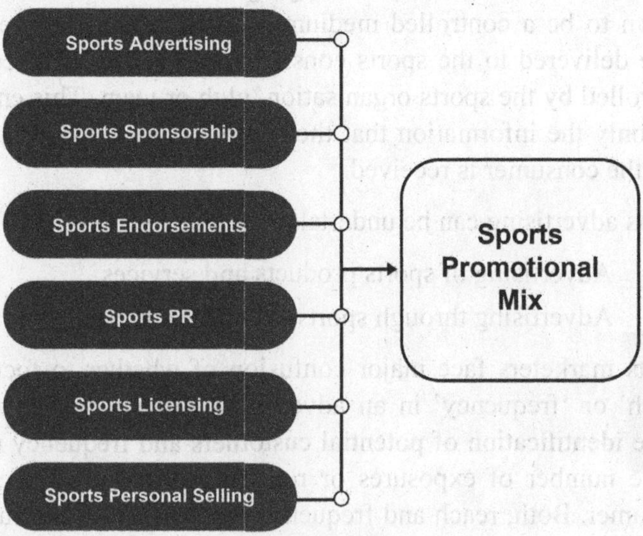

Figure 7.1: Sports Promotional Mix

Sports Advertising

Advertising is a method of communication directed towards the users of a product or service. Advertisements are paid messages by organisations that intend to inform or influence people who receive them.

Advertising is present everywhere, even though people may not be aware of it. Advertising uses every media feasible to get its message through to its target audience. It does this via television, print media – newspapers, magazines, journals, radio, internet, social media, mailers, direct selling, hoardings, posters, contests, sponsorships, merchandise, events, sounds, visuals, colours and even people's endorsements.

In sports, advertising is a paid message about the sports product using various media especially newspapers, television, magazines, radio, social media platforms, OTT platforms, scoreboards, pocket schedules, posters, game programmes, outdoor advertising, in-stadia signages, etc. Advertisement is known to be a controlled medium of promotion. The message to be delivered to the sports consumer is carefully created and controlled by the sports organisation, club or team. This ensures that only the information that the sports organisation wishes to give the consumer is received.

Sports advertising can be undertaken in many ways –

- Advertising of sports products and services.
- Advertising through sports events or athletes.

Sports marketers face major confusion of whether to focus on 'reach' or 'frequency' in an advertising strategy. Reach refers to the identification of potential customers and frequency refers to the number of exposures or repetitions needed to access a consumer. Both, reach and frequency are crucial for the success of an advertising strategy. The sports marketer must finalise on which sports consumers must be targeted (determine reach) and the number of exposures necessary to reach prospective sports consumers (determine frequency).

Sports advertising, a few decades ago, typically meant an ad with the team or club name or logo. But with today's technology advancements, new advertising offerings have emerged. The electronic scoreboard brings high-resolution LED and video which provides a more elegant visual experience of the game. Right messages using high-tech audio with perfect acoustics lead to more impact on the sports consumers. Banners and marketing campaigns complement a better look and feel. Adding internet to the mix, the fan has personal experience through OTT platforms, smartphones, live data feed, etc. This controlled medium of promotion may also lead to credibility loss among the consumers because the audiences may be aware that the advertising and information flow is controlled by the organisation.

Sports Sponsorship

Sponsorship is a form of sports promotion that includes an alliance, association or partnership between sports events or sports organisation and corporate entities. These business associations are centred around the exchange theory. The corporate entities provide finances, products, or services to the sports events or organisations and in return, the sports events or organisations provide varied benefits to the corporate entities. There can be more than one sponsor in any partnership. All the parties involved must perceive the exchange as fair for the sponsorship deal to be successful. A common example is a brand logo printed on a team's jersey. Media exposure and visibility are guaranteed in sports sponsorship allowing corporate entities to stand out and differentiate themselves. Sponsorship agreements may include the following benefits and rights –

- Use of the sports event or organisation's name, logo, or trademark in their marketing communication.
- Exclusive association with the entire sports event or facility.
- Exclusive association within a sports product or service category.
- Use of various phrases in connection with the sports product, sports event, or facility, such as "official sponsor", "partnered with", "official supplier", "supported by", "official product", or "presented by" etc.
- Exclusive use of the sports product.
- Authorisation to organise particular promotional activities such as contests, advertising campaigns, social media campaigns or on-site sports product sales.

Sports sponsorship associations grant the opportunity for all the parties to position/project their brand image, increase their audience and expand the quality of media opportunities. The parties should have a shared understanding of the vision, mission and objective of the sponsorship agreement along with a similar target market.

Business entities make substantial investments in sports for various reasons like –

- To promote their products and further increase sales.
- To display goodwill.
- To establish and improve their image through such high visibility events.
- To obtain exposure and access to the sports event or organisation's markets.

Sports events or organisations gain benefits from sponsorship engagements as corporate entities provide events with financial resources, products and services. Procuring sports sponsorship deals is vital for the overall success of the sports events because such engagements provide necessary resources to promote and deliver the events.

Sports sponsorship is generally separated into three different categories namely –

1. League/ Sport.
2. Team/ Sports organisation.
3. Athlete/ Player.

Each corporate entity interested in sports sponsorship has to choose which category they want to be associated with and pursue it. Each of the above has different characteristics and advantages that the entities will receive after agreeing with them –

- **League/ Sport:** Associating with a *league or a sport* will help a corporate entity increase its brand awareness to large audiences across the whole nation. They will also get access to events for host venue, gain broadcasting and marketing rights, etc.

  For example, Bajaj Allianz General Insurance, a private insurance company owned by the Bajaj Group of India entered into huge partnership deals for sports events like IPL and Indian hockey team. Huawei, a multinational information and communications technology company, provides global sponsorship opportunities to the many popular sports leagues like La Liga, Club América, IPL, etc. Additionally, the company supports a variety of sports events by involving technology and automation in sports. Bisleri, one of the biggest bottled water brands in the country, has been the hydration partner for marathons like the TATA Mumbai Marathon 2018, Adidas Creator Premier League, etc. The brand has sponsored several college sports events as well. IPL has/had sponsors like Dream 11, Byju's, VIVO, Tata and Paytm many FMCG brands, as well as auto and ancillary. ISL has/had sponsors including Dream11 and Policybazaar, while PKL has online pharmacy platforms Netmeds.com and Dream11.

- **Team/ sports organisation:** Associating with a team will help entities reach the regional and local markets that the team associates with. This category is also beneficial for entities that want to raise their reputation without having to pay higher rights fees. For example, HCL technologies, Indian multinational information technology services company partnered with Manchester United FC, a professional football club of the Premier League, as their official Digital Transformation Partner. HCL Technologies created the official Manchester United App for them. They also built the team a website and created an advanced essential platform that would make it easier to adapt to new emerging technologies. ICICI Bank, an Indian financial bank service also has a multi-year partnership with Manchester United offering around 35 million Indian fans of the club two types of credit card, i.e., Manchester United Signature Credit Card and Manchester United Platinum Credit Card. Each card has competitive rates and qualifies for a variety of exclusive privileges, discounts on merchandise from Manchester United FC online store and other associated partners in India. Herbalife Nutrition, a nutrition company has partnered with the JSW group's **Inspire Institute of Sport (IIS), which is India's first** private-funded high-performance training institute. IIS **trains young athletes across five Olympic disciplines** of athletics, boxing, judo, swimming and wrestling and provides over 150 talented junior athletes with residential scholarships. These athletes also have access to world-class infrastructure, technical training and sports science support to help them achieve their potential. Herbalife Nutrition provides nutrition support to athletes who train at IIS through this association.

- **Athlete/ Player:** Associating with an athlete is quite **flexible than with a league or a team. Athletes can be** made brand ambassadors for the promotion of all the campaigns. Sponsoring the right player is vital for the brand as athletes symbolise a very unstable market and may not always be in agreement with the brand objectives and tactics. Herbalife Nutrition also sponsors more than 100 athletes, teams and events. Some of the athletes they sponsor are Virat Kohli – cricketer, Mary Kom – boxer, Lakshya Sen – badminton and Manika Batra – table tennis. Saina Nehwal – a badminton player was sponsored by Iodex, Kellogg, Fortune Oil, Top-Ramen and National Egg Coordination Committee (NECC). Sachin Tendulkar – cricketer, has/had sponsorship deals with Pepsi, Boost, Adidas, Apollo Tyres, Luminous Power, True Blue and NECC apart from several other brands.

Big Brands like Coca-Cola, a well-known multinational beverage corporation opts to sponsor in all of the above categories. Coca-Cola has been sponsoring international sporting events like the Olympics, NASCAR, FIFA World Cup, NBA for many years. They also partnered with the International Paralympic Committee (IPC) for worldwide marketing rights. Coca-Cola is also a prominent sponsor for various events of the BCCI, IPL and various other sporting leagues in the country. They also sponsor college and regional sports events. They also invest heavily in promoting cricket events, brands and players. Coca-Cola is also one of the sponsors for few IPL teams like Punjab Kings, Mumbai Indians, Delhi Capitals. Thumbs Up, which is a product of the Coca-Cola product portfolio sponsors Indian athletes like Bajrang Punia – wrestler, Vikas Yadav – boxer, Deepika Kumari – archer, Manu Baker – shooter and Atanu Das – archer. They also have collaborations with the National Rifle Association of India.

Classification of Sports Sponsorship at Sports Events

The position and the visibility of the brand change depends on various factors like the investment made. The following are the different kinds of sponsors seen at any sporting event –

- **Title/Main sponsor:** The title sponsor is the highest contributor who has the naming rights to the event and acquires the maximum deliverables and branding that can be offered in the event/ league they sponsor. Example – VIVO IPL, Hero ISL, etc.
- **General sponsor:** The huge contributor who invests significant share of the total sponsorship revenues. They enjoy benefits such as extensive media coverage and license rights.
- **Official sponsor:** These sponsors make smaller contributors and could have certain roles to play with fewer benefits. They are acknowledged by their category such as official knowledge partner or official insurance partner etc. For example, Star Sports is the official sponsor for IPL.
- **Presenting sponsors:** The contributor who acquires the rights to position the "presents" or "presented by" within the name and logo of the event. Dream11, PhonePe,

Byju's and Just Dial were co-presenting sponsors for IPL.

- **Informational sponsor:** These are official partners taking care of broadcasting, PR, media coverage and more.
- **Kit sponsor:** A kit sponsor refers to an entity that provides resources like kit, jersey, equipment, etc. in exchange for the right to position its brand image/ logo on the kit or equipment for the duration of the event. Nike and MPL were the kit sponsors for the Indian cricket team.
- **Technical/ Product sponsor:** The sponsor supplies resources during the event and acquires the right to associate its brand with the event's brand image. Technical and product sponsors provide technical or product-related support during the event. These sponsors are generally classified according to the category of the product offered by the sponsor. For example, a beverage company is referred to as the official beverage sponsor, a fashion brand is referred to as the official fashion sponsor, etc. Hence, there are many variations of product sponsors such as official rental sponsor, official coffee sponsor, official smartphone sponsor, official stationery sponsor, official watch sponsor.
- **In-kind sponsor:** A company that donates or provides its products to be utilised by the people involved in the event is called an in-kind sponsor. For example, a packaged water like brand Bisleri or Aquafina may sponsor sports events by providing water to all players and officials during the event. The brand does not provide any financial assistance but contributes through its resources. Many start-ups or medium-level brands also opt for in-kind sponsorship to improve their brand awareness.
- **Media sponsor:** This kind of sponsorship may or may not include any financial transaction, but the event organiser does get special coverage on all the media platforms managed by the media partner. For example, a media

partner promotes the event on all their channels like Star and Disney+ Hotstar for IPL 2021.

- **Financial sponsor:** The sponsor offers an amount of money to the event organisers to become their financial sponsor. In return, they acquire general benefits like reach and engagement through press releases, mentions during and after the official event, in advertisements, vouchers for the audience and other benefits mentioned in their agreement.
- **Location sponsor:** Some businesses may offer their venue as a form of sponsorship. For example, a resort may offer up their premises for the players to reside in.

The event organiser may have many more types of sponsorship titles attached to the event depending upon the proposals from entities, the structure of the event and the requirement of funds. An effective sports branding strategy would include the addition of numerous properties to create maximum credibility for their brand.

For example, Coca-Cola, one of the prominent multinational beverage companies, has been the longest-standing partner of the Olympic Movement making it an excellent example of how a company can amalgamate sports sponsorship within its marketing strategy. Coca-Cola has supported every edition of the Olympic Games in many ways since 1928. It was one of the founding members of The Olympic Partner (TOP) programme and a proud partner of the Olympic Torch Relay for more than 20+ years. Coca-Cola has a renewed partnership deal with them until 2032 to extend the company's association with the Olympic Movement to a remarkable 104-year-old relationship. Apart from providing refreshments to Olympic athletes, officials and spectators with its assorted portfolio of beverages, Coca-Cola assists in generating public excitement before every edition of the Games via its global marketing campaigns and entertaining fans in the host cities on-site with its interactive initiations and platforms. Coca-Cola leverages its Olympic connection by massive advertising tactics through television, radio, social media presence, print, transit, in-stadia, outdoor, etc. They also undertake PR campaigns. For example – teams handing out Olympic branded Coca-Cola merchandise. Cola also has exclusive rights to distribute its products through hundreds of carts and stalls spread throughout all the Olympic venues.

During the Sydney 2000 Olympic Games, Coca-Cola hosted a music event entertainment called Red fest in five prominent Australian cities. The fest was entwined with consumer promotion in a bid to reward customer loyalty. Coca-Cola and Diet Coke products had tokens specially packaged which the customers could collect and use (15 tokens) to gain entry to the Red fest events. A designed website informed consumers about all the Olympic schedules, details and ticket availability. More than 1,00,000 people collected the tokens to party with the celebrities and view the beginnings of the Olympic Games at the Red fest event. Coca-Cola has also exhibited its responsibility to the environment with several initiatives at the Olympics such as recyclable plastic bottles since London 2012 Olympic Games, a water replenishment programme in and around the Pyeong Chang 2018 Winter Olympic Games intending to improve biodiversity and so on.

Coca-Cola reached more than 500+ million impressions for the #ThatsGold campaign on social media during the Rio 2016 Olympic Games. They support Olympic athletes through investment in youth sports initiatives, national Olympics, endorsements and sponsorships. Coca-Cola's pin trading centres are always fun traditions for fans to build existing or new pin collections.

Athlete Endorsements

Endorsements are a type of promotional activity that uses celebrities or famous personalities who have the power to direct a high degree of trust, respect, recognition and awareness amongst an audience. These personalities offer their image, name or network to promote and advertise a product or service for consideration. This consideration may be monetary or non-monetary. Marketers include endorsements in a marketing strategy with the hope that an endorsement, connection and approval of a celebrity or personality will influence the consumers regarding the product or service. The cost of associating with the celebrity or personality for the brand is directly proportional to her/his fame. The more famous the endorser, the more bigger is the endorsement deal.

Athletes are now considered sports stars or celebrities, especially with the boom of mass media. They are seen in different media and advertising campaigns for sporting and non-sporting products. Organisations leverage the level of popularity and fame the star athletes have by associating with the athlete's image and brand for multi-million currency endorsement deals. For example, Sachin Tendulkar endorsing biscuits, hot and cold beverages, etc. will encourage his fans to consider purchasing these products. Such a type of promotion reaches a lot more people than normal advertising tactics because of the popularity of sports stars like Tendulkar. Through endorsements, brands aim to promote aspirations of building a lifestyle instead of just promoting the product or service.

Forming a relationship between a product (sports product or non-sports product), the athlete, and the consumer is very crucial for long-term endorsement attainment. The selection of athletes to endorse are generally characterised by –

- Athletic performance.
- Likeability.
- Social equity and reach.
- Power to influence.
- Credibility.
- Uniqueness.
- Charisma and charm.

Brands consider the above factors while taking strategic decisions of selecting an athlete and the message to endorse. They prefer choosing an athlete based on how well they connect with the brand's target audience in a way that communicates credibility and trust in the product or service. Athlete endorsements also help the sports organisation reach a broader target audience, create brand awareness, generate revenue and differentiate from the competitors.

Sports stars and professional athletes, all around the globe, are the most recognisable personalities. People try to imitate these sports personalities by purchasing the brands endorsed by them. Consumers feel the need to connect and associate with the success and popularity of the athlete and are often persuaded to buy products and services endorsed by them.

Many athletes also endorse various brands at once because of the dynamic nature of the endorsements. Sports marketers should evaluate different markets and endorsement contracts with different niches for brand protections like –

- **Morality:** The morality clause gives the brand the right to terminate an endorsement contract if it would be risky for that brand's reputation or image to continue with the contract. Historically, this clause is the means for a brand to discontinue an endorsement contract if the athlete develops a bad image, is accused of criminal activity, infidelity, malicious practices, etc. For example, Tiger Woods – international golf player – due to his car accident in 2009 followed by his acknowledgement of marital infidelity lost some of the big sponsorship deals like Gatorade, Accenture, General Motors, Gillette and AT&T in 2009 and 2010 worth INR 134 crore. Lance Armstrong – former professional road racing cyclist, lost his brand endorsement contracts with Nike, Trek Bicycle Corp and FRS after the news broke that he had taken performance enhancement drugs in 2012. S Sreesanth –

Indian cricketer lost his Nike and Muthoot endorsement deals after the match-fixing scam broke in 2013.

- **Exclusivity:** Exclusive endorsements are agreements that clearly state which other products or services the athlete cannot endorse. Generally, a competing brand with the same/similar products cannot be endorsed by an athlete. For example, Virat Kohli – cricketer, endorses the brand Puma. Due to exclusivity in their endorsement deal, Kohli would not be allowed to promote/ endorse/ wear Adidas, Nike, or other competitors within the athletic apparel field.
- **Strict Licensing and NIL usage:** Strict licensing clearly outlines the way a brand and the athlete can speak about and activate the partnership between the two regarding the product or service through social media activations, commercial spots, branded campaigns, etc. Names, image and likeness (NIL) usage include the details of how a brand can integrate an athlete's persona within their marketing campaigns and collaterals. NIL usage outlines details of what and how the brand can utilise – face, voice, mannerisms and cannot utilise – specific team apparel, family members, potential catchphrases, or trademarked slogans within their marketing activations.

Examples of endorsement –

Michael Jordan – Nike Air Jordan brand

Michael Jordan, one of the most successful and well-known professional basketball players globally, was the first athlete to take endorsements to a bigger level by establishing himself as a brand, unlike any other athlete. Jordan's association with Nike fashioned the Air Jordan brand. This brand includes markets, designs and focuses only on Michael Jordan. Nike has paid him an approximate amount of $1.3 billion as per Forbes' count since the first deal was signed with Jordan in the year 1984 making him a cultural icon. It is the costliest and richest athlete endorsement *deal ever but one of the biggest bargains as Jordan helped in the transformation of Nike from an underdog to one of the most valuable consumer brands in the world. Jordan has also worked with brands like Coca-Cola, Gatorade, Chevrolet, McDonald's, Hanes, Wheaties, and many more. But none of these deals were as noticeable, prominent and lucrative as his partnership with Nike.*

Nike and Jordan created the Air Jordan brand that initially focused on basketball shoes but eventually expanded to a variety of other athletic apparel. Jordan wore these shoes from the beginning of his career and they were available for sale to the public from 1985. To date, Air Jordan has continuously released new models of shoes, from the Air Jordan 1 to the latest Air Jordan 35 and as of 2021, Air Jordan Brand has developed a durable legacy for the legendary Michael Jordan.

Cristiano Ronaldo – Lifetime deal with Nike

Cristiano Ronaldo, a Portuguese professional football player, has signed up a lifetime endorsement deal with Nike. This endorsement deal has established a direct relationship between Nike and Ronaldo creating a great example of how an athlete, by wearing or using the brand increases the sales because Ronaldo's fans desire the product their favourite player uses and advertises. Nike utilises the credibility and trust of Ronaldo among his fans through this deal.

Michael Phelps – Subway

Michael Phelps, an American Olympian swimmer, who holds the record in the highest number of gold medals at the Olympics endorsed Subway until 2012. Phelps was known as Subway's "famous Fan" in the campaign's commercial ads. Phelps had over 2.15 million followers on Twitter when the deal was signed. His deal was signed before the London 2012 Olympic Games, allowing Subway to gain credibility in advance. One tweet from Phelps during that period gave an instant growth in sales of Subs. This deal ended when people found out that Phelps had never really eaten a Subway sandwich that he endorses which negatively impacted the sales of the brand. Phelps also apologised to his fans for falsely encouraging them to eat the Sub. He also called it "that garbage" which led to the termination of their deal.

Virat Kohli – Indian Cricketer

Virat Kohli has navigated his way to the top post-signing an INR 110 crore deal with Puma and has engraved his name as one of the most marketable athletes in India. Before this, Kohli signed an INR 5 crore 18-month deal with Audi India, an INR 6.5 crore deal with MRF, and in total had earnings of Rs 1.93 million as per Forbes 2020. Manyavar, Fair and Lovely, Vicks, Flying Machine, Fast Track, Cinthol, Munch, Clear Shampoo, Great Learning, Colgate, Hero, Lafarge, Max Life Insurance, Google, Vizecare, etc. are also some of the biggest brands that are endorsed by him. He is also the only Indian to be featured on the Forbes list of the world's highest-paid athletes in 2017. Kohli launched his athleisure brand One8, in collaboration with Puma in November 2017 rapidly expanding its product portfolio by entering the innerwear and men's formal wear market.

Indian Companies Engaging with International Athletes

Many Indian companies also signed up international athletes and sports stars to endorse their products and services. For example –

- Tiger Woods, an American professional golfer, was engaged by the Hero Group.
- Lionel Messi, an Argentine professional footballer, was engaged by Tata Motors as the company's global brand ambassador for two years from 2016 onwards.
- Cricketers like Chris Gayle, Andre Russell, Kieron Pollard, etc. have endorsed their respective IPL franchise teams that they play for in India and globally.

Public Relations/ Publicity in Sports

Public relations (PR) focus on developing a good image of an organisation. A sports organisation or team must foster good relationships with various community groups like the sporting associations, governing bodies, media, local sports centres, and most importantly, fan clubs. The sports organisation or team needs to communicate with these groups regularly to maintain their relationship. It is also important for sports organisations to identify and control the information about their sports product or service in the market. Determining a way to communicate this information will further improve the sports organisations' value and reputation.

PR is slightly different from other ways of promoting a sports organisation. It generally includes processing of information regarding the sports product or service into mass media in form of a news piece. Due to this, sports PR is generally known as publicity. Publicity concentrates on the practice of unpaid and organic promotion of a sports product or service through any third party in the business of publishing print media. It also includes presenting information through television, radio and the internet. The objective of any good publicity campaign is to be viewed as coming from a neutral and unbiased source.

Three common aspects of sports publicity used in the marketing efforts of every sports organisation or team are –

1. Sports Information.
2. Media Relations.
3. Sports Journalism.

A sports marketer must understand and utilise publicity as a critical tool as it helps in the evaluation of public attitudes, articulation of policies and procedures of a sports organisation that might be of public interest. It has to execute programmes of action that need public understanding and approval.

Sports Licensing

Sports Licensing is a contractual arrangement in which a sports organisation or team gives another organisation the license to use its logo, name or trademark on all or some of the company's products. It can also apply to licensing agreements between sports organisations and individual athletes or the manufacturers of merchandise, products and services. The sports organisation or team will be known as the 'licensor' and the company or athlete leasing the rights is known as the 'licensee'. Sports licensing allows reaching out to the local, national or global market of sports fans, subject to the sports organisation.

Around the world, every team uses agreements and partnerships to acquire uniforms or create new kits for athletes and merchandise for fans. This helps reduce the risk of infringement or wrongful fabrication of the trademarks of individual athletes and teams. Licensing gives sports organisations an opportunity to –

- Establish a presence in the marketplace.
- Create a new source of revenue.
- Enhance brand awareness, value, image and appeal.
- Build relationships with sports supporters.
- Protection of the brand and intellectual property (IP) – quality and consistency.

Intellectual properties (IP) are properties that include intangible elements of the brand. The most commonly known IP, which may be registered publicly are patents, copyrights, trademarks to establish ownership rights. IP, which is also commonly referred to as know-how, is based on operational experiences. A patent for creation or development is the grant of a property right to the creator. Discovery of any new and useful process, machinery, a configuration of matter, or any new improvement can be patented. Copyrights protect or safeguard intellectual works like art, content, writing, music, pictures and others. A trademark generally serves as an identifier of the brand, products and business. Images, slogans, colours, etc. can all be trademarked.

Sports organisations or teams can increase their revenue generation potential by acquiring and using these IP rights strategically. Owners of patents, copyrights and trademarks can earn more revenue by licensing these to others. Licenses, without transferring ownership, grants rights to the licensee to use the IP. For example, use of particular technology know-how for entertainment purposes or merchandise of the team.

Many international sports brands like Real Madrid, FIFA, NBA are known to generate retail business and consumer interest in India. English football clubs such as Manchester United have launched licensed academies and sell a wide range of the brand's merchandise in India.

Online and offline platforms have seen an increase in the popularity of sports merchandise. The nation has also made a mindful move towards becoming a multi-sports nation through initiatives like Khelo India by the SAI and the Government of India. India also has properties like the National Games to promote the idea of multiple sports. The Professional Golfers Association of America (PGA) established the Professional Golfers Association of India (PGAI) intending to promote licensing programmes in India. The FIFA World Cup Russia 2018, saw an increase in Indian travellers to Russia despite India not participating in the World Cup. The sales of footballs, jerseys and other FIFA-related merchandise have tremendous sales every year through e-commerce websites.

National cricket sports brand Indian Premier League (IPL) is also a valued sport licensing property in the country. Individual playing teams in IPL like Royal Challengers Bangalore (RCB) capitalise on their brand value and rise as lifestyle brands despite not winning the trophy until 2021.

Sporting personalities like Virat Kohli who launched WROGN and the recent addition of brand One8, in collaboration with PUMA or Yuvraj Singh's brand YOUWECAN have utilised their success of sports licensing by creating their brands.

Licensing and merchandising, thus –

- Allows fans to indulge in their passion for sports.
- Facilitate the support of fans.
- Provide fans with authentic and official licensed products of sports brands.

Personal Selling in Sports

Selling sports products and services through one-on-one communication between a sports organisation representative and the consumer is considered to be one of the most effective promotion strategies. Sports organisations aim to develop strong relationships with existing consumers and potential customers by communicating through approaches like speaking one-to-one or texting via cell phones, the internet, social media platforms, etc. These efforts lead to stimulation of sales of the sports product or service, engagement of their customers, increment in customer retention rate and persuasion of potential customers. Due to the direct buyer-seller relationship established, personal selling is regarded as one of the most widely used and successful ways to achieve organisational goals. Although personal selling is expensive and time-consuming, choosing a structured communication channel that fulfils the goals of the organisation and customers will lead to the desired outcome.

The benefits of personal selling in sports are –

- Opens up two-way communication with the sports organisation and sports consumer.
- Provides personal attention to the sports consumer.
- Receive immediate feedback, questions or concerns.
- Customise individual services as per the requirements of the customer.
- Flexibility in terms of communication, process and convincing strategies as per the customer.
- Boost customer confidence and trust.

Sports retail brands like Nike, Adidas, Puma, Shiv-Naresh, Cosco, etc. use this personal selling approach in their stores. Salesmen in stores are trained to offer assistance to customers by providing information about the brand's products and convincing them to buy these products through direct contact and interaction. They also promote the brand through personalised service to ensure that customers find the right product for themselves.

Sports organisations or teams also indulge in B2B sales, especially when it comes to sponsorship packages. Majorly, professional sports teams focus on sponsorship sales through personal selling. They continuously strive to understand the elements that resonate with the sponsors and what their key takeaways from this sponsorship deal would be. These elements should create an experience for the sponsor beyond the deal offered by the sports organisation.

Focus on Grassroots Sports Development

Traditionally, India has not been a very 'sporty' kind of nation. We love our sports heroes, but when it comes to playing the part on the field, we had other priorities that took precedence. With growing awareness in terms of the benefits of a healthy lifestyle in recent years, we have seen focus shift to the inculcation of an active lifestyle right from childhood. This agenda is closely linked to the needs of enabling participation in competitive sports at a young age. It is heartening to see many corporate entities coming forward to support the agenda of grassroots sports development in India.

There are many brands that have recognised the opportunities involved in integrating sports into their marketing agenda; these corporate entities have many options at their disposal – right from the biggest properties like the IPL and international fixtures of the national teams, to more localised events as well as age-group properties. Many brands have realised the value of associating with grassroots sports, given the reach it could give them in a country as populated as India. This is in harmony with a greater need in the nation, of enabling the development of a generation with strong sporting habits. For instance, the involvement of Coca-Cola with the growth of footballing culture in India is a shining example. Along with the All India Football Federation (AIFF), the soft drink major launched the grassroots football tournament in 2009. The tournament turned out to be a great platform and a launchpad for many talented youngsters, providing them with an opportunity to build on their skills and make a career out of it. This also is in sync with AIFF's goal of bridging the gap between India and strong footballing nations. In fact, in just four years since its inception, the programme has impacted the lives of 41,760 footballers across 86 cities (coca-colaindia.com). This is a truly remarkable initiative in which an MNC is synergising marketing efforts with the sporting agenda of a nation. Another example is Unilever's Malt Food Drink brand Boost, that had been built with strong cricketing associations with some of the most famous cricketers in India like Kapil Dev, Sachin Tendulkar and Virat Kohli endorsing it. Boost also got involved in the agenda of creating the next Tendulkar and Kohli by involvement with grassroots cricket through sponsorships. The brand has also launched Boostcamp – a tech-enabled platform that helps the youngsters in pursuing their dream through assistance in training, nutrition, motivation etc. Having built a reputation as the 'secret of the energy' of our cricketing superheroes, their commitment towards supporting the dreams of the next generation of cricketers, is a good example of how a brand could find the right win-win situation.

SUMMARY

Promotion is a part of the 5Ps of Sports Marketing. In a traditional sense, promotions include strategies and techniques that assist in communicating a product or service to the target audience.

The selection of a correct sports promotion mix might be one of the toughest decisions faced by any sports marketer. The promotion mix should have a blend of promotion tactics that engage and entice the consumer. The mix should reflect upon the type and nature of sports products or services and the specific characteristics of the needs of consumers. Promotion is the method in which sports marketers will communicate with potential consumers to inform, attract, persuade and remind them about a sports product or brand. The objective of promotion is to urge consumers to acquire a favourable opinion about a sports product or brand to stimulate them to appraise it. While sports represents a great platform for non-sporting brands for branding and promotion, we also need to view the sports properties as assets that can be built into strong brands.

Chapter **8**

Five Pillars of the Indian Sporting Industry

INTRODUCTION

The previous units have established that sports is a large global business. Billions of dollars are spent annually on sports teams, at sports events, on athletes, sponsorships as well as on equipment and apparel. Over the last decade, the Indian sports industry has fundamentally grown at a healthy rate. The industry is not only an active platform for creative branding, investments and marketing opportunities but also a platform for fan entertainment in the country.

Sporting leagues in India have paved a way for the promotion of sports like kabaddi, football, badminton, etc. They have also generated an increasing fan base, creating value for stakeholders and ensured financial profitability for the promoters. This has also created an increased opportunity for young talent in many sports at the grassroots level. The government and sporting federations have also improved their schemes and initiatives for the development of sports.

The Indian sports industry has many players who drive, collaborate and regulate the operations in the industry. Without them, the sports industry would be disoriented. They act as 'pillars' to ensure that the sporting industry is moving towards steady growth.

The following are the five pillars of the Indian Sports Industry –

1. Public Sector – Governing Bodies.
2. Private Sector – Brands, Consultancies and Retail players.
3. Physical Education and Grassroots Development.
4. Infrastructure and Sports Events.
5. Sports Media and Broadcasting.

Let us study each of them briefly.

PUBLIC SECTOR – GOVERNING BODIES

Sports is known to be an important component of the socio-economic development of a country. The government plays an important role in encouraging and supporting sports in the country. The government and its organisations represent the public sector of the industry. The public sector is accountable for –

- Creation and establishment of sports policies.
- Allocation of funds for the development of athletes and infrastructure.
- Development and promotion of specialised programmes for the overall development of sports in the country.

The development of sports is a national priority because it promotes –

- Child and youth development.
- Active lifestyle.
- Employment opportunities.

- Peace and development.
- Social inclusiveness.
- Sense of belongingness.
- National pride.

The Government of India focuses on the importance of sports for overall development and excellence by establishing procedures for effective coordination among all stakeholders involved in the promotion of sports. They also extend support with required training, infrastructure and other facilities to the athletes which help them excel at international events.

Following is a chart of the major sports governing bodies that represent the public sector in India –

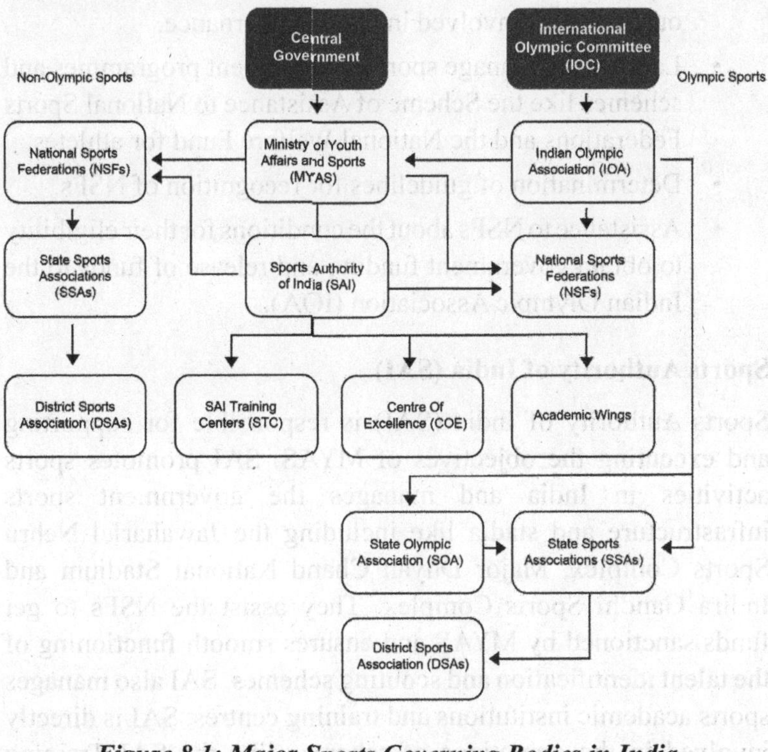

Figure 8.1: Major Sports Governing Bodies in India

Ministry of Youth Affairs and Sports (MYAS)

The Department of Sports at MYAS is the top governing body for sports in India. MYAS focuses primarily on formulating sports development programmes and funding the development and maintenance of sports infrastructure. MYAS also regulates the recognition status and funding of the National Sporting Federations (NSFs) and ensures that they abide by the guidelines stated by MYAS. It also propels the development of sports infrastructure in the nation and creates the competence to nurture elite athletes to represent India at international events. MYAS undertakes the following duties –

- Introduction and implementation of policies like the National Sports Development Code for all NSFs and other entities involved in sports governance.
- Launch and manage sports development programmes and schemes like the Scheme of Assistance to National Sports Federations and the National Welfare Fund for athletes.
- Determination of guidelines for recognition of NSFs.
- Assistance to NSFs about the conditions for their eligibility to obtain government funding and release of funds to the Indian Olympic Association (IOA).

Sports Authority of India (SAI)

Sports Authority of India (SAI) is responsible for supporting and executing the objectives of MYAS. SAI promotes sports activities in India and manages the government sports infrastructure and stadia like including the Jawaharlal Nehru Sports Complex, Major Dhyan Chand National Stadium and Indira Gandhi Sports Complex. They assist the NSFs to get funds sanctioned by MYAS and ensures smooth functioning of the talent identification and scouting schemes. SAI also manages sports academic institutions and training centres. SAI is directly involved in the operations of schemes like the SAI Training

Centres (STC) Scheme, National Sports Talent Contest (NSTC) Scheme and Army Boys Sports Companies (ABSC) Scheme along with academic institutions like Netaji Subhas National Institute of Sports (NSNIS) at Patiala and Lakshmibai National College of Physical Education (LNCPE) at Thiruvananthapuram to produce competent coaches, sports scientists and physical education teachers.

Indian Olympic Association (IOA)

The Indian Olympic Association (IOA) is the representative body for India affiliated to the International Olympic Committee (IOC), the Olympic Council of Asia (OCA) and the Commonwealth Games Federation (CWF). It administers the Olympic Charter over the NSFs of Olympic sports autonomously and is responsible for organising the National Games. IOA handles the following duties –

- Manage the preparation and participation of athletes for all international sports events, including the Olympic Games, Commonwealth Games, Asian Games and South Asian Games.
- Facilitate between NSFs of each Olympic sport and other relevant organisations like the NSNIS.
- Conduct the National Games every two years.
- Act as a liaison between the Government of India – MYAS and NSFs for financial support and promotion of Olympic sports in the country.

National Sports Federations (NSFs)

National Sports Federations (NSFs) are governing bodies responsible for the promotion of a particular sport and organising of tournaments. They play an important role in the development of a particular sport from the base level to the top. They are further supported by state and district sports associations to promote the sport right from the villages, rural level, school level, district level to the national level. For example, the Swimming Federation of India is the NSF responsible for the promotion and development of the sport of swimming supported by each state's swimming associations like Karnataka Swimming Association, Maharashtra State Amateur Aquatic Association etc.

Each NSF generally has a pyramid structure that begins from the district level for any state. Each sport has to have a district body for itself known as the district association which will be the first point of contact for that particular sport in the district. All district associations within a state come together to form a state association for that sport and many such associations from different states and union territories come together to be registered as the National Sports Federation (NSF). All these associations and federations are registered as a trust with the Charity Commissioner and have to adhere to all the norms regarding meetings, accounts, funding and transparency as listed. Once all these compliances are in order, these NSFs can request to gain recognition from the MYAS and further deem eligible for government funding. Once MYAS approves the recognition, each NSF is completely responsible for conducting the various tournaments associated with that particular sport at all levels. They are also responsible for the selection of players and athletes for all the national and international events.

Each NSF is affiliated with international bodies of their respective sport and also abides by the guidelines set by IOA and the Olympic charter of IOC. NSFs undertake talent identification, support the training of these identified athletes and organise championships and tournaments within their respective jurisdictions. They also facilitate the participation of Indian athletes at international events and ensure the rules, eligibility and documentation is in the right order.

Few examples of recognised NSFs in India are Indian Weightlifting Federation, Hockey India, Fencing Association of India, Athletics Federation of India, All India Football Federation, Cycling Federation of India, National Rifle Federation of India, Roller Skating Federation of India, Table-Tennis Federation of India and Rowing Federation of India.

PRIVATE SECTOR – BRANDS, CONSULTANCIES AND RETAIL PLAYERS

The sports industry in India is growing in terms of viewership, participation and sports-related organisation, opening new business opportunities for brands, entrepreneurial ventures, emerging technologies, services, etc. The rising disposable income, outlook towards fitness and overall growing economic conditions has led to the increase in the demand for manufacturing and retail of equipment, apparel besides increase in sports advertising, talent management and training.

The private sector plays an important role in the marketing, promotion and training of sports leading to the commercialisation and privatisation of the industry. They own leagues, teams, sports clubs and also work closely with the government and federations for event sponsorship, event management, equipment procurement and contribute to the development of sports infrastructure. For example, organisations like Puma Sports Pvt Ltd, Reebok India Company, Nike India Pvt Ltd, Shiv Naresh Pvt Ltd, Lotto Sports, Planet Sports – Future group are immersed into the production, sourcing, retailing, distribution, branding, promotions and sponsorship of goods, equipment, athletes and events. Adidas India was the apparel brand associated with the government for the Khelo India Youth Games 2020 and Khelo India University Games 2020.

Millions of viewers across the globe give way to ad revenues, merchandise and ticket sales for Indian leagues and sports. Indian Premier League (IPL), Indian Super League (ISL), Premier Badminton League (PBL) and Pro Kabaddi League (PKL) have generated various opportunities for the private sector through sponsorships, event management, retail, broadcasting rights and digital marketing, opening up new engagements and possible revenue generation opportunities. The private sector supports the sports industry with the following motivations –

- Profit earning objective.
- Non-profit/ Corporate Social Responsibility (CSR) objective.

The private sector also gives a boost to the sport and financial opportunities to athletes by increasing their net worth. For example, kabaddi has always been a well-known sport played by many in India. The broadcasting of PKL by Star Sports has aided the promotion of the league as a brand by utilising the network of sporting and non-sporting channels and focusing on the presence of celebrity team-owners who increase interest, viewership and stadium attendance. Mumbai alone had more than 500+ kabaddi clubs in 2015 (Forbes, 2015). With the popularity of PKL, Mumbai now has more than 850+ kabaddi clubs associated with Mumbai Upnagar Kabaddi Association. Rajesh Kumar, a professional kabaddi player from Haryana was the vice-captain of the Indian team when they won the gold during the 2007 World Cup. He is employed as a senior ticket collector with the Indian Railways. He has been awarded monetarily by the government for his achievements as he was a part of the team that won gold medals at two World Cups, three Asian Games and two South Asian Games. He has also been awarded the Arjuna Award by the Government of India. But it was PKL that actually lifted Kumar's financial fortunes when he was selected by Patna Pirates for the highest bid and paid around INR 12.8 lakh to play for just over a month along with all the training. He also earned a good amount of money through his participation in the reality TV show, Khatron Ke Khiladi.

Private sector engagement in sports governance is limited to deals related to public-private partnerships (PPP) for specific task-related tenders like stadium management or renovation of facilities. We will study the PPP model in detail in the next Unit.

PHYSICAL EDUCATION AND GRASSROOTS DEVELOPMENT

Physical Education

Physical Education (PE) is a course of instruction that focuses on the development of human performance through physical activities. Physical activities include simple walking, running, jogging, sprinting, jumping, throwing, climbing, kicking, pushing, pulling, kicking and so on. The combination of physical, social and psychological elements of human beings through well-directed physical activities is an integral part of the general education in schools, colleges and universities in every country. Improvement in students' physical health and better academic performance are the benefits of PE in educational institutions. Lack of physical activity among youth increases risks of health problems like obesity, diabetes, cardiovascular disease, high blood pressure etc. Through PE, educators aim to promote life-long healthy habits and improve scholastic performance. Various schemes have been introduced in India post-independence to develop physical education –

- The first national plan of physical education and recreation was formulated by the Central Advisory Board of Physical Education in 1956.
- Lakshmibai National Institute of Physical Education (LNIPE) was established at Gwalior in 1957.
- Netaji Subhash National Institute of Sports was established at Patiala in 1961.
- Kunzru Committee was appointed for different youth development activities such as physical education, sports, ACC, NCC in 1959.
- Dr CD Deshmukh's committee was appointed for the development of colleges and universities sports in 1963.
- National Policy on Education was announced by the government to improve physical fitness and sportsmanship in 1968.
- All India Council of Sports was founded which further recommended sports and physical education to be a mandatory subject in schools and colleges in 1980.

- The Government of India established a separate 'Ministry of Sports and Youth Affairs' (MYAS) to focus on the importance of physical education and sports as a nation-building activity in 1982.
- The Sports Authority of India (SAI) was then set up to look after all aspects relating to physical education, sports, adventure sports and other youth development programmes in 1984.
- National Policy of Education focused on the integration of sports and physical education to massive involvement of youth in national and social development in 1986.
- Assistance to Youth Club Scheme was introduced in 1986-87.
- The National Sports University (NSU) was established in the year 2018 in Koutruk, Manipur to impart undergraduate, postgraduate and doctoral programmes in Sports Coaching, Sports Sciences and Physical Education of various sports.

The above-established associations, initiatives and schemes were part of the Indian Government's five-year plans which focused on the promotion of physical education, development facilities for coaching and training, promotion of rural sports and fitness programmes, development of sports infrastructure and centres, nurturing and identification of talent, development of indigenous games and special schemes for coastal, tribal areas, etc. The second Five-year plan included the establishment of the Lakshmibai National Institute of Physical Education (LNIP) at Gwalior and the National Institute of Sports (NIS), Patiala. The third Five-year plan started the National Coaching Scheme and the rural sports programme for allocation towards physical education, sports and games were increased during the fourth Five-year plan. The fifth Five-year plan included the expansion of coaching facilities. The sixth Five-year plan emphasised identifying and nurturing sporting talent. The seventh

Five-year plan directed the creation and development of sporting infrastructure. The national sports policy was also introduced in the seventh Five-year plan. The eighth Five-year plan included the development of schools and sports in rural areas through the creation of playgrounds, funding for sports equipment, etc. Modern sports infrastructure and scientific facilities that focused on sports medicine, sports psychology were a part of the ninth Five-year plan. Promotion of broad basing sports and excellence was sought in the tenth Five-year plan. The eleventh Five-year plan focused on creating facilities, supporting scientific research systems and hosting national and international sports events. The plans also included the establishment of various schemes for the promotion of sports activities and the culture of physical education in India. The twelfth and thirteenth Five-year plans focused on playfield development, the establishment of the Khelo India initiative and community coaching. The establishment of the National Council of Teacher Education (NCTE) which is a statutory body of the Government of India has led to a large number of physical education training colleges all across the country. Physical Education Foundation of India (PEFI) is also one of the apex organisations recognised by the Ministry of Youth Affairs & Sports, Government of India which works towards development and creating awareness of physical education and sports in India. PEFI includes a group of our country's top sports professionals, physical education teachers and officials of the country.

Grassroots Development

The term 'grassroots' in the sporting context is the development of the foundational elements. It consists of athletes, coaches, officials, volunteers' administrators, government and parents who commit to the cause to play an important role in the development and sustainability of the grassroots sports movement influenced by sports experience. Grassroots sports are foundational, community-driven, localised and a social movement focused on the development of sports and fitness. On one hand, it aims towards the development of athletes, coaches, training facilities, clubs and competition while on the other hand, it aims to better the society through sports by regenerating communities, improving the well-being of physical and mental health, enhancing the education of students, reducing anti-social and criminal behaviour to further make a positive impact on the economy of the nation. Grassroots sports is developed at the most basic level and has nothing to do with age restrictions. Considering the age perspective, grassroots development does not aim at producing 14-year-old sports wonders but aims to provide access to basic resources needed to practise sports to every 14-year-old.

The development of grassroots sports also focuses on eliminating the following challenges that hinder the growth and success of an athlete –

- Poor operational practises.
- Athlete drop-out.
- Lack of funding.
- Untrained coaches.
- Poor infrastructure, training facilities and equipment.
- The idea that grassroots development is synonymous with youth development.
- Media representation of sports.
- Unrealistic parent expectation.
- Politics and power.

India is on the path of building a robust grassroots development structure to lead the sporting potential of the nation to success and reap the benefits in the future by establishing numerous policies, programmes and funding programmes for grassroots sports. Grassroots sports development is an essential step to build a strong sporting community in India. Students in private schools get access to good sports infrastructure and coaches as compared to students in government schools. But talent in rural areas goes unnoticed due to lack of facilities.

Private sectors in India play an important role in driving the sports ecosystem. Many organisations contribute a minimum of 2% of the average net profits to the development of sports at the grassroots level as a mandatory CSR activity. Some companies like Tata Trusts, JSW Steel, Aditya Birla Group, Reliance, Adani, PVR group, etc. support the Indian sports ecosystem through their investments and involvement in the development of grassroots sports and support athletes who perform well.

Government initiatives and national sports programmes like Khelo India – Youth Games, University Games, Talent identification, Infrastructure development, school development and Talent Olympic Podium Scheme (TOPS) play an important role in identifying, nurturing and developing athletes to achieve success in their respective sports. These initiatives aim to provide good infrastructure and facilities to identified athletes through coaching, financial support, nutrition and basic education for her/his holistic development. In 2021, the sports minister announced the establishment of 1000 Khelo India centres in every nook and corner to help promote underprivileged athletes.

Such initiatives from the private and government sectors, will not only help India achieve the ultimate goal of winning multiple Olympic medals and becoming a dominant sporting power but will also empower the youth towards holistic development of the nation.

Non-profit organisations like the Society for Transformation, Inclusion, and Recognition through Sports (STAIRS), work towards sports, health, skill development and the education of children across India. STAIRS facilitates the process of creating an environment and support system for children to use their right to play. Their programmes include tournaments, championships, training camps, etc. to provide a platform for the children to develop their skills and talent. They provide opportunities for potential talent to climb up the success stairs leading them to win at the national and international levels. As of 2021, STAIRS is currently the largest National Sports Promotion Organisation recognised by MYAS ensuring youth development and focusing on achieving Sustainable Development Goals through sports. Around 3,00,000+ children play at 400 STAIRS training centres every day in 4,000+ villages across 7+ states.

SPORTS INFRASTRUCTURE AND SPORTS EVENTS

Sports Infrastructure

Sports infrastructure is the physical construction required to facilitate participation and enable the community to participate in sports. It includes stadia, facilities, goods, systems and services that are necessary for every country to enable athletes to practise and compete in tournaments. Sports infrastructure helps develop world-class athletes and urges the youth of the country to actively engage in sports to further build a sporting culture. More than 100 sporting facilities are prevalent in India which fulfil the international standards of sports infrastructure which is either owned by the government or by private organisations, schools and colleges. Sustaining the growth momentum leads to the need to increase sporting facilities which will further enable the Indian Government to achieve its dream of 50 Olympic gold medals. Identifying and consolidating data about existing sporting facilities will help in the upgradation and refurbishment of sports infrastructure. These facilities should further be promoted for better utilisation and training infrastructure for the athletes.

The development of sports infrastructure in India is supported by –

- Government policies.
- Smart city development.
- Support of the private sector.

India's sports industry is very decentralised and fragmented. Increased capital investment into the sports industry has enhanced the development of sports infrastructure to open up to many commercial opportunities. MYAS and SAI have been set up by the ministry to develop and maintain sports facilities and stadiums. Sports are also included in the agenda of every state government and most of the sports infrastructure is funded by the state according to their priorities. The government has launched various initiatives like –

1. **National Sports Policy, 2014**: To raise the standard of sports and promoting the development of satisfactory sports infrastructure across the country.

2. **Khelo India Scheme - National Programme for Development of Sports Scheme, 2016**: It includes appropriate policies for infrastructure development. The government also launched the Khelo India app where an individual can search for an extensive database for sporting facilities all over the country. This database includes SAI facilities, SAI-supported facilities and private facilities. As of 2021, INR 1,756 crore have been allocated and 272 sports infrastructure projects are in the pipeline (News on Air, 2021).

3. **SAI Training Centres Scheme (STC)**: To provide in-house training, coaching and nutritional support to athletes.

4. **Come and Play Scheme:** To ensure optimum utilisation of five stadiums in Delhi and open allocated areas in SAI stadiums to play community sports.

5. **Panchayati Yuva Krida Aur Khel Abhiyan (PYKKA) Scheme:** To provide funding for sports infrastructure development and maintenance in rural areas, villages and panchayats.

6. **National Playing Fields Association of India (NPFAI):** To spread awareness on fitness and to encourage children to play sports by building more playing fields and areas in the country. It also works towards establishing playing fields associations at the state level so that NPFAI can sanction funds to these states for the development of the same.

7. Since 2018, this ministry sanctioned 189 sports infrastructure projects, 360 Khelo India Centres, 24 Khelo India State Centres of Excellence and 160 Khelo India Academies for promotion and development of sports in the country, as of 2021 (India Education Diary, 2021).

Many Indian cities that have been allotted under the smart cities scheme have identified potential opportunities and are developing world-class sporting infrastructure facilities. For example, the Government of Odisha has announced the development of Kalinga International Sports City in Bhubaneshwar, which is also being developed as a smart city, to host mega international events in the future. This sports city will be built near Infovalley and spread over 100-acres about 15 km away from the heart of Bhubaneshwar. Plans for the development of four world-class satellite stadiums in Cuttack, Sambalpur, Berhampur and Rourkela have also been laid out.

The private sector also plays an important role in the development of sports infrastructure by contributing towards the development and maintenance of sports facilities. Redevelopment, maintenance of existing facilities, the establishment of new stadia, setting up of sports universities and training centres need a significant amount of investment from private sectors.

Sports Events

Sporting events, tournaments and championships have played an important role from ancient times in communities and societies around the world. Tournaments and events provide athletes with opportunities to develop sports skills, measure performance and earn rewards for their hard work. Businesses and governments perceive sports events as a good opportunity to invest, promote, expand and generate revenue. As discussed in Unit 1, sports products as provided by sporting organisations can be divided into the core product and product extensions. The core product will be the initial event, game or competition and the product extensions will be all the goods and services that are related to the core product.

Globally, organisations have understood that sports events have the quality to influence people's behaviour and create general awareness regarding their products and services. A significant amount of money is invested by brands in acquiring the rights to use the said sports event to achieve a change in consumer attitude and behaviour towards their products and services. The inspirational, attitudinal and behavioural change driven within a sports consumer has amplified due to the new broadcasting platforms supporting massive reach globally. Major sports events like Olympics, Commonwealth Games, various international and national leagues like FIFA, UEFA, IPL, ISL, PKL, NBA, NFL and international and national championships like Wimbledon, World Cup, etc. also contribute to the increase in tourism and economic development of the host countries. These events are powerful enough to bring an attitudinal and behavioural change in individuals towards commercial products too. This also leads to a change in attitude in people towards the actual sport being played leading them to participate more frequently in those sports events.

SPORTS MEDIA AND BROADCASTING

Media and sports thrive and complement each other globally. In India, the sports media and broadcasting environment have significantly advanced into one of the largest sports media and broadcasting markets globally over the last quarter of a century. The increase in the popularity of sports has led to the increase in the need to ensure fans get live game updates considering the spread of media technology like television, mobile and internet amongst the Indian population. Broadcasters utilise this opportunity to advertise between intervals to generate revenues. Due to this, sports media and broadcasting rights have become expensive.

Sports media and broadcasting in India have progressed since Asian Games were televised on Colour TV in the year 1982. Foreign broadcasters entered India during the Cricket World Cup in 1987 and continued growing with Commonwealth Games and leagues like IPL. TV viewership also started attracting sports such as football, kabaddi, hockey, badminton, etc. in the league format, transforming India from a cricketing nation to a multi-sport nation. India has the potential to gain popularity and revenues like the international sports leagues — NBA, NFL, UEFA — due to its huge population and diverse sporting presence.

According to India Sports Sponsorship Report 2021 from Group M, media spends in Indian sports had doubled in the five years before the pandemic, from INR 2,518 crore in 2014 to INR 5,232 crore in 2019. Digital media has seen a disproportionate growth in the same time period, driven by innovation, technology and improved sports content delivery. The growth of digital media across broadcast, telecom sectors and online videos will drive the premium on sports rights. Younger demographics with the ability to pay, increase in grassroots investments, growth in broadband and improvement of sports infrastructure are the main factors driving the consumption of sports. Broadcasters invest in premium sports rights for scalability and sustainability to drive large-scale internet players in the huge digital ecosystem. This will drive growth in investment of premium content on sports OTT platforms, integrate pure-play entertainment, adopt subscription-based models and advertising content. For example – Hotstar in India. Cable and Satellite TV operators also invest to combine mass reach and premium segmentation with sports networks like Sony Sports and Star Sports. Social media platforms have enabled sports organisations to connect and tell their stories directly to sports fans through various digital channels leading fans to get in touch with their favoured clubs. Corporates also indulge in franchise ownerships and media spends. All these developments in sports media and broadcasting have enabled the industry to be profitable leading to a shift in the relationship between athletes, teams and fans.

SUMMARY

Sporting leagues in India have paved a way for the promotion of sports like kabaddi, football, badminton, etc. They have also generated an increasing fan base, creating value for stakeholders and ensured financial profitability for the promoters. This has also created an increased opportunity for young talent in many sports at the grassroots level. The government and sporting federations have also improved their schemes and initiatives for the development of sports.

The Indian sports industry has many players who drive, collaborate and regulate the operations in the industry. Without them, the sports industry is disoriented. They act as ‘pillars’ to ensure that the sporting industry is moving towards steady growth.

The following are the five pillars of the Indian Sports Industry –

1. Public Sector – Governing Bodies.
2. Private organisations – Brands, Consultancies and Retail players.
3. Physical Education and Grassroots Development.
4. Infrastructure and Sports Events.
5. Sports Media and Broadcasting.

Chapter 9

Promotion of Sports through the Public and Private Sectors

INTRODUCTION

The government is a vital stakeholder in the sporting ecosystem. Phases like the 2020 lockdown could be seen as signs that the government and the sports industry players can come together to support events like National Games and other grassroots events which act as breeding grounds for future Olympic champions. The pandemic has shown us that the rate of recovery of sports as an industry is directly linked to the way the government and rights holders can rally together on matters like international travel restrictions, quarantine rules, etc. which could impact the sports industry. We have seen in the past that sports can lift the morale of a nation in difficult times and can be just the shot of optimism citizens need when the going is tough. The need of the hour is for government and sponsors to work together in Public-Private partnerships. The current times call for many such initiatives.

During the COVID-19 pandemic in 2020, the Government of India announced an incentive structure to offer financial support for 500 private academies, through the Khelo India Scheme. As per the scheme, the academies would be graded into categories based on the levels of the players trained there, the level of the coaches, the quality of the field of play, infrastructure to support the same and capability in the area of sports science. The 14 disciplines seen as a priority for the 2028 Olympics (mentioned below) would be considered eligible for receiving support in the first phase itself. The scheme is expected to help the academies that are engaged in grooming talent from remote areas of the country. As per this scheme, the Sports Authority of India (SAI) would work together with National Sports Federations (NSF) on the categorisation and gradation of the academies. Recent years have seen many flagship initiatives from the Central Government to support grassroots sports, the Khelo India movement being a case in point. The government should support budding entrepreneurs working in the sports and fitness space as a part of the Public-Private partnership agenda. The agenda should be to drive sporting culture in the nation; at one level sports should be seen as an integral part of a child's growing up phase, and at the other end of the spectrum, the state needs to work in alignment with private establishments to enable through infrastructure, a strong pipeline of talent for the future.

GOVERNMENT INITIATIVE FOR PROMOTING SPORT IN INDIA

1. **GOI Identifies 14 sports for Olympic excellence:** The government has identified 14 sports to be developed for the 2024 and 2028 Olympics and started a 'one state, one game' initiative with State Governments. As a part of this, the Central Government has approached State Governments to choose one of the 14 sports. While the Central Government will provide the funding to each

state for each sport, states can contribute too. Shortlisted sports for the 2028 edition include archery, boxing, shooting, badminton, wrestling, hockey, weightlifting, cycling and athletics. Sports like table tennis, swimming, judo, fencing and rowing will be included 2028 onwards.

2. **Bill passed for Sports University in Delhi:** The Delhi Assembly passed a bill to set up a Delhi Sports University (DSU), India's first sports university, which will offer graduation, postgraduation, and doctorate degrees in cricket, football and hockey amongst other sports. Ninety acres of land have been identified for the construction of the university in Mundka.

3. **Expansion of "Fit India Scheme":** To promote the Fit India Movement, the Government of India has made government-owned facilities free of cost for sports federations (national and state), clubs and various leagues from 1 November 2019. The facilities will also be accessible free of cost to non-SAI coaches training athletes, provided he/she has a minimum of at least 10 wards. A coach can book the stadia for training sessions online and can also charge a reasonable training fee from his/her trainees. Even the athletes, who are not training for any sport professionally, can book the stadia online.

4. **Launch of Khelo India Girls League:** Widening the coverage of the Khelo India Games (KIG), the Central Government had decided to launch several leagues across all sports exclusively for girl athletes to encourage them to join sports at the grassroots level and consequently groom them for the future. The leagues titled 'Khelo India Girls League' (KIGL) and all the proposed leagues will be organised in association with national sports federations (NSFs) and respective State Governments.

PUBLIC-PRIVATE PARTNERSHIP (PPP) MODEL

The private sector needs the support of the government bodies to function. They need the backing of sports governance and policies of the existing sports governing bodies to achieve their objectives and run their business effectively. Private leagues like IPL, PKL, ISL, etc. operate in a successful model which is in alignment with the policies established by various governing bodies, especially the technical regulations of each sport established by NSFs and pay license fees to respective governing bodies. The professionalisation of individual sports leagues is still a challenge as private sectors have yet to see the lucrative benefit of investing in individual sports. The Public-Private Partnerships (PPP) model, is a collective arrangement between a government body and the private sector organisation (s) to leverage the strengths and support each other towards a common goal. For example, KOOH Sports Foundation is a startup that aims to provide an opportunity for kids who do not have access to good quality sports education and training. KOOH Sports works with the Athletics Federation of India (AFI) to get technical certification for their SpeedStar initiative, undertaken to identify young runners and is funded by corporate donors and sponsors.

The PPP model in India is still on the road of development due to limited standardised guidelines and incentives for every state to incorporate the PPP model into their sports policies leading to funding constraints. But due to government initiatives like Khelo India Scheme and Talent Olympic Podium Scheme (TOPS) by MYAS, sports have increased their focus on the PPP model. Such initiatives provide grant aids for formation, operation and maintenance of sports centres and academies for selected high-priority sports to Sports Authority of India (SAI), to state governments, private sector clubs and identified athletes under the PPP model to further supplement and facilitate Long-Term Athlete Development (LTAD). The government is supporting

PPP model investments to develop training and high-performance centres in the country. It also includes the creation and upgradation of infrastructure with the latest technologies for the future. NITI Aayog, the public policy think tank of the Government of India has emphasised and encouraged private sector participation in the development of sports infrastructure in their Sports Revitalisation Action Plan.

The PPP model is the best type of collaboration for the bright future of sports. The public sector owns vast reserves of land and can employ the regulatory measures for licenses and approvals to be easily accessible. The government also ensures a lower rate of interest on borrowed funds. NSFs can initiate state funds for sports activity in-stadia along with a source of steady revenue generation, utilisation and maintenance of these projects for greater Return on Investment (ROI). Combining the above with the private sector's specialised expertise, liquidity, ability to absorb risks, management role and ability to provide lower labour costs and benefits, gives a perfect balance for the development of the grassroots talent, infrastructure, elite athletes, etc. For example, a private organisation utilises its partnership with a governing body to gain licenses, approvals and borrowed funds with ease and a lower rate of interest. They may then construct a stadium and then lease it over to the public agency. In India, one of the most popular and relevant forms of PPP is in the establishment and development of sports infrastructure along with the upgradation of the existing stadia by the inclusion of private funds. Traditional PPP forms like Renovate, Modernise and Operate (RMO) and Build, Operate Transfer (BOT) along with modern PPP forms Refurbish, Operate, Maintain and Transfer (ROMT) facilitate the involvement of the private sector in the development, upgradation, maintenance and operation of sporting facilities. They also support risk-sharing among all the stakeholders and ensure the mitigation of these risks for all parties involved.

India's performance at the Tokyo 2021 Olympic Games has been quite successful as compared to the previous games. This can inspire a surge in private investments all the more in Olympic sports due to India's remarkable performance at the games. Tokyo 2021 Olympic medallists Neeraj Chopra – Gold medal in track and field (javelin) and Bajrang Punia – Bronze medal in wrestling, both trained at Jindal Steel Works (JSW)'s Inspire Institute of Sports (IIS). IIS is India's privately funded high-performance Olympic training centre founded by JSW sports and supported by 20 private corporations like Kotak Group, IndusInd Bank, Citibank, Marico, BridgeStone, Borosil, etc. Many experts say that the Odisha State Government has been supporting the national hockey team through the PPP model and has brought them huge success. Currently, Odisha Government has partnered with Reliance Industries for athletics, Tata Group for hockey and JSW sports for swimming, etc.

Karnataka State Cricket Association and GIZ (Deutsche Gesellschaft für Internationale Zusammenarbeit) — a German development agency, have signed an agreement to jointly promote resource efficiency, sustainable development and support measures which contribute to greenhouse gases emission at the M Chinnaswamy Stadium in Bengaluru. GIZ's ComSolar project and Indo-German Environment Partnership (IGEP) programme installed a 400-kW solar power plant on the roof of the stadium to utilise the potential of solar energy.

ELMS Sports Foundation, a not-for-profit initiative committed to the development of sports in India, includes a Public-Private Partnership programme that focuses on the improvement of the overall training experience for coaches and athletes by including the best processes and standards in terms of high performance, nutrition, sports science, sports psychology, etc. This programme complements the policies of sports governing bodies and government academies through the development of frameworks and mechanisms involving all stakeholders to create a change for the better. ELMS has a PPP collaboration with the Sports Authority of Gujarat (SAG) to provide expertise and financial support towards the existing sports complex at Nadiad to make it a high-performance centre. High-Performance Committee (HPC) comprises top officials of SAG, top management of ELMS and ground performance managers who identified the technical and management gaps based on their analysis. The HPC further developed a plan of action called the High-Performance Plan (HPP) to address those gaps. The academy has also been accredited by the Sports Authority of India (SAI) for training Khelo India athletes.

The academy at Nadiad focuses on the following components to create a conducive ecosystem for high performing athletes –

- Common infrastructure and equipment.
- Process and technology.
- Administration.
- Sports coaching.
- Athlete management.
- High-Performance sports consultant.
- Sports science.
- Sports specific infrastructure and coaching.
- Physiotherapists.
- Nutritionists.
- Sports psychologists.

All India Football Federation (AIFF) — the national governing body for football in India that manages the national football team, I-League — and IMG-Reliance — the sports division of the Reliance Industries — now re-branded as RISE Worldwide, signed a 15-year partnership contract in 2019. The objective of this partnership is to capitalise the commercial potential of football in India from the grassroots to the professional level. RISE Worldwide, which initially was a joint venture between

IMG Worldwide and Reliance Industries acquired all the commercial rights to football in India including advertising, new league rights, sponsorship, broadcasting, intellectual property, merchandising, franchising, video, film and data. This deal will also focus on the development of the branding and marketing of Team India, national and domestic competitions and teams along with restructuring, scheduling and reformatting of domestic football competitions. AIFF and RISE will also work with football state associations to develop these proposals.

CORPORATE SOCIAL RESPONSIBILITY (CSR) INITIATIVES IN SPORTS

Corporate Social Responsibility (CSR) is a self-regulating concept through which an organisation can be socially accountable to society, its stakeholders and to itself. CSR, which is also called corporate citizenship, includes activities of an organisation's involvement to make an impact on all aspects of society like economic, social and environmental. In India, the promotion of sports is recognised as a CSR activity. The Companies Act 2013 compels profitable corporates to spend a minimum of two percent of their average net profit of three years towards CSR activities. Statutorily, organisations with a revenue of more than INR 100 crore or net worth more than INR 500 crore or net profit of more than INR 5 crore during the immediately preceding financial year are required to spend two percent of their three-year annual average net profit into CSR activities. Schedule VII of the Indian Companies Act 2013 includes "training to promote rural sports, nationally recognised sports, Paralympic sports and Olympic sports" in their CSR policies. In 2016, the obligations under CSR for sports were expanded to include "construction, renovation, maintenance of stadiums, gymnasiums and sports science support including rehabilitation centres" as permissible CSR activities. Investment in CSR activities in sports is gradually increasing in India where organisations are providing funds in holistic programmes to support the development of sports and athletes in various parts of the nation with facilities such as services of international coaches, nutritionists, sports science trainers, mental health professionals, etc. They are also providing funds to invest in infrastructure, academies and training centres for various sports like tennis, athletics, hockey, football, swimming etc. Through the PPP model, the public and the private sector come together to establish high-performance training centres. Schemes like Khelo India and TOPS by the government support the development of private sports academies and centres to identify and develop grassroots talent in the country. The availability of such schemes is leading to a positive increase in the investment of the private sector in sports as a part of their mandatory CSR activity. International leagues and clubs have established their sports academies in major cities like Mumbai, Delhi-NCR, Bengaluru and Chennai to support grassroots development.

There are different ways in which a private organisation contributes to the development of sports –

- Financial funding for promising athletes through their foundation.
- In-kind to fund infrastructure, training facilities, apparel, etc.
- Invest in non-profit organisations.

Organisations like Tata and JSW have established their training centres as foundations and are looking at diverting their CSR funds towards identifying and nurturing young sporting talent. Many organisations like GoSports Foundation, Olympic Gold Quest (OGQ), Anglian Medal Hunt Company etc. engage in investing as not-for-profit organisations to help athletes who have been taken on board.

Tata Steel Ltd, an Indian multinational company, has built sports academies for archery, athletics, football, hockey and sports climbing. Tata Steel has been consistently involved in creating, developing and nurturing sporting talent through its academies and initiatives for a century. The company's first chairman Sir Dorabji Tata financed India's first Olympic team to Antwerp, Belgium in 1920. Tata Steel established the Jamshedpur Athletic Club in 1927 and also started sports competitions for working women and children. Tata Steel established the Tata Steel Adventure Foundation in the year 1984. They further established Tata Football Academy in 1987, Tata Archery Academy in 1996, Tata Athletics Academy in 2004 and so on. In 2017, Tata Steel stepped into the commercial side of sports through the establishment of Jamshedpur Football Club (JFC), which competes in India's premier football league, the ISL. Naval Tata Hockey Academy was also started in 2017, which was a joint venture of Tata Steel and Tata Trusts, to train the budding hockey enthusiasts to bring back the triumph of Indian Hockey at the international level.

Currently, Tata Steel has also been running training centres of more than 19 different sports disciplines in the JRD Sports Complex in Jamshedpur training close to 2500+ kids every year. Through their investment and involvement to develop the overall sports ecosystem of the country, Tata Steel has produced 1 Padma Bhushan, 11 Padma Shri, 1 Khel Ratna, 5 Dronacharya, and 41 Arjuna awardees in the area of sports.

Indian Super League (ISL) started the ISL grassroots programme as a strategic CSR initiative to allow boys and girls of ages 6 to 14, across the country, to learn football along with a focus on developing their skills and talent. The programme aims to reach out to more than 500,000 children and expose them to the best practices in global football. They also aim to distribute more than 100,000 footballs in various towns and villages across the country as a part of their overall initiative.

Glenmark Pharmaceuticals Limited, an Indian pharmaceutical company, has established Glenmark Aquatic Foundation (GAF), a not-for-profit CSR initiative focusing on the promotion of swimming in the country. GAF aims to improve the swimming ecosystem in India by providing resources to build a core team of highly motivated experts, develop meaningful partnerships with national and international organisations and focus on the potential of every athlete. It has launched the "The Elite Squad" scholarship to provide the Indian swimmers a chance to win medals at the Olympics. GAF has also joined hands with SAI to establish the Glenmark TIDM programme conducted at SAI National Swimming Academy (SAINSA) for talent identification, development and management of swimmers at Dr Syama Prasad Mookerjee Swimming Complex at Talkatora Stadium in New Delhi.

GoSports Foundation is a non-profit venture that works towards the development of India's top talents in Olympic and Paralympic sporting disciplines. They have a variety of athlete scholarships and knowledge-building programmes to achieve their aim of sports excellence for social change and to improve the lives of individuals, communities and that of the country. Many well-known sports stars and successful sports industry professionals like Rahul Dravid – former Indian Cricket team captain, and Pullela Gopichand – former All-England Badminton Champion, are on the Board of Advisors along with the former physiotherapist of the Indian cricket team, John Gloster, who is the Head of Sports Science section at GoSports Foundation. The following are examples of some of the established programmes –

- GoSports Long-Term Athlete Development Programme.
- Para Champions programme.
- Stars of Tomorrow programme.
- Rahul Dravid Athlete mentorship programme.

Credit Suisse Group AG, a global investment bank and financial services firm based in Switzerland, has partnered with Jai Vakeel Foundation, a non-profit organisation to start a sports facility. Their mission is to improve the lives of intellectually disabled children. More than 1,000 Credit Suisse staff volunteer their time to enhance the learning environment at five schools in underprivileged communities in Mumbai (Worli and Powai), Pune and Bengaluru every year. More than 4,000 students benefit from the initiative.

IMPACT OF COVID-19 PANDEMIC ON INDIAN SPORTS INDUSTRY

The COVID-19 pandemic in 2020 affected the sports ecosystem significantly. Games and competitions were postponed or cancelled, creating a disruption for the governing bodies, athletes, coaches, teams and organisers. There was also a pause in the non-stop live sports content consumption. Owners, broadcasters and sponsors had to work together to navigate through the implications of event cancellations and modifications. Significant impact was felt on the following revenue sources coming from live sports –

- Advertising revenue.
- Broadcasting revenue.
- Sponsorship revenue.
- Match day revenue – ticket sales, merchandise, food and beverage etc.

These sources of revenue initially dried up due to cancellation of live events. Even businesses associated or dependent on live events like hospitality, event management, stadium rentals, sporting goods, merchandise suffered losses. Many individuals, who used to work on a per event or per match basis, such as officials, umpires, support staff or athletes with no sponsors were severely affected. One of the major consequences of COVID-19 for the sports industry was the postponement of major sports events, which were scheduled to be held in 2020 like the Tokyo Olympics Games, the Men's T20 Cricket World Cup in Australia, the Euro and Wimbledon tennis championships. The overall Sports Sponsorship Market in India saw a de-growth of 34% (India Sports Sponsorship Report 2021, Group M) as a consequence of the cancellation of many events. With the system of bio-secure bubbles and the elaborate arrangements that came into place as a result of the pandemic, sporting action was back sooner than expected. Many marquee events that 2020 lost, were held successfully in 2021. Of the different franchise-based leagues operating in India, only the IPL (held in UAE) and ISL (held in Goa) happened in 2020. The situation highlighted the need for the industry stakeholders like rights holders, media, franchises and sponsors to work in close collaboration with one another and in strong alignment with the government to see through a difficult phase for the sector.

SUMMARY

The government is a vital stakeholder in the sporting ecosystem. Phases like the 2020 lockdown could be seen as signs that the government and the sports industry players can come together to support events like National Games and other grassroots events, which act as breeding grounds, for future Olympic champions. The need for the hour is for government and sponsors to work together as Public-Private partnerships. The PPP model is the best type of collaboration for the bright future of sports. In India, one of the most popular and relevant forms of PPP is in the establishment and development of sports infrastructure along with the upgradation of the existing stadia by the inclusion of private funds. Traditional PPP forms like Renovate, Modernise and Operate (RMO) and Build, Operate Transfer (BOT) along with modern PPP forms, Refurbish, Operate, Maintain and Transfer (ROMT) facilitate the involvement of the private sector in the development, upgradation, maintenance and operation of sporting facilities.

Corporate Social Responsibility (CSR) is a self-regulating concept through which an organisation can be socially accountable to society, its stakeholders and to itself. In India, the promotion of sports is recognised as a CSR activity. The Companies Act 2013 compels profitable corporates to spend a minimum of two per cent of their average net profit of three years towards CSR activities. Investment in CSR activities in sports is gradually increasing in India where organisations are providing funds in holistic programmes to support the development of sports and athletes in various parts of the nation with facilities such as services of international coaches, nutritionists, sports science trainers, mental health professionals.

Chapter **10**

Recent Developments and Future Trends in Sports Marketing

INTRODUCTION — THE FUTURE OF SPORTS MARKETING

The future of sports marketing centres around human connection. Sports organisations, teams, athletes and brands that can establish connections with the audience, despite the swiftly changing conditions, will flourish. Technology is changing the business landscape rapidly, allowing organisations to innovate new ways to reach consumers. Technology is a means to an end that will constantly variate, but fostering an emotional connection with sports consumers will be constant because connection holds immense power.

Companies are using technology to enhance player performance and fan engagement due to the boom in technology. The Indian cricket team signed a deal with StatSports, a Northern Ireland-based performance tracking, and analysis company, before the 2019 ICC Cricket World Cup. The company produces a small device that measures metrics such as distance covered, speed, acceleration, deceleration and dynamic stress load, allowing coaches to analyse and record data about the players' movements and manage their workload. Athletes, teams and organisations are welcoming technology to improve themselves creating a demand among tech companies to provide solutions for the sports industry. Indian IT companies like Wipro, HCL Technologies and Infosys products are being adopted by the global sports industry for data analytics and tech solutions. In June, HCL became Cricket Australia's official digital technology partner. Infosys partnered with French Open in 2019. Sports technology is predicted to be a US$10 billion market globally by 2024 and although it is in its infancy in India, significant strides have been made over the last few years.

The COVID – 19 pandemic in the year 2020 has had an impact on the sports industry globally. The industry is reliant heavily on in-person engagement and live sports. Although the pandemic created an adverse impact on athletes and live sports in general, it also created new opportunities and exciting avenues for growth strategically paving a path for the evolution of the industry in the future. Sports organisations and brands have developed new directions to find different ways to connect with sports consumers in the wake of COVID. These strategies are reinventing the marketing concept and are appealing to more young viewers through such moves. More than 63% of sports fans aged 13 to 39 state that 'life without sports is boring' (YPulse's special report, 2021).

Brands and sports organisations have accepted the new normal and are innovating by –

- Embracing complexity through the navigation of shifting media distribution landscape: The pandemic has stimulated new viewing habits in sports consumers. Brands and rights holders tailor-make their target packages depending on the evolving preferences of fans by streaming directly to the consumer by engaging in traditional broadcast activities.

- Entertaining the sports consumers with non-live content: Sports organisations, athletes, rights holders and brands are indulging in non-live opportunities like revenue generation, analytics and fan engagement.
- Ensuring performance and flexible partnerships: Sports sponsorship activations are changing face to pursue more flexible, performance-driven, targeted and omnichannel partnerships. They are not just offering visibility for the entities involved.
- Harnessing the growing sports tech market boom to create a competitive advantage in the sports ecosystem.
- Escalating fitness mega trends during social restrictions through innovations like virtual events focused on a healthy lifestyle will lead to growth in this segment.
- The evolution, growth, and opportunities in ESports.

NEW TRENDS FOR SPORTS MARKETING

The sports industry sector operates on fitness, health, entertainment, along with the sections that focus on digital in all its forms. It consists of a vast and diversified audience, in terms of demographics, occupations, geography and society. It is also an industry that is a hyper-dynamic sector and one that welcomes constant change.

Three important concepts drive the fundamental changes in Sports Marketing –

- Digitalisation.
- Individualisation.
- Sustainability.

Sports organisations, athletes and brands must catch up on the new trends that circle the above concepts for continuous growth and transformation to effectively gain a competitive advantage. The following are the trends that have begun changing the dynamics of the industry –

Social Media

Social media platforms have opened doors for sports marketers to allow sports organisations and brands to provide flawless experiences from the stadium to social feeds. These platforms are leveraged by brands, advertisers and sponsors to reach, engage and connect fans with their favourite athletes, teams and sports. Even for top broadcasters like Star Sports, Sony, ESPN to the local news channel, social media these days is mostly the first to break news and share the biggest moments in sports events. Social media has also offered numerous new channels to reach and engage audiences given the possibilities for success to increase numbers of followers, mentions, retweets. It also provides real prospective business outcomes including event promotions, ticket sales, fundraising and community involvement. Sports marketers now have these social channels at their fingertips that offer more effective, measurable and responsive methods to engage with fans. Social media platforms have made –

- Sports marketing more accessible to organisations and brands.
- Omnichannel strategies are more budget-friendly, seamless and easy to adopt.
- Cost of entry and exclusivity more accessible.
- Sports marketing is more measurable through analysis of reach, engagement and measurement of impact for every tactic.
- Sports marketing is more authentic by allowing brands to build a real connection with fans.
- Athletes are more engaging and connect-worthy.

Athlete Influencer Marketing

Athletes have been valuable assets to sports organisations, brands and agencies because of their game as well as their reach with the audience. With the evolution and growth of social media, digital publishing tools, and new trends like Fantasy Sports, all athletes can cultivate their fan audience organically. They can represent and depict whatever they please like — their on-field life, their off-field life, their personalities, their businesses, their charity and so on. This has led to a change in the image of athletes as being trendsetters, entertainers, activists, philanthropists and entrepreneurs, irrespective of their sporting skills, achievements and experience. As they adopt more roles that surpass their sporting persona, their level of reach and influence also increases, making them valuable even off the field.

Influencer marketing refers to the field of marketing in which influencers are paid by cash or other incentives to promote a product, service or brand. Consumers trust references or suggestions from a third party more often than a brand itself. Traditionally, elite or star athletes were leveraged by organisations or brands to sell equipment, clothing, etc. but social media has offered an outlet for athletes to feature their passions other than sports. These passions can include fitness, food, fashion or travel. Athletes bring a fresh perspective to influencer marketing. Athletes, who have dedicated their entire life to a sport leading them to become one of the best in the country, are the best form of influencer. This emerging trend can be seen in the increasing number of influencer activities carried out by famous athletes. In fact, 6% of total endorsement value by Indian athletes in 2021 came purely on account of social media influencer deals (India Sports Sponsorship 2021, Group M). Athletes are not influencers by trade but by nature. A combination of social media and athletes is a new field of competition in the field of sports marketing. Athletes progressively manage to be social media influencers because of their direct line of communication with their followers. Athletes already have a fanbase due to the exposure from their game, team and league. Organisations and brands not only take notice of elite or star athletes but also of lesser-known niche athletes. Niche athletes gain from every day brands because they lead fairly normal lives and a lifestyle that people connect with. Niche athletes also are equally excited to be influencers of a brand and offer a level of personality.

Although the athletes are closely watched, their social influence is no longer only tied to their success in sports. The athlete's attitude towards fans, the social relevance of the brands, engagement levels, etc. are elements that increase their social influence in the eyes of their followers. Many athlete influencers also use social media as a personal broadcast platform to speak out about significant issues. Athletes have a platform to promote themselves and their thoughts without needing to step onto a playing field. These athletes used their platforms to build their secure endorsements, support meaningful social causes and create a personal brand.

For example, the collective voices of athletes was never so loud as when the lockdown was declared. Whether it was to keep fans entertained while they were stuck at home, or help spread awareness for an important cause, the year 2020 has seen more athletes using their social media platforms to connect with their communities than ever before. Athlete influencers all around the world urged their followers to maintain social distancing, stay at home as much as possible and take necessary precautions, if stepping out. They also promoted the importance of mental health, fitness and vaccination drives.

An example of athletes promoting social causes would be Serena Williams, former world no. 1 tennis player with 23 Grand Slam singles titles. She has been very vocal about issues around race and police violence.

Rohit Sharma, Indian cricketer, has been using social media platforms to spread awareness about environmental issues. One of his posts on social media includes a video, he posted during the festival of Diwali, in which he is seen appealing to people to take care of the health of animals and the environment. He posted a tweet to support Greta Thunberg, a Swedish teenager leading a growing youth movement against climate inaction. He also shared a gif on Instagram with a picture of his daughter reading a guide about oceans with a caption that intended to motivate parents to teach their kids to save and protect nature.

MC Mary Kom is an Indian boxer who won an Olympic medal at the London 2012 Games along with winning several World Championships and international meets for the country. Kom not only extended financial support to the COVID-19 relief fund but also urged her followers to donate by spreading awareness through social media. She also posted awareness videos for the government and Delhi Police. She has also posted a thank you message for the Boxing Federation of India (BFI), Sports Authority of India (SAI), her coaches, support staff, and her supporters on her Twitter handle after winning her sixth World Women's Boxing Championship title. She promotes her endorsements on her social media platforms. Kom also used her voice against the International Olympic Committee's Boxing Task Force during the Tokyo 2021 Olympic Games for disputable judgment in her flyweight (51kg) pre-quarterfinal which she lost despite winning two of the three rounds. The International Boxing Association (AIBA) was suspended by the IOC for financial wrongdoing and alleged misgovernance because of Kom's stand.

The goal of a sports marketer while selecting an athlete influencer to promote their brand should be authenticity. The athlete should be allowed to be candid and post content about which they feel comfortable. This feels natural, makes the athletes happy and the promotion feels authentic.

Over The Top (OTT) content

Over The Top (OTT) means any streaming service that distributes content over the internet independently on the terminal device.

The service is carried "over the top" of another platform and is offered to the viewers via the internet. OTT goes around cable, broadcast and satellite television platforms. Disney+ Hotstar, Amazon Prime, Netflix, Sony Liv, YouTube, Facebook channel are examples of OTT platforms.

Platforms like Disney+ Hotstar, Sony Liv, Amazon Prime have upturned the sports rights market. For example, the UEFA Championship 2020 ran exclusively on Sony channels and the Sony Liv platform in India. La Liga, Spain's professional soccer league, runs on Facebook in India. Even Twitter is involved in a short news service in sports rights. An individual can now watch live sports anywhere, anytime and on any device.

The impact of IPL on live streaming was truly phenomenal. It had the biggest impact on Disney+Hotstar's overall subscriber base with viewership escalating and advertising agencies benefitting from the opportunity as well. All parties involved were in a win-win situation due to increased viewership and revenue allocation.

OTT platforms present the possibility to project tailor-made content and formats for sports organisations and brands. This possibility increases as much as the opportunity to earn revenue and involve new partners. OTT platforms also drive subscribers to create profiles to understand who watches what kind of content, which further aids in targeted marketing opportunities. From the moment the user watches the OTT video, she/ he gives back an amount of data to the platform. The data can be analysed and refined through the logged-in experience of the subscribers and users. This refined data allows sports organisations and brands to improve the fan experience. The partners involved can also participate in the creation/production process of content.

Through a partnership with the OTT platforms, sports organisations and brands can capitalise on the opportunities that live streaming offers like Subscription Video On Demand

(SVOD) and Advertising Video On Demand (AVOD). Such opportunities retain greater ad revenue and implement different ways to monetise their content. Partnering with an OTT platform also helps sports organisations and brands effectively manage engaging content for fans without the limitations of traditional broadcasting across live TV. Sports brands can package extra content within a streaming platform such as highlights, stats, replays, documentaries, fan reactions, post-match discussion and more, eventually leading to a stronger fan base.

ESports

ESports refers to a sport that requires competitive gameplay in a league or tournament format. It is very often confused with online gaming but it is not so. ESports is very similar to online gaming but is structured into a professional and competitive video gaming competition format played by professional gamers. It is defined by online games of skills played through leagues or tournaments in different teams or as individuals playing against each other to win the title, championship or league, just like in physical sports. ESports can also include games that are the virtual manifestations of traditional sports. For example, FIFA, Defence of the Ancients (DOTA2), Call of Duty, League of Legends (LoL), Counterstrike, etc.

ESports tournaments vary in operations, scale and frequency from regular sports because of its more versatility and adaptability. Similar to traditional sports, hand-eye coordination, visual processing, attention, strategy development and executive function are required to excel at ESports. Additionally, well-timed responses of athletes to games stimuli also add to excellence and growth in ESports.

ESports has gained sturdy growth, popularity among the youth, and an attractive option for brands to associate with an empowered and young audience over the last decade. It also continues to provide a platform for social gamers as well as hard-core gamers to compete. These competitions may be held online and offline. These games are multiplayer games, where a gamer can form teams and compete online. The most common video game genres of ESports are –

- First-person Shooter (FPS).
- Multiplayer Online Battle Arena (MOBA).
- Real-time Strategy (RTS).
- Fighting.
- Card Games.
- Battle Royale.

The broadcast of the above tournaments takes place along with commentary just like cricket, FIFA, etc.

It has especially gained popularity during the COVID-19 lockdown in 2020 due to its accessibility indoors and on smartphones. Organisations are aiming to engage with existing customers and prospective customers who indulge in ESports by merging it with their marketing strategy. It has the potential to dominate the Indian market due to the massive amount of marketing and advertising on different internet streaming platforms such as YouTube and Twitch. The ESports market in India has grown to be a INR 3 billion industries in 2021 and is expected to reach INR 11 billion by 2025. The ESports industry in India is expected to have 85 million viewers, 1.5 million players, 20+ broadcasters, several brands, publishers and organisers together to define the ESports market by 2025 (EY India report, 2021).

Fantasy Sports

Fantasy Sports is a type of skill-based online gaming where sports fans get the opportunity to build their virtual teams by selecting real-life players. They compete online with others based on the performance of the selected players in the live upcoming game. Fantasy games are an extension of real-life sporting events and are played across many sports like football, cricket, kabaddi for monetary reward. The virtual teams earn points based on the statistical performance of the players during the real-life match. Based on these points, a winner is determined. Fantasy Sports engages and connects sports fans closer with real-time action. While cricket certainly is popular among Fantasy Sports in India based on the number of subscribers and its mass popularity, other sports such as kabaddi, football and basketball (NBA) are also catching up. Dream11, MyTeam11, Howzat, My11Circle, MPL Fantasy Cricket Halaplay, Ballebaazi 11Wicket, MyFab11, etc. are some of the players in the Fantasy Sports sector in India. As per KPMG, the IPL fantasy league will be worth $1 billion alone in the years to come. The gross revenue from Fantasy Sports operators in India in 2020 was INR 2400 crore up from INR 920 crore in 2019.

To gain a share in the market, Fantasy Sports platforms in India focused their marketing strategies towards the Indian Premier League (IPL) 2021. Many new emerging Fantasy Sports platforms also spent their advertising money through tactical digital advertising just like Dream11 and Mobile Premier League (MPL). Dream11, one of India's well-known Fantasy Sports platforms was the title sponsor at IPL 2020 and invested in marketing for IPL 2021, which included official on-ground partner of IPL, co-presenting sponsor on Star Sports & Disney+Hotstar and sponsor of several IPL teams.

The following are the basic elements that generate direct revenues for a Fantasy Sports platform –

- Site margin.
- Number of active users.
- Average monthly spends.

Artificial Intelligence

Artificial Intelligence (AI) is a wide branch of computer science connected to the development of smart machines that are competent in accomplishing tasks that require human intelligence.

AI performs repetitive, detail-oriented projects quickly and with relatively few errors. Tasks like analysing numbers of documents of relevant fields are filled in properly without any errors. AI has helped fire an explosion for efficiency, opening doors for new business opportunities for many corporations. Artificial Intelligence is software that is capable of formulating its conclusions to reach a goal. In this process, AI software can learn, self-optimise, and, ideally, return data output. Some examples of AI that we see around us and use regularly are — Alexa, Siri, and other smart assistants, Email spam filters, Netflix's recommendations, Robo-advisors, Chatbots, etc.

The different types of technology that uses AI are –

- Automation.
- Natural language processing (NLP).
- Robotics.
- Machine learning.
- Machine vision.

Sports at various levels like national, international and Olympic levels have become data-driven. Decisions from scouting to training to in-game tactics rely on statistics of various other variables like performance, game conditions, officials and scenarios. The increase in the analysis of data on-field and off-field has generated scope for AI in the sports industry. Various AI devices are increasing the demand for monitoring and tracing players. This has led to the generation of details about athlete performance and fitness variables data such as speed, heartbeat, acceleration, etc. Technology has become a key contributor in the sports industry evolution, both inside the stadium and outside, enabling each sports organisation, player and team to be their best version of themselves.

Below are a few significant ways AI is changing the sports industry and sports marketing.

Artificial Intelligence –

- Studies the customer data and generates sports consumer-specific context.
- Operates as a chatbot to transmit any type of communication with the sports consumers. Chatbots also engage with fans to offer information regarding ticket status, parking, checking points and the schedule of the game.
- Helps improve athlete training, performance and reduces injury.
- Delivers real-time insights through analysis of data during a game which helps coaches and teams make changes to their strategies.
- Used in advertising to show relevant ads to customers depending on their demographics, tastes and preferences.
- Utilised for streaming and broadcasting.
- Helps in scouting and recruitment.
- Used by referees in a game.
- Boosts automated journalism with software like Wordsmith that produces sports matches summaries by processing the video of the game.

For example, Nike launched a system called the "Nike Makers' experience" in 2017 that allowed customers to design their sneakers in-store. This system allowed the customers to put on blank Nike Presto X sneakers and select their colours and graphics. Using Augmented Reality (AR) and projection technology, the system then exhibited the design on the blank shoes. Within 90 minutes, the created designs were printed on the sneakers and made available to the customer. This feature drove sales and increased customer engagement and aided in further collection of data about customer preferences. Nike used this data with machine learning algorithms to design future products, recommend personalised products and marketing messages to these customers.

The COVID pandemic made people rely on digital experience as sports were allowed to resume after a few months without spectators. For the fans watching games at home, companies with products like HearMeCheer and IBM Watson used assembled sound from all the previous sports matches to embed an AI model to give a crowd cheering sound while live games were aired on television and OTT platforms. Such applications are AI-based which also gather 'crowd noise' from at-home fans and stream them inside the stadium during live games. The AI-powered fake crowd cheering and Virtual Reality (VR) technology have reformed sports completely in terms of the game experience. This also led to a perception that a large number of people attended the games live than the stadium capacity. IPL 2020 incorporated fake crowd cheering. Companies are also studying fans' previous preferences and aim to give them an experience of stadiums with the help of AI, Augmented Reality (AR) and VR.

Wearables

Wearable devices are products structured by electronic components and software that are incorporated into clothing and worn on the body. Nowadays, a variety of wearable devices, such as smartwatches, smart glasses, smart jackets and a wide variety of other gadgets have been invented leading us towards a better-connected lifestyle. These wearable devices are utilised for tracking and collecting information on a real-time basis. They include motion sensors that map the outline of an individual's day-to-day activity to further sync them with their mobile devices or laptop computers.

The following are the various wearables devices present in the market today –

- **Smart watches:** A watch that provides users notifications about their calls, emails, messages, social media updates along with the basic functions of a watch like telling the time and date.

- **Fitness tracker:** A fitness tracker device keeps track of the count of steps each day and monitors the heart rate of the user. The device also calculates and analyses accurate data on the exercise and calorie burning by the user.
- **Sports watch:** Sports watches are specially built for athletes or individuals who indulge in sports like swimming, running, cycling, etc. These devices include a GPS tracker and records information on the user's heart rate, pace, etc.
- **Head-mounted display:** Head-mounted displays are devices that offer virtual information directly to the eyes of the audience. It includes aspects from the world of virtual reality.
- **Smart clothing:** Smart clothing includes electronic devices that are incorporated into the wearable clothing of the user. It also gives an interesting and fashionable look.
- **Smart jewellery:** Smart jewellery is designed similarly like smart watches especially targeting women. These smart jewelleries alert the users of their text messages, emails, calls when their phone is out of reach.
- **Implantable:** Implantable devices are wearable electronics that are surgically implanted under the skin of the user. These are generally used for medical reasons like tracking contraception, insulin levels, etc.

Wearable devices in the sports markets are segmented based on the –

- **Type of device:** Wearable devices in the sports market has been segmented into pedometers, smart fabrics, activity monitors, fitness and heart rate monitors, sports and running computers, etc.
- **Component:** Wearable devices in the sports market are segmented as hardware and software products.

- **Application:** Wearable devices in the sports market has been segmented into consumer electronics, industrial application, healthcare and enterprise.

Wearable devices in sports are utilised for monitoring the physicality of athletes and assist in analysing the elements that affect performance. These devices are constantly upgraded with easy attachments to carry the body weight and give better stability to the athlete. The devices also focus on materials and design advancements. Apart from lightweight, water-resistant and durable wearables in sports, manufacturers are also aiming towards cost-effective solutions which consumers are generally inclined towards. The easy availability of wearable devices on diversified platforms has resulted in the growth of the global market through modern trade and online channels. The availability of these devices on e-commerce platforms has led to convenience buying due to no physical constraints for the consumer. E-commerce has also helped consumers conduct a comprehensive evaluation of the wearables and research about product information, benefits, price, etc before the purchase. Further, an increase in competition for better technology will continue to boost the market for wearable devices in sports.

The drivers of the wearables in the market are –

- Adoption of digital payment.
- Transportation service on-demand.
- Enhanced growth in telecom industries.

The limitations of the wearables in the market are –

- Lack of awareness associated with benefits of wearables for non-sports consumers.
- Concerns regarding the security of information and data privacy.
- High prices and large levels of investment.

The following are some of the current key market players in the wearable technology space – Nike, Apple, Adidas, Under Armor

Inc., Garmin Ltd, Catapult Sports Pvt Ltd, Zepp Labs Inc., StretchSense, Qualcomm Technologies Inc., Sony, Lifesense Group, Xiaomi Technology Co. Ltd., Samsung Electronics, Huawei, HTC, Fitbit, etc.

Dark Social

Dark Social refers to the invisible shares that take place through channels like text messages, emails, WhatsApp, messengers and other social texting applications. The term 'Dark Social' was first introduced by Alexis Madrigal in an article in 2012. People share a lot of content via private channels like instant messaging programmes, messaging apps and email. The private characteristic of these channels makes it nearly impossible to track the source and traffic of the content. According to RhythmOne, 84% of the content sharing globally happens through Dark Social. This traffic comes from an unknown source and such shares cannot be tracked through web analytics applications and software such as Google Analytics. Content shares on public platforms like Instagram, Twitter, Facebook are easier to track than private sharing making Dark Social, a big dark slice in the social media sharing pie.

Following are some of the common Dark Social channels –

- Messaging apps: WhatsApp, Text messages, Instagram and Facebook messenger, Telegram, etc.
- Emails.
- Native mobile apps.
- Secure browsing: Incognito mode or use of HTTP instead of HTTPS.

The concept of Dark Social defines any web traffic that is not certified by a known source. Referral traffic is usually classified by 'tags' attached to the content or link, whenever it is shared. But Dark Social does not contain such referral data. It includes copy-pasted links and messages shared via messaging platforms.

These channels do not attach any tags to track the link or content, except when the shared link was copied and pasted with the tag included. For example, copy-pasting a URL of an article found on Twitter with UTM parameters included.

Some tools help track this Dark Social traffic. Link shorteners like 'Owly' or 'Bitly' give a better understanding of the clicks for a link by using a tracked link. Tools like 'Sharethis' help implement sticky or inline share buttons for easy tracking of the content shared through messages, email, texts, etc. The sports industry has entered the WhatsApp era and is utilising Dark Social traffic to build a genuine relationship with the sports organisation's audience to create a link with their brand. WhatsApp has more than 2 billion monthly active users with more than 100 billion messages sent each day (Backlinko LLC, 2021). Adidas has set up dedicated groups in the form of 'Squads' in some European cities to involve the younger generation and start connecting with them as a part of marketing on Dark Social channels. Adidas's Tango Squad is a group of football influencers purely operating on Dark Social platforms, especially on WhatsApp.

Consumers are always going to share with friends and family privately. Interacting directly with consumers in these private spaces, creating more relevant and worth sharing content is the way forward for all sports organisations.

Blockchain Technology

Blockchain is a technique of detailing information that prevents changing, hacking or cheating the system. A Blockchain is a distributed digital ledger of various transactions that are replicated across the complete network of computer systems on the Blockchain in a permanent and verifiable way. Information is stored in the form of blocks that are identical throughout the Blockchain network making it uncontrollable by a single entity and with no single point of failure.

This will offer the capability to today's sports industry globally to address many issues related to the liquidity. Blockchain will facilitate complex smart investment contracts, types of detailed smart sponsorship contracts along with donations where another sports organisation, a brand, a club or an athlete will offer a deal for a long period to receive a share from other streams of revenue or a future income in return for a capital investment before time.

Below are some potential opportunities of Blockchain technology in the sports industry –

- **Performance metrics and statistics for development and utilisation of big data:** The sporting world generates a massive amount of data that has yet to be applied to its full potential. Performance metrics of athletes can be very beneficial to develop training and coaching plans to further attain better results. Blockchain technology provides a reliable data bank collected from trusted sources like biometric measurements and mapped directly into the ledgers. Athlete data like pulse rates and biometric measurements can be directly added to the database from verified and credible devices. This will help coaches plan training effectively and enable athletes to understand their abilities.
- **Anti–doping:** Doping is the use of banned substances in competitive sports by athletes to gain an unfair advantage. Anti-doping involves activities that are focused on eliminating doping along with protecting clean athletes and the integrity of sports. Many doping scandals have taken place in recent years. During the Rio 2016 Olympic Games, hackers leaked medical files of many top-performing and highly regarded athletes from the United States with claims of evidence of doping. The use of Blockchain technology will safeguard such files from being leaked ensuring fairness in sports and preventing manipulation of doping data. Blockchain will provide a better-structured system of recording test results and prescriptions because the accuracy of the data will be

checked, present protocols will be set before logging in making the data impossible to change.

- **Fan engagement and fan identity:** Fans, as we are aware, are required to monetise sports. They spend money on merchandise, tickets to games, watch games on TV, other platforms and also boost TV rights and advertising revenues. Sports organisations have embraced the use of social media to reach out to potential fans and engage existing fans. Blockchain technology can further help sports teams and clubs introduce their currencies or virtual token of specific teams which the fans can spend on match tickets, merchandise, food and beverages, etc. The system can facilitate peer-to-peer ticket exchange which can be popular among fans enabling ticket re-sales. This can be fairly administered between clubs and fans to avoid dealing with the fake-ticket market. Loyalty schemes managed by the Blockchain technology that is explored in other sectors could help sports organisations and clubs benefit from it to engage with fans all over the world. Blockchain eliminates many third-party agents leading sports organisations and teams to get directly connected to their fans. Blockchain-based identities create a new scope for athlete and player interaction. Fans could receive verified profiles or non-fungible tokens (NFT) of their favourite player which represents their fan status and can be valued based on their performance. This fan data through these profiles can further be analysed by sports organisation to plan their marketing strategy to offer personalised and customised experiences to engage fans.
- **Sports broadcasting rights management:** Sports viewership habits are constantly changing due to the advent of new technologies. Due to such advancements, the broadcasting rights market is increasingly divided. Fans are consuming sports on live streaming platforms over social media and clip-format content on smartphones instead of traditional TV. The

broadcasting rights holders can utilise Blockchain networks for tracking their licensed rights to identify unexploited rights. They can also enable automatic rights payments through smart contracts.

- **Cryptocurrency advertising**: Blockchain technology has recently been used in the form of cryptocurrency advertising. Cryptocurrency (also called crypto) is a digital currency that uses an online ledger with strong cryptography to secure online transactions. Cryptocurrency uses Blockchain technology and is a mode of payment that can be exchanged online for goods and services. Crypto payments company called Zumbo appeared on pitch-side sponsor boards during the Euro 2020 qualifier round in a Scotland vs Serbia football match. This space of advertising is still being explored.

Blockchain technology is still in its budding stage in India. Many industries are trying to understand this concept but the Blockchain opportunities for the sports industry look promising. Blockchain will benefit and foster the potential of many sectors, investors and startups along with sporting sectors like ESports, sports investments, anti-doping, etc. Blockchain-based sports betting has also been a means for the adoption and use of cryptocurrency in sports and ESports. Professional athletes are now being paid in crypto like Bitcoin, sponsorships, top-tier endorsements and fan initiatives, leading Blockchain technology to thrive in the sports industry.

Women in Sports

The rise of women in sports has been very impactful for sports marketing trends globally, not only in terms of participation but also for creating history. This increase in female athletes has created a new audience for Women's sports. Sponsorship deals, TV rights, endorsements for Women's sports are on the rise. Globally, since 2018, revenues from Women's sports have increased over 45% in 2021 and will continue to grow in the years ahead. Women's sports have the potential to generate extensive TV audiences, increase fans per event and deliver value to sponsors. A recent multicounty study found that 66% of people expressed interest in at least one Women's sport of whom 49% are female. This indicates that women are no longer a minor target audience but also play an important part of the target audience (Deloitte group, 2021).

In India, so many sportswomen have not only participated and won Olympic medals but have also broken gender stereotypes along the way. From PT Usha – track and field, participating in the Los Angeles 1984 Olympic Games to Mirabai Chanu – weightlifting, PV Sindhu – badminton, Lovlina Borgohain – boxing, winning medals at the Tokyo 2020 Olympic Games, Indian female athletes have come a long way. These female athletes have opened various opportunities for themselves as well as sports organisations and brands in form of endorsements, sponsorships, etc.

Adidas India's #FasterThan campaign is a great example of how sports organisation and brands globally and in India are focusing their marketing activities on female athletes. This campaign focuses on celebrating women in sports, aims to inspire other women and young girls along with celebrating sports. In this campaign, Adidas featured the inspirational stories of real women, influencers and athletes from various age groups and fields through the film medium. The brand collaborated with Mirabai Chanu – weightlifter, Himanshi Goyal – promoter of body-positivityand Nishriin Parikh – a professional body-sculptor aged 53. #FasterThan campaign also focuses on mental and emotional state rather than just physical fitness. It also includes a cross-section of various stories using real people and athletes to establish the power of sports to break down cultural and gender barriers.

SOCIAL, ETHICAL AND LEGAL ISSUES IN SPORTS MARKETING

Sports Marketing strategies sometimes knowingly or unknowingly, cross the social, ethical and legal boundaries. It is an implied code of business that sports marketers have to follow certain values and principles like fairness, honesty, respect and responsibility. These values must apply to all functions carried out by the sports organisation. Whether it's communicating the right details of the sports product to the sports consumers, ensuring not to offend anyone, not undertaking an illegal approach and creating a positive ethical image about their management, athletes, coaches, fans; the sports organisation should ensure to take the right path socially, ethically and legally.

Sports marketers should refrain from including the following in their marketing campaigns –

- Sexism.
- Racism.
- Duplication and fabrication.
- Misrepresentation of facts.
- Character assassination and defamation of competitor brand.
- Association with controversial individuals.
- Malicious activities.
- Immoral and illegal activity.

2021 AND BEYOND: THE WAY THE SECTOR EVOLVES

The Indian sports industry has been in a phase of growth and quick scaling up since the advent of the IPL in 2008. With the commercialisation route being adopted by other sports thanks to the learning curve from cricket, the industry has seen many initiatives that engage the fans, resulting in the success stories of many business models. The COVID pandemic has, no doubt, been a speed-breaker, but it has only made the sports world stronger. The market is in a state of constant flux and in light of the turns it has taken in recent years, we could see a few trends for the future –

Fantasy and sports data: Gone are the days when the fans who viewed sports on media were passive spectators. Today we like to comment, interact and pass our verdict on the happenings on the field. The past couple of years have seen Fantasy Sports platforms investing more in major sports properties, and in 2020 we saw Dream XI winning the title rights for the IPL. Fantasy Sports is a cluttered space in India; currently, there are at least 30 of them with decent scale, with more of them coming up regularly with innovative engagement models. This would certainly necessitate regulations to safeguard consumer interest and to ensure best practices. The fulcrum of this business rests on sports data and there are currently no clear protocols on monetary arrangements between governing bodies and the platforms. The rate at which this business is growing would soon lead us to a point where we need "official league data" to be procured from governing bodies and rights holders, with mutually agreeable pay structures for the fan data.

Premium for category exclusivity: Recent years have seen the emergence of many tech companies in the area of sports sponsorship in India. These organisations are agile and are quickly able to get into business adjacencies. For example, an e-commerce player can easily slip into the role of a payment platform and then could pivot into being a content company. The investors love this and these companies enjoy fast growth, with many of them becoming unicorns. When these businesses switch rapidly across categories, it makes matters difficult for the sports associations as the lines between different sponsor categories start getting thinner, making the promise of category exclusivity a tricky area to handle. Without clear visibility on the evolution of the tech industry, the drive to block off unheard-of business categories is likely to push up the premium for the live sports industry.

Problem of plenty and the subscription drive: More on-field action indicates better signs for the sports industry. With many top-notch events like Tokyo 2020 and Euro 2020 getting pushed to 2021 and closer home, with a T20 fiesta on the cards with the IPL and ICC T20 World Cup being held in India, there is a lot on the plate for the sports fans making it a lucrative proposition for broadcasters too. With so much on the plate, the Indian sports fan will be forced to make choices in terms of what, when and how long to subscribe. Hence the subscription game will be driven up and with live sports demanding appointment viewing, we might finally reach a point where there could be consensus on the fact that Indians are indeed willing to pay for content!

Platforms driving sporting content: Many online players introduced innovative content as the sporting world experienced a dearth of live sports content in the days of the lockdown; as a result of which we saw the emergence of many innovative streaming and content services. With new content platforms entering the game, there was a need for newer sporting content. It is this trend that has led to the birth of properties like Jharkhand Premier League and Lanka Premier League. It needs to be seen if the lower tier cricket leagues will provide enough content affinity, the same being the case with newer non-cricketing leagues too. It is clear, however, that newer content platforms will certainly heat the battle for media acquisition rights in near future.

Prize money and career opportunities in ESports: The prolonged lockdown due to the Corona threat has accelerated the growth of ESports in India through habit formation. At the peak of lockdown in April in 2020, while there was a good increase in users per week, we also saw an upswing in the average gamer time; the live stream viewership also grew by 61% and 66% respectively in the first two weeks. As we look forward to 2021, the ESports ecosystem in India is reaching an inflection point and is readying for a giant leap. At this stage, organisers need to focus on building career opportunities and improving prize monies.

In the sports industry, the prime mover for business is always the action on the field. The more the number of games that catch the attention of the fans, the better it is for the entire ecosystem. Many iconic sports events including the Olympics, Euro and World T20 were postponed and are expected to be played now. In that context, 2020's loss can be viewed as 2021's gain. This is the time for rights holders, broadcasters, athletes, sponsors, franchises and others stakeholders to work with a strong sense of alignment towards the common good. While the collaboration among private parties has to be optimal, we also need the governmental machinery to work hand-in-hand with the sports industry players to assist the sector which is gearing up to pick momentum. We have exciting activities to look forward to with a lot to gain for the industry players, and most importantly, the fans too.

SUMMARY

The future of sports marketing centres around human connection. Sports organisations, teams, athletes and brands who can establish connections with the audience, despite the swiftly changing conditions will flourish. Technology is changing the business landscape so rapidly allowing organisations to innovate new ways to reach consumers. Technology is a means to an end that will constantly variate, but fostering an emotional connection with sports consumers will be constant because connection holds immense power. The sporting world experiences constant change. Three important concepts drive the fundamental changes in sports marketing – Digitalisation, Individualisation, Sustainability. The following are the trends that have begun changing the dynamics of the industry –

- Social Media.
- Athlete Influencer Marketing.
- Over The Top (OTT) Content.
- ESports.
- Fantasy Sports.
- Artificial Intelligence.
- Wearables.
- Dark Social.
- Blockchain technology.
- Women in Sports.

About the Author

Vinit Karnik has over 25 years' experience in Media, Entertainment and Sports Management. He has essayed leadership roles in areas related to business growth and strategic thinking. Marketer and team player at heart, Karnik has built a reputation of being an industry thought leader, drive business results and building long term relationships with key stakeholders. A radical thinker with a proven track record of ameliorating new business models, streamlining workflow and creating a team work environment to enhance profitability for the organisation and clients, Karnik has been a decisive leader at the forefront of conceptualising projects and deliver end to end execution solutions. In a diverse market like India, he has deftly handled emerging market dynamics and has immensely contributed to the evolution of Sports Management and Consulting, Media Strategies and the Business of Entertainment. He is therefore the best professional to comment on Sports Marketing in India, its evolution, trends and opportunities going forward.